TOYBOX
AL SARRANTONIO

LEISURE BOOKS NEW YORK CITY

LEISURE BOOKS ®

September 2003

Published by

Dorchester Publishing Co., Inc.
200 Madison Avenue, Suite 2000
New York, NY 10016

If you purchased this book without a cover you should be aware that this book is stolen property. It was reported as "unsold and destroyed" to the publisher and neither the author nor the publisher has received any payment for this "stripped book."

Copyright © 1999 by Al Sarrantonio

All rights reserved. No part of this book may be reproduced or transmitted in any form or by any electronic or mechanical means, including photocopying, recording or by any information storage and retrieval system, without the written permission of the publisher, except where permitted by law.

ISBN 0-8439-5174-5

The name "Leisure Books" and the stylized "L" with design are trademarks of Dorchester Publishing Co., Inc.

Printed in the United States of America.

Visit us on the web at www.dorchesterpub.com.

RAVE REVIEWS FOR *TOYBOX* AND AL SARRANTONIO!

"Gems of weirdness."
—*Publishers Weekly*

"Will linger long after you've closed the book."
—*SF Chronicle*

"Each and every one a gem."
—Joe R. Lansdale

"These stories sneak up on you, then slam down on your head when it's too late . . . a dark treasure chest full of incomparable horror fiction."
—Edward Lee, author of *Monstrosity*

"A very talented writer."
—*Washington Post Book World*

"A writer of great stories."
—Raymond E. Feist

"A true creative wonder, an artist."
—Thomas F. Monteleone, author of *The Reckoning*

Introduction copyright © 1999 by Joe R. Lansdale

"Pumpkin Head" copyright © 1982 by Al Sarrantonio. First appeared in *Terrors*.

"The Man With Legs" copyright © 1983 by Al Sarrantonio. First appeared in *Shadows 6*.

"The Spook Man" copyright © 1982 by Al Sarrantonio. First appeared in *Twilight Zone Magazine*.

"Wish" copyright © 1985 by Al Sarrantonio. First appeared in *Shadows 8*.

"Under My Bed" copyright © 1981 by Al Sarrantonio. First appeared in *Shadows 4*.

"The Big House" copyright © 1999 by Al Sarrantonio.

"Bogy" copyright © 1987 by Al Sarrantonio. First appeared in *Whispers VI*.

"The Corn Dolly" copyright © 1984 by Stuart David Schiff. First appeared in *Whispers 21-22*.

"The Electric Fat Boy" originally appeared, in a substantially different form, as "The Meek" in *Cemetery Dance Magazine*. Copyright © 1990 by Al Sarrantonio.

"Snow" copyright © 1996 by Al Sarrantonio. First appeared in *Realms of Fantasy* magazine.

"Garden of Eden" originally appeared, in a slightly different form, in *Cemetery Dance Magazine*. Copyright © 1995 by Al Sarrantonio.

"The Dust" copyright © 1982 by Al Sarrantonio. First appeared in *Death*.

"Father Dear" copyright © 1983 by Al Sarrantonio. First appeared in *Fears*.

"Children of Cain" copyright © 1989 by Al Sarrantonio. First appeared in *Stalkers*.

"Red Eve" copyright © 1991 by Al Sarrantonio. First appeared in *Under the Fang*.

"Pigs" copyright © 1987 by Al Sarrantonio. First appeared in *Shadows 10*.

"Richard's Head" copyright © 1991 by Al Sarrantonio. First appeared in *Obsessions*.

"Boxes" copyright © 1983 by Al Sarrantonio. First appeared in *Shadows 5*.

*For my Aunt Josephine and Uncle August
who many, many Christmases ago gave
me those Alfred Hitchcock anthologies
and put ideas in my head.*

Contents

Introduction by *Joe R. Lansdale*	9
Pumpkin Head	19
The Man With Legs	33
The Spook Man	47
Wish	59
Under My Bed	69
The Big House	75
Bogy	85
The Corn Dolly	95
The Electric Fat Boy	111
Snow	123
Garden of Eden	135
The Dust	149
Father Dear	157
Children of Cain	175
Red Eve	195
Pigs	209
Richard's Head	231
Boxes	249

AL SARRANTONIO, SHORT STORY BARON

an introduction by Joe R. Lansdale

When I first started trying to write seriously, I encountered stories by Al Sarrantonio, and as I began to sell, I encountered even more of his work, and always in better places than where I was appearing.

Perhaps I should have been jealous. But I wasn't. It was obvious that he belonged in better places.

He knocked me out. I wanted to be able to do the tricks he did with words. I looked everywhere for his stories, and though I can't say (sadly), that I found a lot of them, because I don't believe there are that many, each and every one I found was a gem.

Later, when Al turned to novels, his short story production waned. There's a reason for this. Novels give you more bang for your buck. Meaning, a short story seldom made a writer more than a few dollars back then, and a novel paid better. Not a lot better, but better. And it had greater potential. Sadly, more people read novels than short stories, and are more willing to lay their money down for a novel length tale than a book of short ones.

Books, at least theoretically, mean you have the chance of royalties. (Hah!) A following. A publisher that wants you to do more novels. A solid product that's more likely to be kept and held onto than a magazine containing one of your stories. Library space. And books help keep the family happy because they get to eat, have a roof over their heads, and don't have to use a bucket to tote water from the stream. Or another bucket into which to deliver their morning constitutional and tote out of the house. Preferably not to the stream where the other bucket goes.

If this sounds like I'm running the novel down, I'm not. I love them. But I'm saying this: the novel is not ignored. The short story is.

That's the sad truth, brothers and sisters. But it's the truth.

So, if you're gonna survive, you got to write novels.

But, Al, though a solid novelist, is to my mind, at heart, a short story writer. Sure, his books are entertaining, but there's a unique magic, a special attitude, a personal stylistic attack, that belongs to his shorter fiction; he's one of those handful of writers who actually owns a big patch of the short story real estate. It might be said, as a novelist, Al rents out space. He certainly improves the property, but as a short story writer, well, we all have to back off and consider.

For there, in short story land, he is a powerful land baron.

I wanted desperately to wrest away a little of that real estate from him for myself.

So I studied and probed his stories. Poked them with mental pokers, sliced them with imaginary scalpels, and finally came to the conclusion that there was no way I could understand his method. It was not mechanical. It was not something that could be dissected, examined, understood. It was, literally, just what it appeared to be.

Magic, baby.

Voodoo.

Dat ole hoodoo from beyond that's got no explainin'.

Yet, in spite of his tremendous magic, Sarrantonio is one of our most ignored short story writers. One of our most ignored writers.

Shame on everygoddamnbody. He da man, dear hearts, and you got to know that.

Maybe it's because his magic has appeared in so many places, and has never—I really find this hard to believe—never been collected.

This book, I hope, I beg, I plead, will remedy that lack of awareness.

All you got to do folks is open the cover, get past this introduction, and get to the words.

And then, the magic takes over.

Sometimes, it's dark magic. Nasty magic. Sometimes it's white magic. But it's always magic.

Let me point out my special loves.

Pumpkin Head. Boxes. Richard's Head. The Man With Legs. The Dust. Father Dear. The Spook Man.

Good grief. I'm going to name every story in the book. Who cares about my special loves. They are all tremendous.

What Sarrantonio does in nearly all the aforementioned stories, is either make you feel like a child again, or he looks at his story with child-like eyes. And so do you. Everything is rich and bright. It's as if all the sensations you feel while reading his tales are being felt for the very first time. Sweet and sour. Hot and cold. Dark and light. Sad and happy.

His prose is often poetic. A touch of Bradbury's poetry perhaps. The Bradbury of THE OCTOBER COUNTRY. A bit of Charles Beaumont's sly meanness. A lot of Robert Bloch's cleverness. Fred Brown's too. But, finally, and without question, these stories are Al Sarrantonio's.

As, I said, in the real estate of the short story, he does not rent out space. He owns it.

But let me tell you, dear hearts. To enter into these stories, to stand on their terrain, even if you are trespassing, is more than worth it. You may not own the land beneath your feet, but by being here in this magical place, you will be transformed, and you will never be able to leave.

You can close the book, of course, but it's too late. Al's done done his thing.

The man with legs will tap about in your head, pumpkin head's noggin will loom forever, and you'll never quite think of boxes in the same way. Or even little wads of dust.

That's a writer, dear hearts. That's what it's really about. He or she doesn't merely entertain you. They own a part of you.

Forever.

Look, I know I just said it, but it bears repeating, and I'll say it again. A good writer, and Al Sarrantonio is that, owns you.

Because you become part of their real estate. No matter where you go, after reading these stories, Sarrantonio's got a piece of you.

It's worth the slavery.

It has its benefits.

So don't be afraid.

And to make the rest of us writers feel even more frustrated, Al's a pretty nice guy.

But take this book and turn the page and trespass on Al's property.

Go ahead. Take the step.

TOYBOX

It was In-Between time.

In-Between time: a brown and gray morning, somewhere in the middle of January slush and March's chill-rain. December was dead; the Christmas tree was firewood, and the ornaments—the delicate glass bulbs, the shining tin angel, the flickering tinkerbell lights—were packed away. The presents were scattered to the four corners of the shimmer-glass house, some broken, others broken, mended, and broken again. Thanksgiving was dead, Easter unborn. New Year's had been put to bed, growing old. Summer was decades away; the 4th of July a hazy, distant dream.

It was In-Between time: and Selene brooded all morning, pacing from top to bottom of the shimmer-glass house, shaking her raven curls, stamping her slippered feet. "Bored, bored," is what she said, moving with a sigh from the stuffy attic to the cold-smelling cellar. The playroom was boring, the kitchen boring, the teleview room boring. Outside, dull-barked, unleafed trees, drooping, waiting for gray rain, were boring. The other shimmer-glass houses, lined up like crystal dominoes along the block, were boring.

Selene settled on the living room floor, brushed the fibers of the cranberry rug first this way, then that. She would wait for the boring morning to turn to boring afternoon and then boring night. Then she would climb into her boring bed and sleep dull sleep. Thus would pass In-Between time: sleeping at night, by day brushing the dull rug until either spring came or she brushed her way right down to China—which was probably boring too.

But then—

The doorbell rang!

Ding-Dong!

Bing-Bong!

A thrill went up little Selene's spine. That was *not the way doorbells in shimmer-glass houses usually rang—usually they buzzed with the vapid sound of a weak mosquito.*

It rang again: Ding-Dong!

And again: Bing-Bong!

This was *not boring.*

Selene almost reached the door before her legs did. "One, two, three," she counted.

She threw open the door—

Christmas assaulted her eyes—and Thanksgiving, Halloween and the 4th of July. There was a whirlwind of holiday colors, green, red and orange and black, a tornado of sparkler lights and circus bulbs. The cyclone moved by, off into the living room, and when Selene ran in puffing with excitement it settled, right on the cranberry rug where she had started her boring trip to China.

The whirlwind of light subsided.

And there stood...a man.

He wasn't a man, exactly. His face and hands were painted too brightly white, his boots were too black, his pants and vest and tall cap too red. His buttons were large brass sunsets. His eyes were flat black circles, and his lips red brushstrokes that looked still wet.

In his hands he held...a BOX.

There was surely black enamel somewhere in the world that looked as bright and liquid and deeply painted as this, but Selene hadn't seen it till now. This black enamel looked like deep midnight itself, splashed on and somehow sticking. The box had blinding silver hinges and a lid attached, and on the lid, in bright yellow letters, was the word:

T*O*Y*S

"Who—" Selene began.

But her mouth fell open silent as the figure suddenly bent, stiffly at the waist, like a soldier, and set the box before her.

"Not *boring*," he said, in a voice like Father's when something good happened. He turned his head sideways to regard her with his flat black eyes. "Would you like to see?"

And before Selene could answer he had pulled the lid up on the toybox so that Selene could look down into it.

It went on forever. There was a toyshop down there—a toyshop so wide and especially long that Selene could not see the end of it. On shelves and in glass cases toys sat, some crowded so close together they touched like kisses. Everything was amber lit, the color of dust motes.

TOYS.

There were drums and planes and wagons and blocks. And where there wasn't one toy there were three.

"Would you like to play?" the Toyman whispered, bending his voice close to Selene's ear. "Would you like to see what these toys can do?"

And, again, before she could answer "Yes!" the Toyman read her mind.

"See," he said.

Selene gasped happily.

And there, down at the far reaches of the toyshop, in the dim recesses, something floated off a dusty wood shelf. Something orange, bright and round, with a cutout mountain-peak grin and two triangle eyes, something burning bright and strong within that flew at her down the corridor like a live and screaming thing....

Pumpkin Head

An orange and black afternoon.

Outside, under baring but still-robust trees, leaves tapped across sidewalks, a thousand fingernails drawn down a thousand dry blackboards.

Inside, a party was beginning.

Ghouls loped up and down aisles between desks, shouting "Boo!" at one another. Crepe paper, crinkly and the colors of Halloween, crisscrossed over blackboards covered with mad and frightful doodlings in red and green chalk: snakes, rats, witches on broomsticks. Windowpanes were filled with cut-out black cats and ghosts with no eyes and giant *O*'s for mouths.

A fat jack-o'-lantern, flickering orange behind its mouth and eyes and giving off spicy fumes, glared down from Ms. Grinby's desk.

Ms. Grinby, young, bright, and filled with enthusiasm, left the room to chase an errant goblin-child, and one blackboard witch was hastily labeled "Teacher." Ms. Grinby, bearing her captive, returned, saw her caricature, and smiled. "All right, who did this?" she asked, not expecting an answer and not getting one. She tried to look rueful. "Never mind; but I think you know I don't *really* look like that. Except maybe today." She produced a witch's peaked hat from her drawer and put it on with a flourish.

Laughter.

"Ah!" said Ms. Grinby, happy.

The party began.

Little bags were handed out, orange and white with freshly twisted tops and filled with orange and white candy corn.

Candy corn disappeared into pink little mouths.

There was much yelling, and the singing of Halloween songs with Ms. Grinby at the piano, and a game of pin the tail on the black cat. And then a ghost story, passed from child to child, one sentence each:

"It was a dark and rainy night—"

"—and...Peter had to come out of the storm—"

"—and he stopped at the only house on the road—"

"—and no one seemed to be home—"

"—because the house was empty and haunted—"

The story stopped dead at the last seat of the first row.

All eyes focused back on that corner.

The new child.

"Raylee," asked Ms. Grinby gently, "aren't you going to continue the story with us?"

Raylee, new in class that day; the quiet one, the shy one with black bangs and big eyes always looking down, sat with her small, grayish hands folded, her dark brown eyes straight ahead like a rabbit caught in a headlight beam.

"Raylee?"

Raylee's thin pale hands shook.

Ms. Grinby got up quickly and went down the aisle, setting her hand lightly on the girl's shoulder.

"Raylee is just shy," she said, smiling down at the unmoving top of the girl's head. She knelt down to face level, noticing two round fat beads of water at the corner of the girl's eyes. Her hands were clenched hard.

"Don't you want to join in with the rest of us?" Ms. Grinby whispered, a kindly look washing over her face. Empathy welled up in her. "Wouldn't you like to make friends with everyone here?"

Nothing. She stared straight ahead, the bag of candy, still neatly wrapped and twisted, resting on the varnished and dented desktop before her.

"She's a faggot!"

This from Judy Linthrop, one of the four Linthrop girls, aged six through eleven, and sometimes trouble.

"Now, Judy—" began Ms. Grinby.

"Faggot!" from Roger Mapleton.

"A *faggot!*"

Peter Pakinski, Randy Feffer, Jane Campbell.

All eyes on Raylee for reaction.

"A pale little faggot!"

"That's enough!" said Ms. Grinby, angry, and there was instant silence; the game had gone too far.

"Raylee," she said, softly. Her young heart went out to this girl; she longed to scream at her. "Don't be shy! There's no reason, the hurt isn't real, I know, I know!" Images of Ms. Grinby's own childhood, her awful loneliness, came back to her and with them a lump to her throat.

I know, I know!

"Raylee," she said, her voice a whisper in the party room, "don't you want to join us?"

Silence.

"Raylee—"

"I know a story of my own."

Ms. Grinby nearly gasped with the sound of the girl's voice, it came to life so suddenly. Her upturned, sad little face abruptly came to life, took on color, became real. There was an earnestness in those eyes, which looked out from the girl's haunted, shy darkness to her and carried her voice with them.

"I'll tell a story of my own if you'll let me."

Ms. Grinby almost clapped her hands. "Of course!" she said. "Class," looking about her at the other child-faces: some interested, some smirking, some holding back with comments and jeers, seeking an opening, a place to be heard. "Raylee is going to tell us a story. A Halloween story?" she asked, bending back down toward the girl, and when Raylee nodded yes she straightened and smiled and preceded her to the front of the room.

Ms. Grinby sat down on her stool behind her desk.

Raylee stood silent for a moment, before all the eyes and the almost jeers and the smirks, under the crepe paper and cardboard monsters and goblins.

Her eyes were on the floor, and then she suddenly realized that she had taken her bag of candy with her, and stood alone clutching it before them all. Ms. Grinby saw it too, and, before Raylee began to shuffle her feet and stand with embarrassment or run from the room, the teacher stood and said, "Here, why don't you let me hold that for you until you're finished?"

Raylee stood silent, eyes downcast.

Ms. Grinby prepared to get up, to save her again.

"This story," Raylee began suddenly, startling the teacher into settling back into her chair, "is a scary one. It's about a little boy named Pumpkin Head."

Ms. Grinby sucked in her breath; there were some whisperings from the class which she quieted with a stare.

"Pumpkin Head," Raylee went on, her voice small and low but clear and steady, " was very lonely. He had no friends. He was not a bad boy, and he liked to play, but no one would play with him because of the way he looked.

"He was called Pumpkin Head because his head was too big for his body. It had grown too fast for the rest of him, and was soft and large. He only had a little patch of hair, on the top of his head, and the skin on all of his head was soft and fat. You could almost pull it out into folds. His eyes, nose and mouth were practically lost in all the fat on his face.

"Someone said Pumpkin Head looked that way because his father had worked at an atomic plant and had been in an accident before Pumpkin Head was born. But this wasn't his fault, and even his parents, though they loved him, were afraid of him because of the way he looked. When he stared into a mirror he was almost afraid of himself. At times he wanted to rip at his face with his fingers, or cut it with a knife, or hide it by wearing a bag over it with writing on it that said, 'I am me, I am normal just like you under here.' At times he felt so bad he wanted to bash his head against a wall, or go to the train tracks and let a train run over it."

Raylee paused, and Ms. Grinby almost stopped her, but noting the utter silence of the class, and Raylee's absorption with her story, she held her tongue.

"Finally, Pumpkin Head became so lonely that he decided to do anything he could to get a friend. He talked to everyone in his class, one by one, as nicely as he could, but no one would go near him. He tried again, but still no one would go near him. Then he finally stopped trying.

"One day he began to cry in class, right in the middle of a history lesson. No one, not even the teacher, could make him stop. The tears ran down Pumpkin Head's face, in furrows like on the hard furrows of a pumpkin. The teacher had to call his mother and father to come and get him, and even they had trouble taking him away because he sat in his chair with his hands tight around his seat and cried and cried. There didn't seem to be enough tears in Pumpkin Head's head for all his crying, and some of his classmates wondered if his pumpkin head was filled with water. But finally his parents brought him home and put him in his room, and there he stayed for three days, crying.

"After those three days passed, Pumpkin Head came out of his room. His tears had dried. He smiled through the ugly folds of skin on his face, and said that he wouldn't cry any more and that he would like to go back to school. His mother and father wondered if he was really all right, but secretly, Pumpkin Head knew, they sighed with relief because having him around all the time made them nervous. Some of their friends would not come to see them when Pumpkin Head was in the house.

"Pumpkin Head went back to school that morning, smiling. He

swung his lunch pail in his hand, his head held high. His teacher and classmates were very surprised to see him back, and everyone left him alone for a while.

"But then, in the middle of the second period, one of the boys in the class threw a piece of paper at Pumpkin Head, and then another. Someone hissed that his head was like a pumpkin, and that he had better plant it before Halloween. 'And on Halloween we'll break open his pumpkin head!' someone else yelled out.

"Pumpkin Head sat in his seat and carefully brought his lunch box up to his desk. He opened it quietly. Inside, was his sandwich, made in a hurry by his mother, and an apple, and a bag of cookies. He took these out, and also the Thermos filled with milk, and set them on the desk. He closed the lunch pail and snapped shut the lid.

"Pumpkin Head stood and walked to the front of the room, carrying his lunch pail in his hand. He walked to the door and closed it, and then walked calmly to the teacher's desk, turning toward the class. He opened his lunch box.

"'My lunch and dinner,' he said, 'my dinner and breakfast.'

"He took out a sharp kitchen knife from his lunch pail.

"Everyone in the classroom began to scream.

"They took Pumpkin Head away after that, and they put him in a place—"

Ms. Grinby abruptly stepped from behind her desk.

"That's all we have time for, Raylee," she interrupted gently, trying to smile. Inside she wanted to scream over the loneliness of this child. "That was a *very* scary story. Where did you get it from?"

There was silence in the classroom.

Raylee's eyes were back on the floor. "I made it up," she said in a whisper.

To make up something like that, Ms. Grinby thought. *I know, I know!*

She patted the little girl on her back. "Here's your candy; you can sit down now." The girl returned to her seat quickly, eyes averted.

All eyes were on her.

And then something that made Ms. Grinby's heart leap:

"Neat story!" said Randy Feffer.

"Neat!"

"Wow!"

Roger Mapleton, Jane Campbell.

As she sat down Raylee was trembling but smiling shyly.

"Neat story!"

A bell rang somewhere.

"Can it be that time already?" Ms. Grinby looked at the full moon-faced wall clock. "Why it is! Time to go home. I hope everyone had a nice party—and remember! Don't eat too much candy!"

A small hand waved anxiously at her from the center of the room.

"Yes, Cleo?"

Cleo, red-freckled face and blue eyes, stood up. "Can I please tell the class, Ms. Grinby, that I'm having a party tonight, and that I can invite everyone in the class?"

Ms. Grinby smiled. "You may, Cleo, but there doesn't seem to be much left to tell, does there?"

"Well," said Cleo, smiling at Raylee, "only that everyone's invited."

Raylee smiled back and looked quickly away.

Books and candy bags were crumpled together, and all ran out under crepe paper, cats, and ghouls, under the watchful eyes of the jack-o'-lantern, into darkening afternoon.

A black and orange night.

Here came a black cat walking on two legs; there two percale sheet ghosts trailing paper bags with handles; here again a miniature man from outer space. The wind was up: leaves whipped along the serpentine sidewalk like racing cars. There was an apple-crisp smell in the air, an icicle down your spine, here-comes-winter chill. Pumpkins everywhere, and a half-harvest moon playing coyly with wisps of high shadowy clouds. A thousand dull yellow night-lights winked through breezy trees on a thousand festooned porches. A constant ringing of doorbells, the wash of goblin traffic: they traveled in twos, threes, or fours, these monsters, held together by Halloween gravity. Groups passed other groups, just coming up, or coming down, stairs, made faces, and said "Boo!" There were a million "Boo!" greetings this night.

On one particular porch in all that thousand, goblins went up the steps but did not come down again. The door opened a crack, then wider, and groups of ghosts, wizards, and spooks, instead of waiting patiently for a toss in a bag and then turning away, slipped through into the house and disappeared from the night. Disappeared into another night.

Through the hallway and kitchen and down another set of stairs to the cellar. A cellar transformed. A cellar of hell, this cellar—charcoal-pit black with eerie dim red lanterns glowing out of odd corners and cracks. An Edgar Allen Poe cellar—and there hung his portrait over the apple-bobbing tub, raven-bedecked and with a cracked grin under those dark-pool eyes and that ponderous brow. This was his cellar, to be sure, a Masque of the Red Death cellar.

And here were the Poe-people; miniature versions of his evil creatures: enough hideous beasts to fill page after page and all shrunk down to child size. Devils galore, with papier-mâché masks, and hooves and tails of red rope, each with a crimson fork on the end; a gaggle of poke-hole ghosts; a mechanical cardboard man; two wolfmen; four vampires with wax teeth; one mummy; one ten-tentacled sea beast; three Frankenstein monsters; one Bride of same; and one monster of indefinite shape and design, something like a jellyfish made of plastic bags.

And Raylee.

Raylee came last; was last to slip silently and trembling through the portal of the yellow front door; was last to slip even more silently down the creaking cellar steps to the Poe-cellar below. She came cat silent and cautious, holding her breath—was indeed dressed cat-like, in whiskered mask, black tights, and black rope tail, all black to mix silently with the black basement.

No one saw her come in; only the black-beetle eyes of Poe over the apple tub noted her arrival.

The apple tub was well in use by now, a host of devils, ghosts, and Frankensteins clamoring around it and eagerly awaiting a turn at its game under Poe's watchful eyes.

"I got one!" shouted one red devil, triumphantly pulling a glossy apple from his mouth; no devil mask here, but a red-painted face, red and dripping from the tub's water. It was Peter, one of the taunting boys in Raylee's class.

Raylee hung back in the shadows.

"I got one!" shouted a Frankenstein monster.

"And me!" from his Bride. Two crisp red apples were held aloft for Poe's inspection.

"And me!" "And me!" shouted Draculas, hunchbacks, little green men.

Spooks and wolfmen shouted too.

One apple left.

"Who hasn't tried yet?" cried Cleo, resplendent in witch's garb. She was a miniature Ms. Grinby. She leaned her broom against the tub, called for attention.

"Who hasn't tried?"

Raylee tried to sink into the shadows' protection but could not. A deeper darkness was what she needed; she was spotted.

"Raylee! Raylee!" shouted Cleo. "Come get your apple!" It was a singsong, as Raylee held her hands out, apple-less, and stepped into the circle of ghouls.

She was terrified. She trembled so hard she could not hold her hands still on the side of the metal tub as she leaned over it. She wanted to bolt from the room, up the stairs and out through the yellow doorway into the dark night.

"Dunk! Dunk!" the ghoul circle began to chant, impatient.

Raylee stared down into the water, saw her dark reflection and Poe's mingled by the ripples of the bobbing apple.

"Dunk! Dunk!" the circle chanted.

Raylee pushed herself from the reflection, stared at the faces surrounding her. "I don't want to!"

"Dunk!..." the chant faded.

Two dozen cool eyes surveyed her behind eye-holes, weighed her dispassionately in the sharp light of peer pressure. There were ghouls behind those ghoulish masks and eyes.

Someone hissed a laugh as the circle tightened around Raylee. Like a battered leaf with its stem caught under a rock in a high wind, she trembled.

Cleo, alone outside the circle, stepped quickly into it to protect her. She held out her hands. "Raylee—" she began soothingly.

The circle tightened still more, undaunted. Above them all, Poe's eyes in the low crimson light seemed to brighten with anticipation.

Desperate, Cleo suddenly said, "Raylee, tell us a story."

A moment of tension, and then a relaxed "Ah" from the circle.

Raylee shivered.

"Yes, tell us a story!"

This from someone in the suffocating circle, a wolfman, or perhaps a vampire.

"No, please," Raylee begged. Her cat whiskers and cat tail shivered. "I don't want to!"

"Story! Story!" the circle began to chant.

"No, please!"

"Tell us the rest of the other story!"

This from Peter in the back of the circle. A low voice, a command. Another "Ah."

"Yes, tell us!"

Raylee held her hands to her ears. "No!"

"Tell us!"

"No!"

"Tell us now!"

"I thought you were my friends!" Raylee threw her cat-paw hands out at them, her eyes begging.

"Tell us."

A stifled cry escaped Raylee's throat.

Instinctively, the circle widened. They knew she would tell now. They had commanded her. To be one of them, she would do what they told her to do.

Cleo stepped helplessly back into the circle, leaving Raylee under Poe's twisted grin.

Raylee stood alone shivering for a moment. Then, her eyes on the floor, she ceased trembling, became very calm and still. There was a moment of silence. In the dark basement, all that could be heard was the snap of a candle in a far corner and the slapping of water against the lone apple in the tub behind her. When she looked up her eyes were dull, her voice quiet-calm.

She began to speak.

"They took Pumpkin Head away after that, and they put him in a place with crazy people in it. There was screaming all day and night. Someone was always screaming, or hitting his head against the wall, or crying all the time. Pumpkin Head was very lonely, and very scared.

"But Pumpkin Head's parents loved him more than he ever knew. They decided they couldn't let him stay in that place any longer. So they made a plan, a quiet plan.

"One day, when they went to visit him, they dressed him up in a disguise and carried him away. They carried him far away where no one would ever look for him, all the way across the country. They hid him, and kept him disguised while they tried to find some way to help him. And after a long search, they found a doctor.

"And the doctor did magical things. He worked for two years on Pumpkin Head, on his face and on his body. He cut into Pumpkin Head's face, and changed it. With plastic, he made it into a real face. He changed the rest of Pumpkin Head's head too, and gave him real hair. And he changed Pumpkin Head's body.

"Pumpkin Head's parents paid the doctor a lot of money, and the doctor did the work of a genius.

"He changed Pumpkin Head completely."

Raylee paused, and a light came into her dull eyes. The circle, and Poe above them, waited with indrawn breath.

Waited to say "Ah."

"He changed Pumpkin Head into a little girl."

Breath was pulled back deeper, or let out in little gasps.

The light grew in Raylee's eyes.

"There were things that Pumpkin Head, now not Pumpkin Head any more, had to do to be a girl. He had to be careful how he dressed, and how he acted. He had to be careful how he talked, and he always had to be calm. For his face was really just a wonderful plastic one. The real Pumpkin Head was still inside, locked in, waiting to come out."

Raylee looked up at them, and her voice suddenly became something different. Hard and rasping.

Her eyes were stoked coals.

"All he ever wanted was friends."

Her cat mask fell away. Her little girl face became soft and bloated and began to grow as if someone were blowing up a balloon inside her. Her hair began to pull into the scalp, forming a circled knot at the top. Creases appeared up and down her face.

With a sickening, rubber-inflated sound, the sound of a melon breaking, Raylee's head burst open to its true shape. Her eyes, ears, and nose became soft orange triangles, her mouth a lazy, grinning crescent. She began to breathe with harsh effort, and her voice became a sharp, wheezing lisp.

"He only wanted friends."

Slowly, with care, Raylee reached down into her costume for what lay hidden there.

She drew it out.

In the black cellar, under Poe's approving glare, there were screams.

"My lunch and dinner," she said, "my dinner and breakfast."

Little Selene shivered. Silent and cold, the toy pumpkin lay on the living room floor beside her.

There the toybox loomed, a gaping rectangular mouth full of night.

"Go on," the Toyman urged, as she bent her head over the box once more.

Before she could reach in, something leapt out onto the floor beside her.

Two somethings—miniature men: one furtive, drawing back within its own cape; the other stiff, awkward, dressed in rags as it stilt-stepped toward her....

The Man With Legs

"I don't believe you."
"You must."
"I don't."
"You will."

The proof, Nellie said, was a bus trip away.

"I have the fare," said Willie, his eyes brightening, "and I'll pay our way, and I don't believe you, and I'll make you say he isn't there."

"He is."

"Prove it."

"Only one way."

"One way," Willie sang. "One way," he said again, rolling the words over his tongue, around his lips, breathing them moist into the air.

Nellie's eyes were shadowed against his younger ones.

"I'll prove it," she said, unsmiling.

"You will," Willie echoed.

After Willie went off to the bathroom (he *always* had to go to the bathroom) they set off surreptitiously. Mounting thick winter coats and mufflers, thick steamy mittens and black shiny boots, they sneaked from the house by the back door. Mother would be in the front, in the warm light of the television, watching her shows.

"We have two hours," Willie said, in a tone that hinted it made no difference how much time they had, their quest was so foolish.

"Plenty of time," Nellie answered.

The Saturday bus was late. They waited at the second stop from the house so Mother or one of her friends wouldn't see them. Willie fingered the piggy bank in his pocket, turning open the tab that would release the money within, then turning it closed again. He stamped his feet in the cold. Nellie stood rigid, her shiny blue ski parka giving her the proportions of a snowman. Her eyes were squeezed to a squint by the hood, which she had tied tight around her face, and she avoided Willie's eyes.

"He's not there," Willie said in a slow, irritating voice.

"He *is*," Nellie replied through clenched teeth.

"It was only a dream."

"I saw him when we went by in the school bus yesterday," Nellie replied sharply. "I saw him as plain as the lips on your mouth. He was standing on the porch of his house, and he looked at me as the bus went by."

"You dreamed it."

"Didn't."

"You'll never find the house."

"I marked it in my mind."

"'Nuff said."

She turned to hit him, but her bulky swing made her miss. That only made Willie grin.

"Does. Not. Exist," he said, waving his hands at her in a taunting way.

She scooped up snow and heaved it awkwardly at him.

"You'll see plenty."

They stood silent in the snow, waiting for the bus, slapping at their bodies. The temperature had dipped. The light was bright off the crusted snow; if they hadn't liked snow so much it would have hurt their eyes.

"I don't believe you," Willie said.

At that moment the bus came.

They climbed on huffing, and Willie broke open his bank, spilling the change into his palm. They had just enough. He held back a quarter a moment, scaring Nellie into thinking there wasn't enough, and then dropped it into the receptacle, smiling at the driver. The driver didn't smile back. They moved to the middle of the bus, choosing two seats on what Nellie said was the "right" side.

"Why not the other side? We're not going to see the house anyway."

"Sit," Nellie said.

The bus was warm. They contented themselves by watching the patterns of snow outside. There were snow valleys and peaks and stiff, hard drifts of white that sloped up the sides of buildings and stayed there. Willie watched the passing houses, dreamlike in their frosting; he enjoyed especially the upside-down ice-cream-cone icicles that hung frozen from all corners, some dipping to just touch the drifts below.

"Brrr," Nellie said, looking at the same scene and at the ring of frost around the bus window itself.

"It's beautiful," Willie sighed, turning to frown at her.

"Brrr," she said again, challenging him. "You're just too young to know how cold it is."

He shrugged and turned back, admiring the rainbow sheen of ice on a line of row houses. In his mind, all the world became a snowball, an ice shell four inches deep made of snowmen and newspaper delivery boys in parkas and ski boots.

"There it is," Nellie said suddenly, giving him a hard shove. "That's it."

Willie looked along her finger, out past the tip, through the ice-free hole in the window to the spot she indicated.

"I still don't believe you," he said, but his voice was a whisper and he knew he was lying.

There lay a house different from the others, set alone on a small lot with space on either side. Though surrounded by row houses, it stood squarely out. It looked like a boarding house, blocklike and looming, its windows making a face and its porch, stretching from end to end, making a mouth. The house stood off the ground on stilts and, in the snow, looked like a brooding, sly white spider.

"I'll make you believe me," Nellie said. She was already reaching for the pull-cord to let them off the bus when Willie's hand reached for hers. He wanted to stop her. He wanted to stay on the warm bus and look at the frosty world outside and then take it around the circle of its route back to his own house and get off. Then he wanted to make a quick snow fort and get inside in time for supper.

"I believe you, let's go home," he said.

Nellie stood, smiling a smirk down at him.

"I told you it was real."

"You're older than me," Willie said in answer.

"I know," she said, pulling the cord and beginning to walk up the aisle as the bus pulled to a puffing halt at the curb.

He pulled on his mitten, which he had taken off to empty his bank and which had swung loose on its tie to his snowsuit cuff, and ran after her as her head bobbed out of sight down the steps of the exit.

They stood alone at the corner as the bus coughed away.

The afternoon was deathly still. Even the noise of a car with clanking chains on its wheels would have disturbed the Universe at this moment, and both of them knew in their hearts that no such car would come by. Even the frozen telephone wires stood still, the breeze that had whistled them all day quieting in respect.

"Let's go," Nellie said, stepping into the street. Her foot made an agreeable crunch.

Willie stepped hesitantly after her.

They crossed the street hand in hand, and only then, when they stood on the opposite curb in front of the white spider house, did the world begin to turn again.

A car with chains on its wheels churned by.

"I told you I believe you," Willie said, trying to put his hand back into hers.

She wouldn't take it.

"But I don't know if I believe myself," she said tentatively.

They crunched up the porch steps, which creaked woodenly, even under their coating of ice. Someone had salted the steps liberally, and their boots gripped so well on them that Willie imagined that hands had grown up out of the wood and were pulling his boots up, plank by plank.

When they reached the top step Nellie pointed.

"That was where I saw him," she said, "right in front of that window next to the door."

"I . . . don't know," Willie aid.

She reached for the bell, and this time his found hers first and held it tight.

"*Please.*"

She turned her eyes on him, and her eyes said, Tell me the reason, the only reason, why I should stop.

"Because I don't want to know," Willie said in a small sob.

"You do want to know," she said evenly. "And I have to."

Her hand slipped through his and hit the bell solidly.

Somewhere deep within the house a deep, deep chime sounded.

Dong. Dong.

Silence.

Nellie hit the bell again, longer this time, keeping her mitten on it.

Dong. Dong. Dong. Dong.

Deep within, footsteps.

Hesitating at first, the steps of someone unsure, and then firmer and more resolute.

They took a long time to reach the door, but Nellie and Willie waited.

Dong. Dong.

Nellie pulled her hand away from the bell.

The door, a narrow tooth in the house-spider's mouth, opened.

Someone stared out at them and said, "Yes?"

Nellie stumbled back, her eyes wide.

"Fa-" she began, faltering.

"-ther," Willie finished, his mouth hanging open.

Before them stood a young man with black tousled hair and a boyish expression on his open face. His mouth was half-smiling, ready for anything. There was a faint tobacco smell about him and about his flannel shirt. He wore suspenders.

"Pardon me?" he said, a look of bemusement crossing his features.

"I, you—" Willie began.

"*Father,*" Nellie stated simply.

The man's eyebrows went up, but the smile did not leave his lips.

"What she means is, we *thought* you were our father," Willie said. He took his sister's hand, started to pull her back down the porch steps.

Nellie's feet resisted in the snow.

"*No,*" she said. "I was right." She turned back to the man in the doorway. "You're our father."

"Oh? Can that be possible?" The man was staring down past their faces, at their rubber boots.

"Can it?" Nellie said, faltering. She stood with her hands at her side, suddenly becoming conscious that they were hands and that she must do something with them. She put them into her pockets.

"Mother told us you died," Willie blurted out.

The man considered for a moment, then opened the door wider.

"Come in out of the cold," he said.

Nellie began to tramp her feet on the mat, but Willie held back.

"I really didn't think it could be you," Willie said, mostly to himself.

"Come in," the man said softly.

There was the sound of him closing the door behind them with a chilly whoosh, and then the warm of the house began to seep in. It was almost too warm.

"Into the living room," he said, moving in front of them.

It was now that Willie saw his limp. He moved stiffly, like a man on stilts, and though the expression on his face didn't seem to change, Willie could sense an effort behind it, a grunt held back at each step.

"Sit down," the man offered. They settled into a huge green sofa that gobbled them up halfway in oversoft cushions. "Take your coats off." The man sat on a stiff-back chair, pulling it up opposite them across the polished floor. He lowered himself onto it with strain. A fire, a large fire, burned off to their right, and the room was dark but for its amber light and the hint of blue snow-illumination that seeped in from the wide window by the front door.

Neither moved to take off their coats.

"We have to get back on the bus soon," Nellie explained. She wouldn't take her eyes off him. "She told us you died."

"Did she," the man said, meeting her eyes and holding them. "That's interesting." The smile softened around his mouth, making him look even more like a boy.

"Were you hurt in a train wreck," Willie said tactlessly. "Is that why you limp?"

The man's eyes darted to the floor before rising to meet his.

"No," he said simply. His eyes lingered on Willie's legs before moving back to Nellie.

"He was too young to remember when it happened," she explained. "But I remember. They all said you were killed when the train you were on missed a signal and hit the back of another train. They . . . said your legs had been cut off."

"Is that what they said?"

"Yes."

"I suppose they were wrong then."

"*Father,*" Nellie breathed, trying the word on.

The man nodded slowly in answer.

"How long have you been hiding?" said Willie. He was beginning to grow uncomfortable on the couch, and unzipped his parka halfway. He still looked sullen.

"We can't stay long," Nellie scolded, "at least not this time."

The man smiled.

"How long hiding?" Willie insisted.

The man drew his breath in and considered. "Let me see," he said. "It must be . . ." He counted on his fingers. "Five years."

As he said this his fingers tapped lightly on his legs.

"Why?" Nellie said. "Why did you have to hide?"

"I had to go away." He suddenly slapped his knees, making as if to get up. "Why don't I get us some hot chocolate at least? You must still be cold. We can talk more then."

"We really have to go soon."

"*Please?*" The pleading in his voice was startling, it came so sudden.

"All right," Nellie said quickly. "We . . . really don't know you very well."

"That's true."

He got up with a nonfluid motion, gasping as he stood finally on his feet, using the back of his chair for support.

"Are you all right?" Nellie asked.

"Yes," he said. His eyes seemed glued to her foot and then he hoisted himself erect, like a straw man. "I'll be back in a moment."

He disappeared into the rear of the house.

"Do you believe me now?" Nellie said.

"He does look like the picture in Mother's bedroom," Willie admitted sulkily. "But I don't like him."

"I *do*." She overemphasized this last word. "He just hasn't seen us in a long time."

Willie rose. "I don't like the way he walks. Like a stiff man."

"Where are you going?"

"Bathroom," Willie stated.

"Wait till he comes back."

"If he's really Father, I can go to the bathroom."

"He has to be."

Willie moved off, shaking his head.

He quickly became lost. Going through the door the man had gone through, he found himself in a mazelike corridor unlike the rest of the house. Cracked green and white tiles covered the floor, and the walls were peeling with paint. One corridor led off to another, and another, and soon Willie found himself surrounded by branching passageways in an ever-increasing darkness; dim fireflylike bulbs overhead gave illumination.

Willie moved slowly, fingering the walls, until a sound down one corridor pulled him toward it.

A high, singing sound and, behind that, the sound of metal against metal.

Willie stopped before a door, eased it open a crack and peered in.

There were steps leading down, faintly lit, and an area below with more light spread around it.

Down there, someone was singing.

A happy voice—but like the sound a cat makes when you step on its tail accidentally.

The clashing metal stopped.

The singing stopped.

There was a grunt and the sound of something being lashed and tied, the whipping of ropes, and then footsteps.

Little, dancing footsteps, more grunting, and then steadier steps.

Someone was on the stairs.

Willie arched back around the doorway, leaning into the darkness.

After a long, long time, in which Willie counted twenty slow steps, the door was eased open in front of his face. It was closed, and Willie found himself staring at the back of the man who was Father. The man's flannel shirt was hiked up, and Willie could see a network of fine straps crisscrossing his back, pulled tight.

The man moved off toward the front of the house.

Willie counted to fifty and then emerged from the shadows. Holding his breath, he edged open the cellar door and peered down. The light was still on. He edged himself down two steps and crouched, cocking his head. There were no sounds in the cellar.

He went all the way down.

Gasped.

Though he knew she wasn't there, he called out involuntarily, "Oh, Nellie."

On the walls of the room, on every wall in the room, hanging on pegs, in rows, sticking out from boxes, piled in corners, were—

Legs.

There were hundreds, maybe thousands of pairs of legs. In all lengths and sizes, they were squatty and wrist-thin and beefy and babylike. Each was dressed appropriately, in pants and stockings, socks and shoes, ballerina slippers, bedroom slippers, Italian leather shoes or cordovan penny-loafers. Willie could almost see the rest of the people they should be attached to: bankers and bakers and newspaper delivery boys; shoe salesmen; funeral directors. There was a pair with big brown thick boots that looked like they belonged to the man who cleans sewers. There were two or three tap dancers. A gas station attendant. A janitor. All had straps at the top and fine webbings and clasps and snaps and thongs.

There was just about one pair of legs for anything you could imagine.

"Oh, Nellie," Willie breathed, wanting his sister to be there, to hold his hand.

The only other thing in the room besides legs was a small table in the far corner, laid out neatly under a low neon lamp which caught the clean white light off its racks of toothy blades, perfectly outlining them.

Saws. Racks and racks of long and sinewy saws, special bright silver ones that liked to do their work.

"Oh Nellie, Nellie," Willie whispered.

From above, a sound sounded.

A light step on the stair.

A sneaky step.

Holding his breath, Willie turned.

A face peeked under the stair at him, upside down.

"Nellie!"

"Shhh!"

She disappeared back up the stair. Willie heard the click of the closing door, and then she was down in front of him.

Willie began to pull her toward the walls of legs. "Nellie, he—"

"He told me," she said, hushing him. "He told me everything."

"Where is he?" Willie gasped.

"Upstairs." Her eyes got a sly look. "I told him the bus driver was Mother's boyfriend and that he'd be coming for us now unless someone waved him on."

"What are we going to do?" Willie said fearfully.

"He wants us to stay," Nellie said simply.

"No!"

"He's not bad, Willie. Most of his legs he dug up, or found on people who were already dead."

"But—"

"If we stay, he says he'll be Father most of the time. I want him to be Father."

"But Nellie—"

"I *need* that, Willie. Just like he needs to be the people whose legs he puts on."

"I want to go home! I don't want him!"

Trembling, Willie grabbed his sister round the waist and hugged her.

On her back, beneath her hiked-up ski parka and blouse, Willie felt clasps and buckles and straps.

"*You!*" he cried, pushing her away.

"Yes," Nellie said icily. Willie saw now how stiffly she moved.

"*Nellie!*" Willie sobbed.

"I can be anything in this room," Nellie said, turning stiffly and stabbing her finger at the walls and boxes. "I can be the man who delivers flowers, the woman who gives piano lessons. I can be the mailman one morning, the insurance man who comes to your house the same night. Your teacher. Priest. Dentist." She loped toward the neon-lit workbench and lifted with a click from its rack a crystal-fine saw.

"I can be," Nellie said, rocking rigidly on her legs and tossing her diamond sawblade into the air, catching it nimbly, "a little girl. Or little boy."

Willie leaped for the stairs, landing painfully on his knees on the second step from the bottom. Scrambling up them on all fours, he hit the closed door at the top.

It wouldn't open.

Nellie came slowly up after him. There was a smile on her face that the real Nellie had never worn—an ancient smile, nothing even like the meanest smile she had put on when doing the meanest big-sister thing to him.

When she was two steps from him, Willie kicked out at her legs.

"Nooo!" she cried out, falling backward.

Dreamlike, Nellie's body split in two. The bottom half, two leaden appendages trailing snapped strings and wires at the top, clacked dully down the steps to land dead at the bottom.

The top half changed into something else. No longer Nellie, no longer anything human—mailman, priest, or dentist—it turned into a screaming white thing, a shriveled form that scooted down the stairs like an albino insect on two deformed hands.

"Noooooo!" it cooed, moving past the two legs at the bottom of the stair toward the back of the room.

Willie pushed desperately against the cellar door, and with a sudden jerk it opened. Once again he found himself in a maze. Green and white tiled floors assaulted his feet, trying to make him trip. He made turn after turn and found himself back in front of the cellar door. From below he heard a high keening scream that made his bones rattle. He stumbled on, pushing at the walls, trying to find a way out.

Abruptly, Willie found himself in the living room. The same hot fire roared in the fireplace, the same overstuffed olive furniture squatted in front of it.

He ran past, out to the front door.

There it was, and next to it the wide window to the outside

world. Where snow forts waited, and television, and dinner, and Mother.

Miraculously, as he looked, the bus chugged to a halt at the stop outside the house, waiting.

His hand was on the doorknob.

Pulling it open.

A foot stepped around him to press the door closed.

And a voice, the puffing voice of someone who had run very fast very quietly, the voice of someone he might have known, said, "Walk with me, won't you?"

The Spook Man

The Spook Man came to town.

Mothers and fathers locked their doors. Dogs hid in doghouses. Mailmen, ignoring their credo, left mail undelivered and went to bars or home to scolding wives. Schools closed up, locked and bolted their playground gates and sealed their windows. The grasses turned brown; even the weather changed, trading warmth for sudden chill and seeping sunshine for blustery blocks of gray-black clouds. The town tried to hide.

The Spook Man set up on the edge of a baseball field. His rolling home was a brooding many-wheeled thing in All-Souls' colors; those that chanced to look at it said it was as big as a house or as small as a horse-trailer. No two gave the same description. Some said it had a hundred windows, hung with black lace and with flowerpots filled with dead daisies; others described it as sad and shallow, a hobo's retreat. There were gables and then there weren't. A turret and then not. A porch with a jet-black rocking chair that vanished into thin air. A steeple that became nothing. Soon no one looked at it.

The waiting began. Children were locked in cellars, kept in tight bedrooms, told to glue themselves, literally, to television sets. Children were overfed, told to eat and keep their eyes off the windows. Most boarded up their windows, sealed them tight against the dim brown light that suffused everything and tried to leak in. Telephone games became the rule of the day: Susie called Billie called Carl called Maisie. Parents kept a watchful ear to see that games and tv were all that were talked about. Parents were everywhere children were; there was more parent-love exhibited than ever before, and this made Susie and Billie and Pete and Jerry and all the rest nervous.

The Spook Man waited.

Four houses kept four children locked up especially tight. Those were Harry and Brenda and Chubby and Larry—the four who lived, breathed, and ate monsters. When the new werewolf movie came out they were first on line; when the binding wire was snipped from the new eerie comics, they were hovering there with greedy eyes. No plastic creature model escaped them; no fright mask wasn't in their possession. Wax fangs covered their cavities; they walked in shuffling limps; spoke in Igor voices or baying howls.

Harry and Brenda and Chubby and Larry plotted. Each in their own house, with parents floating like balloons nearby, they used their Code.

"I loved the tv I saw last night," Harry told Brenda.

"We'll meet tonight to see the Spook Man," is what he meant.

"I ate a dozen cookies at one sitting yesterday," Chubby told Larry.

"Tonight the Spook Man," is what he said.

"Good books to read," is what Harry told them all.

"Ten-thirty by the playground gate," is what they knew.

As obedient as ever, the four watched television, read books and played games. They smiled like they always did. Then bedtime came, and the light went off, and each in turn climbed carefully out of pried-open windows.

They arrived in concert as a quarter-moon broke through the low sky. The clouds scudded, making the moon blink, and as it shone again, their eyes turned like pin-magnets on the Spook Man's place.

It was a house. This was no hobo's retreat. It was a house as sure as any of them lived in one. There were windows and a steeple and gables and a porch, and there was that jet-black rocking chair. It was magnificent and frightening. Victorian, Georgian, Tudor. Massive.

Bleak.

"Where are the wheels, how did it get there?" asked Chubby.

"I don't want to be here," said Larry.

"Come on," said Harry and Brenda at the same time.

There was only one door, a dark one of metal, and they crept up to it. The sky overhead played tricks, turned bright and dark and all the colors of a thunderstorm. A thunderstorm threatened, went away, came back. Went away.

They reached the door.

The door opened.

The Spook Man was there.

"Ah," he said, from somewhere beneath his cape. The cape fluttered, twirled, snapped. A face was revealed, quickly hidden. Powder-white, red-tinted, empty, sharp. Behind him a thousand fireflies seemed to hover, blinking Christmas tree colors. There were mirrors back there, and curtains, and strings of hanging beads that tinkled in the swirling bellows breeze. And other things lurking.

"Come into my ghost cellar," the Spook Man breathed at them. "Come see my ghosts and ghoulies. I have things that bump in the night and all day long. I have men with rubber faces. I have orange and black bats, and a hag with fingernails ten inches long. I have cats galore, with eyes so bright green and teeth so sharp you'll shudder. I have skeletons of white bone marble, bones that clack one against the other like graveside cymbals. There are red crisp Halloween apples with fang marks in them, dunked for by vampires. The vampires are there too, red and black and hidden in upper corners with the spiders. There is something that looks like jello that oozes when you speak to it; something else so horrible that I've left it unnamed. *You* can name it," he said, pointing one long and insubstantial finger into Chubby's jacket-covered belly. "Or you or you or you," he continued, pointing to them all. He pulled his finger back, making a steeple with all of his fingers and leaning down over it to hover, helicopterlike, above them. "Won't you *please* come in?"

"Sure we will," Harry blustered, pushing in front of the rest. He was brown, crisp haired, and bold, leader of the Four. "That's why we're here, isn't it?"

No one challenged him, but no one moved to follow either.

He mounted the short steps, passing under the Spook Man's cape. "Come on," he said.

They did.

"Excellent!" the Spook Man hissed, rolling his cape over each in turn like a bullfighter, counting each upon the head as he passed. He tapped Brenda twice, causing her to look at him from beneath her red hair.

"Twice knocks for red locks," the Spook Man said, smiling a grin that put wonderful goosepimply hands round her heart.

They found themselves in a black hallway, and when they looked back for guidance the Spook Man was gone. A black wall cutting off the outside world was in his place.

"He's just trying to scare us," Harry said, some of the bluster gone from his voice.

"D-doing a good job," said Larry, youngest and least true of the quartet.

"Ahh," was Harry's reply, and they proceeded.

They felt along the walls, and the walls were damp and slippery. They were crypt walls. They gave off the smell of underground, as underground they went in a gentle slope.

Suddenly, piling one on the other in the darkness, there was a door with a white face on it.

Larry screamed, and Brenda and Chubby and Harry merely shivered.

The face looked through them with the bottomless holes of its eyes.

And said, "Quiet."

It was a Marley face, a face cut from the cloth of ghosts. It shimmered in and out of vision, now sharp, now wavering, now sharp again. It asked them their business. When they didn't answer, it asked who had sent them.

"The Spook Man," Brenda said in a rush.

"The *Spook* Man," the face intoned.

The door melted away, showing a stairway of glowing green steps leading down into absolute black. There could have been a great and deep hole in the earth on either side of those steps, for all they could see. There were steps, and nothing else.

"Let's," Harry said tentatively, meekly, maybe-we-shouldn'tly, "go."

"No," breathed the other three, but again they followed.

The steps sang like chimes. Soon, as the four of them stepped down, a harplike mix of bells rang out. The tones became deeper as they sank into the darkness, turning by sneaky degrees to the middling screech of a stepped-on cat and then to the deep bellow of a funeral mass organ. The tones grew so low and thundering their stomachs rumbled. They looked back to see that the lights disappeared as they left them behind, and, to their horror, they found that along with the lights the steps disappeared too.

They found themselves at the bottom, huddled together, four bodies in the dark trying to fit into the space of one.

"I'm *scared*," Larry said.

"Don't be," Harry countered.

"Why not?" asked Chubby.

"Don't know," Harry admitted.

"Come on," said Brenda this time.

The darkness drifted before them. They sensed something just out of reach, taunting them, debating whether to move back or strike. Things ticked along the floor, brushed at their legs. Chubby felt a clawed thing grab his ankle and release it in the same movement. Dusty things brushed their faces. When they covered their faces, dusty things brushed their hands.

"I'm *scared!*" Larry repeated.

"You're supposed to be," Harry tried, as all around them it grew lighter.

They could see themselves now, their trembling arms and deliciously knocking knees. They could see each other's wild faces. With quick eyes they looked down for the crawling, drifting things, but saw nothing.

A door creaked open in front of them.

"I'm scared! I'm scared!" Larry screamed, turning to flee.

Something held him back. There was a wall a foot behind them moving up on them all the time, compelling them to move on. Larry scratched at it, beginning to cry. Harry and Chubby grabbed him, pulled him through the doorway after them.

A voice sounded, the Spook Man's voice, and Larry quieted immediately.

"Welcome to my cellar," it said.

Blackness descended then. And then a cacophony of lights. Fangs, radium-bright, flew at them from every corner. Deep and ponderous chains were dragged before them, around them. A cauldron made its appearance, bubbling and rolling green-hot liquid. It stirred itself, and then was stirred in turn by the vilest of witches—warts, cackle, and all. The cauldron evaporated, and then the witch was on her broom, coming straight at them and veering up and over at the last second in a steep angle. Skulls appeared at the four corners of the room, at headheight, and then skeletons winked into view below them. A skeletal rattle-dance commenced.

Harry and Chubby and Brenda danced with it. All hints of fear were gone, replaced by wild abandon. They danced like wood creatures, aping the gestures of their bony mates. They laughed.

Larry tried to laugh. Instead he made a compromise, painting his mouth with a horrible rictuslike smile that did little to hide his paralysis. He was paralyzed by fear; horrified by the revel of his wild friends. He wanted to be home, under the sheets and under layer on layer of patchwork quilt, listening to nothing but his own even breathing and the silence of his self-made night. He wanted Mother and Father to be out in the living room, further boarding the windows. He wanted Sis to be in the bedroom next door, sleeping safe with her lemon-yellow duck clasped under her sucking thumb. He wanted the tv to be on; the radio to be on; he wanted to play games, Scrabble and Parcheesi and hearts and rummy. He wanted, along with everyone else, the Spook Man to be gone.

Larry's grin grew wider.

The monsters came now.

Brenda and Harry and Chubby cheered. Here they all were, the models they had built and the comics they had collected come to life. They came in a dancing procession, out of the dark and back into it again. First Frankenstein, green, square, and parading false life, his arms frozen in front; then Dracula—no, *two* Draculas, snarling and circling each other like caged tigers, each seeking to snap redly at the other's neck. Mummies followed; then wolfmen howling at artificial moons that blinked on above; then sea creatures of all sorts, dripping seaweed and smelling of salt and rotting fish. Then the invaders from Space, each more tentacled and more colorful than the one preceding, with breathing apparatus and bulging eyes. There were bat-men and bat-women, giant insects galore, a gaggle of hairless beasts slowly diminishing in number as the gluttonous blob-creature behind them ate them off one at a time. There were men with pumpkin heads and men with fly heads, men with dogs' heads, men with no heads. Growling rabbits. Mammoth frogs. Titanic rats, some so crazed they were eating themselves. Armless, legless, eyeless things; things that crawled and snapped and clicked; slimy things; things that went *flit* and were gone before they could be identified. Creatures of the night. Creatures of every underground imagination.

Horrid things.

Chubby and Brenda and Harry celebrated each monster's passing. With each new fright their huzzahs grew. Here was every nightmare they had ever dreamed about served up like breakfast, the nastiest breakfast there ever was. The monsters came and went, invoking death and rot and damp earth.

Chubby suddenly stopped cheering.

As if a spell had broken, he looked at the faces of his three friends and found only on Larry's what he wanted to see.

"I don't think this is so much fun anymore," he said in a bare whisper.

Larry looked to him with hope; Harry and Brenda were lost in the procession of evil.

"I think I want to leave," Chubby said a little louder.

"I want to go home," Larry joined in without hesitation.

Harry and Brenda showed no interest in them.

"I don't want to be here!" Larry shouted above the flapping of batwings, the bellowing of the not-alive.

Brenda grabbed him and howled, demonlike, into his face.

Chubby momentarily lost himself again, becoming a wild thing. The three of them danced a witches' ring around Larry, screeching and tearing at their hair. The other monsters were gone. They formed a wider circle, and fairy lights, wisps of pale bright shooting stars, twirled round with them.

The terror burst out of Larry.

"I don't want to be here!" he screamed, "I never meant any of it, never believed any of it! I don't like spiders and toads and snakes—I'm scared of mice! I built monster models, but I built model cars and ships and planes too. I read *Creepy* and *Strange* and *Ghoul* and *Monster* comics but I also read *Archie* and *Superman*. I snuck out to the movies to see Westerns and funny movies, instead of always watching the Wolfman. I threw out the model guillotine you made me build; I like to collect coins and baseball cards and stamps." He was crying now. *"I don't even like the night-time—I'm afraid of the dark!"*

The wild dance stopped. Chubby stepped over with Larry, hung his head.

"Me," he muttered, "too."

Brenda and Harry stood, unmoved. There was a wild ruby gleam in their eyes; their faces seemed more elongated, their ears sharper edged.

"We want to go home!" Chubby and Larry begged.

A door opened in the darkness.

It was a rectangle cut out of nothing, leading to the outside night. There was the baseball field, there the chainlink fence they had climbed, a few bare trees all bathed in velvet moonlight.

Larry and Chubby ran through the door.

All around Brenda and Harry there was a booming laugh.

The Spook Man appeared.

His face was less indistinct now, yet still indescribable. He seemed less sinister, more of normal heights and painted in daytime colors.

"Two is more than I ever hope for," he said, almost gently. He made a cape motion at the two fleeing figures outside, now climbing like quick monkeys over the fence and away. "They won't be scared for long. In time it will be almost a pleasant memory for them, a visit to a funhouse."

He turned that elusive face on Brenda and Harry.

"Which is what this is—a funhouse—if you've the right stomach for it." His voice became both echoes and hushed. "Town to town, and hardly ever more than one. Many times none at all." His eyes, piercing, hooded, seemed to be searching for something in their faces, a beacon. "They really don't know me, all the little people in these little towns. They're afraid of me and my little family. But they don't know."

He leaned down over them, a midnight hawk looming over its brood or prey. "Little red and little black," he continued, looking from Brenda to Harry. "Are you ready to join my family? You saw them, all the goblins and fiends and ghosts and demons there are. Once all of them looked just like you, little pink or yellow or ebony people with creature model kits and monster magazines. But something breathed inside them, behind the ghoul costumes and playthings, something locked in the crypts of their human bodies and straining to get out. They loved monsters so much they wanted to *be* monsters. I gave them the chance. I called them—never took them, only called—away from their creature features and werewolf masks and horror novels, and gave them the chance to join their real family. The one that would make their lives complete. Only the true ones stay, of course. Here they breathe with their real lungs and fly with their real wings, cocooning into the beautiful little horrors they want to be."

He leaned even closer, his face becoming the shifting meadow of monstrous shapes, a nightmare triptych mirroring the life he offered. "So, little ones," he said, his voice echoing all around them as his cape flowed out to encircle, hold them fast to his world, "are you ready to become my tiny son, my baby daughter? Do you want to see how much you really love monsters?"

"*No!*"

Harry pushed out at the cape, ducking under its strong black wings and out through the doorway. Soon his feet made the chainlink fence jangle as his sneakers carried him up, over, and gone.

The Spook Man laughed softly. "Hardly ever more than one," he said, half to himself.

He turned slowly back to Brenda.

"And you, little crimson, have *you* made up your mind?"

Brenda made no answer.

The Spook Man laughed a booming laugh then, and the doorway to the world zipped shut, and the brothers and sisters of the night came from their caskets and damp niches and dusty tombs to meet their new sibling, the creature of teeth and claws and wild red eyes that danced before them.

Other toys flew, fell, jumped from shelves and spilled out: a dollhouse bed, a candy-filled cauldron, a rubber axe, a thing dry as tooth-grass and crackly as a drywood fire.

And: from far-off Christmas, a red glass ornament that roundly mirrored Selene's face as she stared wide-eyed into it...

Wish

Christmas.
A baby-blanket of snow enfolded the earth, nuzzled the streets. Great lips of snow hung from gutters, caps of snow topped mailboxes and lampposts.

Christmas.
Dark green fir trees stood on corners, heavy with ornaments and blinking bulbs, dusted with silver tinsel that hung from each branch like angels' hair. Great thick round wreaths, fat red bows under their chins, hung flat against each door. Telephone poles sprouted gold stars; more lights, round fat and bright, were strung from pole to pole in parallel lines. The air, clean and cold as huffing breath, smelled of snow, was white and heavy and fat with snow.

Christmas.
Christmas was here.
It was April.

Daisy and Timothy hid tight in the cellar. Tied and dusty, April surrounded them in fly-specked seed packets, boxes of impotent tulip bulbs, rows of limp hoes and shovels. Spring was captured and caged, pushed flat into the ground and frozen over, coffined tight and dead.

Above them, out in the world, they heard the bells. A cold wind hissed past. The cellar window shadowed over as something slid past on the street.

Ching-ching-ching.

They held their breaths.

Ching-ching.

The window was unshadowed; the hiss and bells moved away.

The bells faded to a distant rustle.

They breathed.

Timothy shook out a sob.

"Don't you touch me!" he bellowed when his sister put a hand on his shoulder. "It's your fault! All the rest are in that *place* because of you—don't you *touch* me!" He pushed himself farther back between two boxes marked "Beach Toys."

Outside, somewhere, a mechanical calliope began to play "Joy to the World."

Winter silence hung between them until Timothy said, "I'm sorry."

Daisy held her hand out to him, her eyes huge and lonely, haunted. He did nothing—but again when her fingers fell on his shoulder he recoiled.

"No! You wished it! It's your fault!"

Daisy hugged herself.

Timothy's face was taut with fright. "You said, 'I wish it was Christmas always! I wish this moment would last forever!'" He pointed an accusing hand at her. "I was there when you said it. By the fireplace, while we hung our stockings. I heard that voice too—*but I didn't listen to it!*" He pointed again. *"Why did you have to wish?"*

"I wish it was April! I wish it was spring!" Daisy screamed, standing up. An open carton of watermelon seeds, collected carefully by the two of them the previous summer, tilted and fell to the floor. Unborn watermelons scattered dryly everywhere. "It was just a voice, I don't know how it happened," she sobbed. *"I wish it was spring!"*

Nothing happened.

Outside the frosted cellar window, the calliope finished "Joy to the World" and went without pause into "Silver Bells."

"You wished it and now you can't unwish it!" Timothy railed. "That voice is gone and now it will always be Christmas!"

Daisy's face changed—she ignored his squirming protest when she clamped her hand to his arm.

"Listen!" she whispered fiercely.

"I won't! It's your fault!"

"Listen!"

Her wild, hopeful eyes made him listen.

He heard nothing for a moment. There was only Christmas winter out there—a far-off tinkly machine playing Supermarket carols, the sound of glass ornaments pinging gently against one another on outdoor trees and, somewhere distant, the sound of bells.

But then there was something else.

Warm.

High overhead.

Blue and yellow.

A bird.

Daisy and Timothy raced for the window. Daisy got there first, but Timothy muscled her away, using the pulled cuff of his flannel shirt to rub-melt the frost from a corner of the rectangular glass. He put his eye to the hole.

Listened.

Nothing; then—

Birdsong.

He looked back at his sister, who pulled him from his peephole and glued herself to it. After a moment—

"I see it!"

Mountain-high overhead, a dark speck circled questioningly.

It was not a Christmas bird. It had nothing to do with Christmas. It was a spring bird, seeking April places—green tree branches and brown moist ground with fat red worms in it. A sun yellow and tart-sweet as lemons. Mown grass with wet odors squeezed out of each blade. Brown-orange baseball diamonds and fresh-blacktopped playfields smelling of tar.

The bird whistled.

"April!" Timothy shouted.

He pulled frantically at the latch to the window, turning it aside and pulling the glass panel back with a winter groan. Cold air bit in at them. Snow brushed at their foreheads, danced and settled in their hair.

Timothy climbed out.

High up, whirling like a ball on a string, the bird cried.

"Yes! Yes! Spring!" Timothy yelled up at it.

Daisy climbed out beside him.

"You did it!" Timothy said happily. "You undid your wish!"

The cellar window snapped shut.

Something small plummeted.

Frozen white and silver, the bird fell into a soft death-coverlet of snow.

"It was a trick!" Timothy screamed. "What are we going to do?" He turned to the locked window, tried frantically to push it in. When he opened his mouth, puffs of frosted air came out with his words.

"We've got to get away!"

Timothy and Daisy looked to the horizon. A huge red ball was there, a second sun, an ornament a hundred stories high, and from it came the faint jangle of bells, the smooth snow-brushed sound of sleigh runners.

"We'll be brought to that place—we've got to get away!"

The sleigh bells, the glassy sound of sled-packed snow, grew toward them. Before Daisy's hands could find Timothy, could pull him against the side of the house, he tore away from her. The bells rose to a hungry clang; Daisy could almost hear them sing with pleasure.

Timothy's fading voice called back:

"Why did you listen to that voice...."

The bells grew very loud and then very soft, and moved away.

Christmas continued. In the sky, a few hearty snowflakes pirouetted and dropped. Tinsel shimmered on tree branches. The air stayed clean and cold, newly winterized. Balsam scent tickled the nostrils. Christmas lights glowed, blinked.

From the horizon, from the giant red Christmas ball, came a sound.

Bells.

Soft silver bells.

"No!" Daisy's feet carried her from the side of the house to the white-covered sidewalk. She left tiny white feet in a path behind her.

The bells belled.

Daisy ran.

The lazy bells followed her. Like a ghost's smoky hands, they reached out at her only to melt away and re-form. Daisy passed snow-white houses, with angels in the windows and mistletoe under the eaves.

Daisy stopped.

The bells hesitated. There came a tentative *ching*, followed by silence and then another *ching-ching*.

Daisy ran, her yellow hair flying.

The houses disappeared, replaced by a row of stores with jolly front windows and Christmas-treed displays. Lights blinked. Above one store a plastic Santa drawn by plastic reindeer rose, landed, rose, landed.

Ching-ching.

The library budded into view. White-coated brick, its crystal windows were filled with cutouts of Christmas trees and holly.

At the top of the steps, the doorway stood open.

Daisy climbed, entered.

Outside, the ghoul-bells chimed.

Ching-ching.

Ching-ching.

Ching.

She heard the smooth stop of sleigh-skis in the snow.

The library door loomed wide.

Someone stepped into it.

"Daisy?" a voice called coldly. It was a voice she knew.

"Daisy?" it spoke again. Icicles formed in the corners; snow sprinkled down from the ceiling. It was the voice that had spoken to her.

Daisy pushed past the empty librarian's desk, knocked over the silver Christmas tree on the counter. She dove under the tasseled red rope into the children's section. Bright book covers glared at her. Babar the elephant walked a tightrope, the bulb-like faces of Dr. Seuss characters grinned, Huckleberry Finn showed off his inviting raft to his hulking friend Jim. "I wish I could be with them," Daisy thought; but nothing happened.

Behind her, the voice, closer, called again in chilly sing-song:

"Daisy, Daisy, it's Christmas always!"

"No!" Daisy hissed to herself fiercely. She crawled under one stack of books that had been left to spill against a bookcase, making an arch. Behind it were more books—Hardy Boys and Nancy Drews, two *Treasure Islands*, one *Robinson Crusoe* tilted at an angle. Behind them a pile of *National Geographic* magazines, with color covers.

Daisy burrowed her way into the magazines, covered herself with books and periodicals, made a fort of the Hardy Boys with a fortress gate made of *The Wind in the Willows*.

Steps clacked closer against the polished oak floor.

"Where are you?" the cold voice sang.

"Christmas all the time!

"Always Christmas!

"Daisy . . ."

The footsteps ceased.

The Hardy Boys were lifted away.

"Daisy . . ."

A hard hand reached down to fall on her. She felt how death-cold he was. His suit was red ice; he wore a red cap at a jaunty angle.

His face was white, his ice-blue eyes were arctic circles filled with swirling frost.

"I wish it was spring! I wish it was April!"

"Christmas always," he said, smiling a sharp blue smile.

"I wish I could kill you!"

With her two small hands Daisy threw *The Wind in the Willows* up at him. A corner of the book hit his cold, smoky eye and he staggered back.

Miraculously, amazingly, he fell. There was a shatter like an icicle hitting the sidewalk. There was the *ching* of a million tiny bells.

He lay silent.

He lay...dead.

Daisy got up to see a dying blizzard blowing in his eyes. A cold blue hand lifted momentarily, reached towards her—and fell back, cracking up and down its length.

He dripped melting water.

Daisy breathed.

Outside, a bird sang.

Daisy crawled under the book arch, under the red tassel. She ran past the empty desk, the fallen silver tree, out the yawning door.

The sky was growing blue. A squirrel ran past. A blackbird dipped low, squawked and didn't fall.

It was April.

Spring.

Christmas was leaving the world.

Balsam scent grew sour and stale. The snow grew old-gray and slushy. Winter was old; the house lights, round wreaths, tinsel grew dim and left-out-too-long. In the middle of "Have Yourself a Merry—" the calliope ground to a halt.

At the horizon, the huge red ball was less shiny-bright.

His sleigh stood in front of the library. It was ice-white and red, lined with ice bells, pulled by ice reindeer. It shivered as Daisy climbed into it and snapped the reins.

"Take me to them," she said.

The sleigh shuddered into melting life.

Spring was exploding around her. They went over miles of white earth turning to green. The air was warm as hay. Fish leaped in blue-clear ponds, orange-yellow flowers burst from the ground, leaves generated spontaneously. Daisy wondered if, back in her cellar, watermelons were sprouting everywhere and hoes and shovels were dancing up the stairs to reach the loamy soil.

Beneath Daisy, the ice sleigh dripped into the ground. The soil drank it up—bells, reindeer and all. Daisy leaped from the last puddle of it, new green grass like springs pushing at her feet.

Over a short hill, touching the spring sky—and there was the red ball.

It was a blown-glass Christmas bulb halfway up the sky. Its glossy crimson was tarnishing. Winter rushed out the tiny door at the bottom, howling, eaten alive by spring. Daisy hugged herself as it blew past.

The dying snowstorm engulfed her, pulled her inside.

She sobbed at what was there.

The ball was filled with frozen Christmas. A *Nutcracker* Christmas tree, with a thousand presents underneath, filled the center of the orb. Its branches sagged. Lights were everywhere, winking out. And lining the walls all the way to the top, were frozen people keeping frozen Christmas.

A spidery white stairway wound up and around, and Daisy stepped onto it. There was the snap of melting ice. She looked in at each block, wiping warm tears of water away with her fingers. In one there was a man with a beard she knew who watered his lawn in the summer each Saturday, even if it rained. His beard was frozen now. He knelt before a Christmas tree, fitting it into its stand. There was a boy who delivered newspapers, caught removing a model airplane from its Christmas wrap. A woman was ice in her rocking chair, a mince pie cradled in her pot-holdered hands—the pie looked good enough to eat. A little girl made garlands out of popcorn. A mother and daughter exchanged Christmas cards.

At the end of the winding stair, at the very top, was—

Timothy.

Daisy gasped. Timothy stared out at her like wax. In his hand he held a limp, flat stocking; he bent to tack it to a rich-oiled mantel above a fireplace. A log fire burned snugly in the grate.

The ice shimmered and softened; Timothy moved.

Beside him, there was an empty space.

As Daisy reached out, the ice hardened again.

"Can't...unwish . . .," Timothy said before his mouth froze closed.

Outside, she heard the bells.

Winter came rushing back. The air glinted like clear cold crystal. The tarnished ball grew metal-shiny. On the Christmas tree, limp pine boughs stiffened, grew tall. Nearby, in the walls, in the air, the calliope played "God Rest Ye Merry, Gentlemen."

Ching-ching.

The sleigh moved over the snow with a sound like *wishhhhhhh*.

Ching.

Daisy looked up, and in the red metal glass above her, someone was reflected from far below.

Someone tall and white, with red-ice coat, blue-ice eyes, black-ice boots.

"Ice is water," he explained, in his voice; "water makes ice."

"I wished you were dead!" Daisy screamed.

He put his boot on the stair.

He climbed.

He stood before her.

As he finally put his cold hand on her; as she felt Christmas brighten and stiffen around her; as she felt the red velvet stocking caress her hands, and smelled the wood smoke from the fireplace, and felt Timothy's hand on her arm, telling her not to listen; as ice filled around her and hardened and froze her forever, she heard whispered close by, in a voice she now knew might have been any of a thousand cold or hot voices, a voice that might become any of a thousand cold or hot things, a laughing voice, a voice that was ancient, persistent and patient in its longing for release, "Make a wish."

Under My Bed

When Daddy says I'm bad, he puts me to bed and turns out the lights. He does that a lot, and I don't like it, but at least I've got somebody to talk to when I'm in here. Daddy thinks I'm alone, but there's a man under my bed.

He only comes up out of the trapdoor after the lights go out and Daddy shuts the door and goes away. The man says he doesn't like lights; he says he doesn't like Daddy much either, and I have to smile when he says that.

He lives somewhere down below the bed, though I'm not really sure where. The living room is downstairs below my bedroom, so he can't really live there or Daddy would see him; he must live in the little space underneath the floor.

He talks to me about things when I'm shut up in here because Daddy says I've been bad. Daddy says I've been bad a lot, every time I do something he doesn't like. Daddy doesn't smile a lot and I don't think he likes me very much anymore.

There was a time when Daddy did like me, but that was a long time ago, when Mommy was still here. I even remember Daddy picking me up and swinging me through the air, letting go and then catching me again, with a big smile on his face. He called me his "little Billy boy." He must have liked me, or he wouldn't have called me that. I even had friends then, and I remember Daddy taking me and all my friends to the ball game once. I spilled soda on myself, and Daddy didn't even get mad; he just smiled and said, "Let me give you a hand there, Billy boy," and helped me clean it up. I spilled soda on myself last week when Daddy's girl friend was here and I thought he was going to kill me.

I remember things began to change just about the time me and Pete Cochran became best friends. Pete's father worked at home, and Mommy used to come over to Pete's house to pick me up after we finished playing. Pete and I played super-heroes, or Huck Finn and Tom Sawyer, or the Hardy boys, and one of us would make believe he was in trouble and the other one would save him. It was fun, and we almost always played it at Pete's house.

But after Daddy and Mommy started fighting I couldn't go to Pete's house anymore, and then Pete couldn't come to mine, and after a while Daddy wouldn't let me go out at all. The fighting got worse and worse, and most of the time I stayed locked in my room. Daddy stopped calling me "Billy boy," and they both started putting me to bed a lot, sometimes in the middle of the day. I almost always had my pajamas on. I think they wanted to get rid of me so they could fight, and I used to lie in bed and listen to them yell at each other and sometimes throw things around. Once, the police came, and that was exciting, but otherwise it wasn't very good. They started to hit me sometimes, too. Mommy hit me once and told me that she and Daddy never wanted to have me, and that the only reason they had me was because Daddy thought it would keep him and Mommy together. She smelled like whiskey when she said it. "At least Pete Cochran's father knows what love is," she said.

After Mommy left, I asked Daddy if that meant that Mommy was Pete Cochran's mommy now instead of mine, but the way he looked at me made me never ask him that again. Things got very lonely after that, and I never went out and didn't see my friends anymore.

The man under my bed came out for the first time right after

Mommy left. A few nights I heard sounds down there, like mice or squirrels, and I hid under the covers. Then, one night after Daddy shut me up in here and it was real dark, I heard the trapdoor open and the man came out. I heard him puffing as he pulled himself out of the hole, and then he lay there for a while breathing hard. I was scared stiff and yelled for Daddy to come and when he did come and turned on the light the man was gone, back down in the hole; but as soon as Daddy turned out the light and left, the door opened again and the man pulled himself out. I yelled for Daddy to come back but he wouldn't, so I pulled the covers up over my head and listened through the mattress. I could hear him moving around down there. After a while I couldn't hear him moving, so I pulled one side of the sheets up over the edge of the bed and made a hole so I could listen out.

He started to talk to me then, and for a minute I was afraid since his voice sounded a little creepy, like squashing bugs; but he wasn't saying mean things so after a while I stopped being scared.

"I know how you feel, Billy," he said from down under the bed. "I'm on your side." Then we talked for a while about things I like to do, and what I don't like and things.

After that night, he climbed out of his door and lay down there talking to me every time I got put to bed. You could say he became my best friend, like Pete Cochran used to be. I could talk to him about anything at all. And he really understood how bad Daddy is to me, and he felt sorry for me about it. "I don't like your Daddy," he told me once.

I could imagine him down there lying on his back with his hands behind his head, staring up at the bottom of my bed like it was blue sky with clouds blowing across it. I sort of got the picture of him like Tom Sawyer, with blue jeans on and a straw in his mouth and freckles and a big smile. Even though he told me he didn't look like that and that he couldn't let me see him, the picture I got of him lying down there with freckles and grinning was so strong that I sneaked Daddy's flashlight under the covers with me one night and leaned down over the side of the bed and shone it on him. I had some trouble with the switch, though, and by the time I got it on he was pulling the trapdoor closed behind him. All I saw was his hand on the door rope and the top of his head; he didn't have any hair and was kind of wrinkly-looking. And I got the feeling he wasn't smiling. Then the switch went off and Daddy heard me moving around and came and took the flashlight away.

The man under the bed wouldn't come out for a week after that, and I realized just how lonely it was in the dark without him. I slept most of the time with the covers over my head; I was scared to be in the dark without him, even if he didn't look like Tom Sawyer.

But he did come back a couple of nights ago, just when I needed him most.

Daddy hit me that night, harder than he ever had before. He had his girlfriend home with him and he was drinking whiskey and I asked if I could watch the TV a little longer, and he hit me. Then he put me in my room and turned off the lights and said that if I made any noise he'd beat me some more. I lay under the covers, and I was crying, and then I heard the trapdoor squeak open, slowly, and I heard the man dragging himself out. He sounded tired, but when he started talking to me I could tell he wasn't mad at me anymore. He almost sounded happy. He said he was sorry Daddy hit me and that he wanted to help; he said he might even let me find the trapdoor. He stayed up with me almost all night, until I fell asleep. The next morning after he left I crawled under the bed and, sure enough, I could feel the edges where the door must be; I'd never been able to find them before, no matter how hard I tried. And last night he said Daddy would never hit me again. "Things are going to be all right, Billy boy," he said, and that made me feel warm all over, because I knew he was my friend.

Tonight Daddy's coming home late, and I got into bed by myself just like the man under the bed told me to. He told me to turn out the light and wait for Daddy to come home. He's been under the bed for more than an hour, telling me funny stories that make me laugh, about other kids' daddies and about the things that happened to them. Some of the things are real funny, like what happens in the cartoons I watch in the morning after Daddy goes to work. Even though I know what the man looks like, I still can't help thinking of him lying down there under my bed like Tom Sawyer, with his legs crossed and laughing, telling those funny stories.

It's late now, and I just heard Daddy come in. He's alone, but he sounds like he's been drinking whiskey again. He's bumping into things and cursing.

I can hear Daddy looking for me, since he thinks I'll still be up; he'll probably think of looking in my bedroom any minute. The man under the bed says to be quiet; he says he may even take Daddy through the trapdoor with him to where he lives. Wouldn't that make a funny story, he says, and he laughs. I laugh with him. He says he won't even let the light bother him this time, that he'll come right out from under the bed.

Daddy's outside my door now; I can hear him fumbling with the handle, trying to open it. He finally does, and now his hand is searching for the light switch. He finds it and turns it on, and he looks very surprised to see the two of us in bed, waiting for him.

Hi Daddy.

The Big House

Chattering with fear, squirrels ran down the boles of oaks. A deeper night fell cold as an ax. The sky roiled like freezing fire: orange, white, black; leaves fell deadened and whipped themselves, tiny tornadoes—then stopped in place, windless, and fell crackling to sidewalks. Sidewalks heaved and split, puffing concrete breath; the sky clapped its hands, booming deep and ominous thunder.

The last day of October.

Halloween.

Biff and Buff, costumed as clowns, red-nosed, white-faced, red-lipped, peaked-hatted and wide-eyed, flattened themselves shaking against a house front to either side of a rattling door. From within came shouting, the crash of fallen candy bowls; when Biff chanced a look through the door's neighboring window he saw the tatters of a ripped witch's costume fly by within and the air filled with candy corn and Milky Way bars. Furniture danced a St. Vitas dance, teacups in cupboards rattled like bones, the very floorboards curled and cracked, stepping up out of the floor before stomping back down again. The neighbors inside clung to whatever wasn't moving and each other; their little girl, costume-less, only the brim of her witch's hat still rimming her head, held to her mother who held to her father who held to the dog who gripped the hall rug howling. The rug rolled up and they all flew away, circling the room, still clutching.

Above the wind, above the greater howl of the night, Biff turned to Buff and shouted, "It has to be the Big House! We'll have to go there!"

Buff's eyes went wide; she gripped Biff's arm with a clutch like an iron vise. "No one goes there! I don't want to!"

"We have to try!" Biff answered, putting his mouth close to Buff's ear to be heard.

Buff turned frightened eyes from Biff to the night, which seemed to tumble in front of them; away from the porch trees swayed on the tips of their roots, bent one way and then back again. Pumpkins blew by, grinning, still winking from their candles within. Clouds were covered by darker clouds; the Moon, full and manly, seemed to throw his head back and laugh.

"It's out of control—we've got to go!" Biff said.

Buff, eyes frightened, turned at a sound from the house and saw the little girl, the brim of her witch's hat flattened against the window above her face, mouthing, "Help! Please save us from the Big House!" before the demon winds within whipped her away, parents and dog trailing behind, into deeper darkness and chaos.

Buff turned to Biff and nodded.

"We have to," she said.

The House was immediately visible from the street. Buff and Biff, bent like old beggars against the night's debris and whipping winds, clutching their trick-or-treat bags to their breasts, knew the direction and knew the sight. Up under the Moon it stood, on the highest hill, towering the tallest trees; it loomed over oaks older than the town itself, black and batwing-like, tall and wide and ponderous, made of heavy wood and stone. Black in the daytime and blacker at night; no flowers grew around it in summer, when even the oaks stayed leafless yet alive. Its windows were black glass; its door a hole of darkness, huge and rectangular, sharp-edged. At its roofline four gargoyles, blank-eyed, of black marble, guarded; two onyx lions, also eyeless, protected the entry. A wall of dark stone, with black iron gates topped by twin blind owls, encircled the House and kept it tight.

DON'T COME IN, a sign on one gate read.

DON'T, read the sign on the other.

The gate was locked with a lock as big as Buff's head.

Bent double against the wind, Biff and Buff climbed the long hill upward. Soon there was no pumpkin debris; the town lay behind them in the bowl of the valley, below the Big House and the surrounding smaller hills. They stopped to look back; saw house lights blinking on and off, telephone poles rattling, wires whipping, streets buckling, a counterclockwise dervishing of dead leaves and gourds, pumpkins smashed to pies, lawn figures (newspaper-stuffed ghosts, a headless horseman without his headless horse, a scarecrow scared, his straw body pulled to weeds) and the occasional caught trick-or-treater. Below the streets the ground earthquaked—and there came the lower sound of deeper things rising, booming up from the Earth's underground.

The far hills shook and trembled, prepared to be swallowed.

"We've got to hurry!" Biff said.

The Big House didn't breathe. Dead as the air around it, it loomed impenetrable.

DON'T COME IN.

DON'T.

No one ever had.

The owls stared down at them blindly.

"How do we get in?" Buff asked, shaking but not cold. She could hear herself speak here, and wished she couldn't. The air was still in the House's domain; still and dry as death.

"We'll climb," Biff said. "Give me a hand up."

Buff, still clutching her treat bag, cupped her hands and vaulted

Biff up as high as he could reach. His fingers brushed the beak of one blind owl, held for a moment.

With a yelp he let go.

"It bit me!" he protested, dropping to the ground.

Buff regarded the owl, which stood poised for flight, frozen.

"Nonsen—" she began.

The owl hooted, spread its wings as if stretching, took off in flapping flight to veer toward the house, where it disappeared into the darkness of the door.

After a moment, with a hoot of release, the other owl followed, after giving Buff and Biff an ominously blank-eyed stare.

There was a ponderous creaking sound.

The gates opened inward.

Biff, standing in awe, clutched Buff's hand.

"Should we—"

"We have to," Buff said, stepping forward, drawing the boy with her.

The gates shut behind them with a ponderous clang, and as they turned to regard this, they saw that the owls were once again in frozen position: though facing inward now, toward the house, staring down at them blankly.

Biff shivered, sure that one of them grinned.

Buff pulled him toward the house.

There were paving stones beneath their feet, so black they appeared empty. Buff thought she and Biff might drop at any moment into one of the seeming holes, though their feet continued suspended over each abyss.

Above them, gargoyles regarded them, turning their heads.

The onyx lions rippled their muscles, began to stretch tautly, attention focusing on the two intruders.

A rumble of roar began deep in the lions' stone bellies, trembled up toward their throats and opening jaws—black fangs glistened.

"Run forward!" Buff said.

They reached the porch, jumped steps as the lions swiped, heads shaking with rage; claws barely missing—

Then: Buff and Biff were inside, though the dark rectangle of door, the sharp-edged opening, into...

Dark.

Blacker than black. Biff felt Buff clutching, Buff felt Biff trembling. She knew if she reached down there was nothing beneath them now; knew there was nothing ahead or behind.

She reached slowly down, drawing Biff's hand with her.

There was no floor beneath them.

The two of them made simultaneous mewling sounds—

—then suddenly they were tumbling, falling, floating all at once, connected by handgrip only.

Lights blinked on, dim but still blinding.

Buff blinked, expected lions charging, gargoyles capering, owls flapping, claws extended—

They found themselves in a perfect front parlor on Halloween, strung with orange and black crepe. Cardboard skeletons on the walls were jointed into dancing poses; the largest of happily grinning cutout pumpkins were taped to the black windows; autumn leaves—red yellow and golden—were scattered artfully on the floor; straw broomsticks leaned in the corners; a straw-stuffed scarecrow stood guard in the center of the room, arms folded, head tilted, one button-eye missing to make a wink, lipstick smile under a smaller button nose, hat cocked jauntily...

...and guarding the largest candy bowl Biff and Buff had ever seen. A cauldron of candy it was, a huge open gourd bursting with gumdrops and twisted paper bags, candy bars of every wrapper color, popcorn balls and candy apples so sticky-shiny they hurt the eyes to look at them; and Neco wafers and jujubees, Atomic Fireballs and giant lollies shaped like Martian monsters (black and orange and *green*), crisp apples stuffed with crisper coins (quarters not pennies!), coupons for milkshakes and hamburgers, gum and more gum, tootsie rolls and pops of same, tiny raisin boxes, Mary Janes and Turkish Taffy, more popcorn balls, candy corn in *fifty* colors: yellow/white, orange/brown, brown/white, purple (!)/green (!), etc. etc.! Candy corn pumpkins with green sugar stems, candy pellets on paper rolls like checkout receipts, pink gum shredded like chewing tobacco, yellow and pink faux cigars, hard candy cigarettes in suspicious brands, candy in boxes, wrappers, cellophane, naked! Candy in every mixed color of the rainbow!

"Help yourself!" a voice invited; Buff saw the scarecrow wink its good button-eye to match its other and point with a rustle at the cauldron.

"It's...alive!" Biff cried.

The scarecrow became inert again; they cautiously approached and discovered that it was indeed stuffed with straw, unmoving, inanimate.

"*I said...help yourself!*" a deeper voice came from another part of the room; Buff and Biff tracked the ventriloquist's voice to one of the cardboard skeletons on the wall, which made its joints dance, its eyes glowing like coals and its jaw jabbering.

Then it stopped as a deeper voice yet, thrown from one of the broomsticks jumped up from its corner, a wide mouth stretching out from the top of its wooden handle. Eyes goggled, then disappeared; the splinter mouth, in mid-voice, was cut off: "Help—

"YOURSELF!"

The lowest of low voices spoke, a bass rumble that seemed to come from the floor itself, which quaked, throwing up leaves.

Biff and Buff quaked too.

"Let's get out of here!" Biff cried, and found no protest from his companion.

The floor steadied, and they ran for the door.

The basso-profundo voice bellowed from everywhere at once, a singsong: "Leave if you must; if you must all is lost."

The door flew open, showing them the town below.

Lightning bolted through the streets. Steam vented from heaving ground, which threatened to swallow houses whole. At the circumference of the town itself a gorge had appeared, a grinding moat, a line of demarcation as the town began to screw down into the depths of the earth.

"*Stop it! Stop it!*" Buff shouted, turning angrily toward the basso voice, which chuckled deeply.

"ONLY...YOU...CAN...STOP...IT...." the voice rumbled and laughed.

"*How?*" Buff pleaded.

The town was disappearing in a heaving, crying hiss of smoke and grinding rock.

"YOU...ALREADY...KNOW...."

"Buff!" Biff cried, "the town is gone!"

Buff saw only a roil of lightning filled smoke where once houses and streets and trees and parks had been.

"*No!*"

Buff ran to the cauldron, reached high and in, dug out a fistful of candy.

"Quick! Biff!" she shouted, and Biff joined her, following her example.

"Put it in your bag!"

Biff did as he was told, thrusting the candy bars and popcorn balls and tootsie rolls and Mary Janes and candy corn (purple/green! yellow/white!) into his trick-or-treat bag.

Buff did the same.

There was a groan from the deepest depths of the house, a satisfied, "AHHHHHHHHHHHHHHHHH...."

The house steadied.

The door slammed shut—

—with Biff and Buff on the outside. They stood on the porch and saw now that the dark of the door's opening really was a parlor door, a black one. The stone lions were stone only, sitting still and silent vigil.

Down below, as if by miracle, the town was back. Telephone poles stood tall, streets lay flat and houses were plumb. Trees dropped leaves as if nothing had happened. Pumpkins glowed in windows, and trick-or-treaters rang doorbells and laughed and filled their bags with treasures.

Biff and Buff rubbed their eyes, looked again.

Everything was back to normal.

"I can't believe it," said Buff.

"Neither can I," said Biff. He began to descend the steps, eyeing the lions with suspicion.

Buff held him fast.

"Wait!"

Questioning, Biff looked at her.

"I have to know why."

She turned back to the dark door, put her hand out even as Biff sought to hold her back.

The Big House reared up with a roar, shaking wide its door like a mouth. From within came fire and smoke. The parlor was gone, along with the cauldron and paper cutouts and straw man and broomsticks. In their place was a hole: deep and widening, with a sour green light and the deep boom of laughter.

Biff pulled Buff back; the lions reared up on their hind legs, leaped up the porch steps as the two children ducked under swiping paws.

Biff and Buff ran, nearly dropping their trick-or-treat bags; the gates were open but closing, the owls swooping, claws extended. At the house's four corners, gargoyles hooted, throwing down stones yanked from their own bodies.

Buff pushed Biff past an attacking owl and scooted out through the gate herself.

The gate clanged shut with a funereal sound.

With roaring in their ears and imagined pursuers behind, Biff and Buff continued to run.

They ran to normal Halloween in the town below.

And in the Big House, something said, as it settled down into its foundation, and threw up its blackened windows to the world, and closed its dark and sharp hole of a door, and froze its gargoyle guards in place at its four corners, and replaced its vicious owls with blank watchful eyes on top of its gates—something said, before settling back into its hole with satisfaction, "I just wanted to see what it was like to *play at it*."

Bogy

It was Old October, but no one was scared.

Pumpkins sat rotting on doorsteps. The air was cold but not crisp; apples wouldn't bob in tubs, and the trees held their wet green leaves and wouldn't let them fall, brown and whipping, to the ground. The Moon rose each night, but pale and quiet: a sick Man. Children were bored and lazy, their Halloween costumes—white plastic bone suits, coal-black witch cones and flapping ghost sheets—neatly folded in boxes on the top shelves of hall closets.

It was Old October, but there were no *Boos* in the air.

No silvery shudders at midnight.

No howling wolf-dogs, wax fangs, velvet capes.

No creaking doors, opening coffins, dropping spiders.

No Telltale hearts.

No clouds; no wind.

It was Old October and something was wrong.

Fear was fading from the world.

Here were four Bogy-boys, count 'em: Spook and Butch and Bill and Augie the new boy: four Bogy-boys more bored and tired and unghoulish than the rest. Here were four Bogy-boys in their Bogy Clubhouse, cheats to their name: surrounded by the implements of their fraternity collecting dust. Boxes of rubber things—worms and centipedes and snakes and green glowy doo-dads with eyes all over—went unused in one corner. Crepe paper, orange and black and orange again, dangled limply, half-hung from the dry rafters. Frankenstein boots went unshined; ghost tarps gray and unwashed; coffin nails rusted in their unopened boxes. Creature models sat half-finished on neglected workbenches, glue-smeared, forlorn; and, worst offense of all, a life-size mummy stood uncoiled, revealing a real, smiling human face, a plaster of Paris head of some long-forgotten celebrity revealed in all its obscene unfrightfulness.

"We've got to do something scary," Spook said to Butch, and Butch nodded lazily. Bill nodded too, his tall straight back against the cool but unclammy wall. He stretched and said, "Yes," but the word didn't quite make it to his lips and rolled back down his tongue to disappear somewhere in his throat.

Augie, the new boy, yawned.

Spook, lean and long with wild, uncombed hair, leader of the Club, began (though he wanted more than anything to just lie down, to nap, to yawn) to speak.

"We went down to the golf course and prayed for lightning to strike."

A slight, tiny, almost happy smile played around Butch's lips for a moment as he remembered two years before, when that Shriner almost got hit. The smile went lax.

"But there wasn't any lightning," he said. "There weren't even any dark *clouds*."

"We went up to the Old home to scare be-Jesus out of Miss Hammer," Bill went on, his voice climbing up from the chasm of his chest, slowly, the words falling to the cement floor as they left him. He was big and wide and bound someday for the army like his three brothers before him.

"And found that Miss Hammer passed away in April," Spook finished sadly, and then he continued weakly, as a pall of exhaustion overcame his words, "I don't know what else there is...."

They tried to move but could not. Even the comic books at their feet, the *Creepies* and *Scaries* and vintage *Eeries*, along with the single thumbed *Popular Photography* with the two frayed pages where artfully naked ladies against sand dunes were printed, seemed to sink deeper into the dry floor at their feet. The day outside, like high summer, was clear and still, bright as a photograph, unghastly. There was a high slim sliver of afternoon Moon that lost mightily to the renewed October Sun.

The day, the season, the battle—all were lost.

"Maybe," Augie, the new boy, said, his mouth forming a presleeping "O" as he spoke, "there's something wrong with Bogy."

A spark—small, incandescent as a candle before a star—danced up into his companions' eyes. Butch said, "Ah." Suddenly, Spook felt almost renewed. Bill pushed himself back up straight against the wall and flicked away the *Eerie* lying like a sleeping dog against his leg.

"Maybe," Butch said, his small eyes glinting in his face, "there is." Spook began to catch fire. Before the other three could move he was up on his feet, standing over them, his hands moving through his hair, pushing it up into straight static shock lengths, his eyes bug-bulbs, his legs twitching.

"What's the motto of the Bogy Club?" he said in a rallying cry.

Without pause, his companions shouted:

"To fright and scare

"No matter where!

"To scare and fright

"Day or night!"

Spook twirled away, throwing himself into the boxes around them: one from this, one from that: when he twirled back he was decked out head to toe in black and red—cape and hat, shoes and buttons, bushy eyebrows and white fang-teeth.

"So?" he shouted; and then he hissed, one word at a time, into their faces: "We'll-go-see-if-something's-wrong-with-Bogy!"

"Yes!" Butch and Bill cried.

"But—" Augie, the new boy, suddenly protested.

"What's the matter?" Spook said in his best Bela Lugosi voice, looming over Augie as the new boy tried to cover his face with a comic. "You believe all those stories we told you?" He pulled the comic away, and it fluttered like a bat into the far corner of the cellar. "You believe Bogy is the source of all fear? That his face is wild, and hairy, and wide-eyed; that his hands are long-nailed and dirty and creased deep with earth, with worms crawling over his knuckles and around his wrists—that his feet are covered with spiked boots and his mouth is cavernous and sharp-toothed? You believe that he howls at the Moon, swims in foul water? That he lives deep in the woods in a moldy hut? That he changes shape and throws his voice? That he can only eat what he kills, and that he only kills"—Spook lumbered around, brandishing an imaginary weapon, stopping abruptly before Augie to haul it high above his head and then bring it down *chop*—"with his long tall axe?" Spook brought his face so close to the new boy that his wax fangs filled the other boy's eyes. "You afraid that fear is fading because Bogy is dying, and that Bogy is dying because he hasn't eaten in so long—that he's so hungry he'd eat even *you*?"

"*No!*" Augie screamed.

"Maybe," Butch screamed, jumping up and moving his legs like a wild man, "you *should* be afraid!"

"Bogy!" Bill shouted, jumping up next to him and howling.

"But you said it was just a story!" Augie whined as they danced around him. "You told me he wasn't real!"

"Maybe we lied!" Spook whooped, and then they put masks and wild wigs and teeth and warts on Augie.

And then they sang their Bogy song:

"To fright and scare
"No matter where!
"To scare and fright
"Day or night!"

And then they dragged the new boy out, to find the inspiration for their Club.

Old October was tight as calcium in the bones of the town. They passed everyday things—soda fountains, the movie theater with "Fright Movie This Friday!" on its marquee in tired red letters that either dangled or were missing. They passed the school, with dusty, peel-taped, faded orange neglected pumpkin cutouts in the windows. They passed the mask shop, the well-known-to-them shopkeeper leaning in the doorway, threatening to doze off. Even Mad Lady Pinkerton, the town prophet, lay asleep under the slowly rotating barber pole, propped up like a scarecrow made of wet oats. She cocked a heavy eye at them as they passed, tried to raise a finger to exclaim something but instead fell back to sleep.

Even the dogs eyed them indolently.

Strange October tried to get at them. Once more they felt weak, drooped, lazy and unscared. They wanted to crawl back to the Clubhouse and sleep the whole season off.

"Fright and scare, scare and fright," Spook mumbled at their lead, but even he didn't believe it now.

"Fright and—" Butch began, but the rest was stifled by a yawn.

They pressed on.

In back of the old ball field, brown with October grass that even now looked ready for summer baseball, they passed into the outer reaches of the town. Now, abruptly, something woke within them. They passed an abandoned horse stable that threw long shadows out at them and seemed to creak louder from its leaning joints, just for them.

"Fright and scare, scare and fright," Spook tried again, and this time they began to believe it.

There was something present now—not strong, but getting stronger. With each step they took, their skins began to tingle and tiny icicles crawled up their backs.

Fear was returning.

"It's getting stronger as we get close to Bogy," Butch said mischievously, turning his eyes on the new boy. A delighted grin spread over his wax teeth.

"Maybe—" Augie began, turning around to look back toward the town, the safe, unscary town, but Bill cut him off.

"Look."

They looked at the wide high wall of woods in front of them, felt a dark and cold and creeping feeling when they looked at it, and then Spook said, "Wow."

"Maybe—" Augie tried again, but they took him by the arms as he held back, and, above them, as they melted into the woods, the Moon brightened and the Sun was truly gone.

There were *real* bats in here, not comic book bats, and other frightful things. There were real bats around them, big brown leathery hinged things with sharp teeth and red rats' eyes, and though they didn't see those wings or teeth or ruby eyes they knew they were there just the same. Then one of them *was* there, breaking out of the dark to slap at Bill's head and then wheel flapping away.

"Wow," Spook said.

They fell deeper into the woods. A heavier darkness came down upon them. Each stepped-on twig called out, "Here we come!" and they found themselves huddled together. Their knees began to knock; their teeth began, imperceptibly at first and then like wind-up novelties, to chatter. Butch laughed nervously. Spook said, again, "Wow," only some of the amusement had vanished from his voice.

There were other creatures around them now, just out of sight, lurking. The Bogy-boys knew they were there. There were big things— things with green seaweed or damp soil hanging off their limbs, things with big saucer eyes and big thick black boots and crimson-lined capes and pointed ears. *Things* that were too white or too black. *Things* that slithered along the ground and dove clacking from tree to tree—*things* with long snouts that liked to bore into soft flesh; *things* the Bogy Club had talked about, dreamed about, now saw in snatches.

Their footsteps, like cannon, boomed around them. Up ahead, the darkness shifted.

"I don't like this," Butch said, and this time Bill did not cut him off.

"You know, I wouldn't mind going back to town," Bill said, but as he turned Spook held him.

"Fright and scare, scare and fright," Spook pleaded.

For a long moment Bill hesitated, and then he nodded and they crept on.

The darkness was different now. It was velvet curtains enfolding them, not only making night but something deeper than night, more final. There was no Moon here; no promise of even a tired Sun rising the next morning. It was as if they had stepped into a rip in the fabric of night, behind which the real darkness crouched waiting.

Once again Bill turned to leave, and once again Spook had to restrain him.

"Fright and scare," he said.

The four boys stepped ahead.

"Forget fright and scare," Bill said suddenly, and then he was gone, running back to town.

The three remaining looked one to the other. Butch's feet began to shift of their own accord, back toward Bill. Spook held him fast. Augie, the new boy, merely trembled.

The darkness darkened even more, and then they burst into a shallow valley with stark, nude tree branches twined like bone-fingers above them. They stopped abruptly, as one, at the sight of a mad jumble of bark and tar shaped into a hut. It was a dark igloo with eyes—tilted to one side with two hollow ovals and a grinning mouth doorway. The ground around the hut was brushed clean of leaves, leaving the stark black forest floor gleaming like dried ebony mud.

"Bogy," Augie breathed.

In answer, something sounded within the hut, a low, crawling cough.

In a flash Butch was gone, moving as fast as his shaking legs could crash him through the woods, shedding his costume, cape and wax teeth on the way.

Spook looked at Butch's retreating frame, and then at the new boy, who was shaking from head to sneakers.

Again a cough came from within, lingering and low, gravelly as the packed earth around them.

"I thought we made him up but he's *real*," Spook said. His eyes behind his mask were wide and white and he began to turn away.

Just then there came a strangled weak sound from within the hut, and Augie's chattering voice said, "It sounds like he's dying."

Spook looked at the new boy, saw his own wild fright mirrored there and was ashamed. "Fright and scare," he said and he grabbed Augie's arm, high above the elbow and tight, and they stepped toward the doorway.

It was darker inside than out. Maybe it was a trick of the darkness: but one moment they were standing at the threshold of the door and the next they had been swallowed by that mouth and were inside.

Spook put his hand on the wall and there, leaning like a man with a pipe in his mouth and arms folded, was an axe handle a good four feet long and a blade sharp as the Sun's edge.

The cough came once more, off in a far corner, and when Spook looked in that corner something was there.

It was a bundle of rags. No, it wasn't that—it was a pile of clothing with something underneath. No, it wasn't that, either—it was a man, or something manlike, huddled or bent or collapsed, with arms and legs and trousers and coat attached here and there in the reasonably correct positions. Spook's eyes became used to this deep darkness, and now the man became more of a man: sitting with his back in the *V* of the corner, his legs pulled up to his chin and his arms, too long, they seemed, wrapped around his knees. His head was lowered.

The figure coughed once and then again—low, rattling sounds now, more far away than near.

"So hungry," the figure said, in a voice so weak and hoarse and artificial it sounded like something from a ventriloquist's dummy.

Spook edged closer.

"So," the figure said, "hungry."

"Fright and scare," Spook began, but even as he said this he knew the thing before him was dying. Around Spook, in the air and trees and soil, fear was truly fading away. He took another step forward and said, his voice filled almost with pity, "Bogy."

"All true," the thing before him said; its voice sounded even more hollow and false. "All the stories true. I'm the source of all fear. I howl at the Moon"—he made a sickly, sad try at a wail—"and swim in foul water. I live deep in the woods in a moldy hut. I . . ." The voice trailed off into a reedy gasp and then there was dry silence.

Around Spook, the fear was just about gone.

He reached out slowly, carefully, inch by inch, and put his hand on Bogy's shoulder. The thing before him crumbled into a pile of rags and empty spiked black boots.

"Fright and scare—" Spook began, but then he called, "Augie?"

There was only silence behind him.

"All true," Bogy's voice came, but not from the rags and empty boots.

It came from where Augie should be.

Like a stretching, waking cat, fear began to return. Shadows pushed out from the wall, making the room become long and sinister; things dropped down from the ceiling and the corners became places you wouldn't want to back into. Spook got the shivers, and now when he got them they only got stronger and wouldn't go away. Fear was growing, and very fast. He looked at the pile of Bogy's clothing and a cold hand clamped over his heart and he was more frightened and scared than he had ever been.

"Augie?" he called once more, not wanting to turn around.

"I change shape and throw my voice," the new boy's voice said, not hollow anymore, "and I kill with my axe and eat what I kill—*so hungry*."

Spook knew that fear would return to the town. He felt it radiating out from the hut, pushing out into the woods and beyond. Butch and Bill, wherever they were, would tremble in their boots. All the Halloween costumes would be yanked down from closet shelves; dogs would bay at the Moon, become mock wolves; and Mad Lady Pinkerton would rise from her sleep in front of the barber shop to cry doom upon all who passed.

Fear was back.

"Augie?" Spook called one final, desperate time, but he didn't turn around. He knew Augie was there. As he ran for the door he saw the monstrous shadow rising against the wall, saw the outline of huge clawed hands and heard the tread of monstrous feet. He heard the cavernous, sharp-toothed jaws behind him.

When he thought he was far enough away for his heart to beat slow and let him hesitate and turn, he saw the glint of the huge axe against the bursting bright October Moon.

The Corn Dolly

Come to me, lad.

The voice, a whispery October rattle, called to him at the edge of the forbidden field.

Corn is ripe, lad.

A thousand dry stalks ticked, one against the other. Traced in the stark gray-white of the suddenly-appearing moon, they appeared to the boy as the heads of so many thousand dried-corpse soldiers, snapping brokenly back and forth in the wind in stiff perfect ranks.

Behind and below him, his mother called.

"Robert!" she summoned, and her voice could not hide its anxious tone, "Supper is waiting!" She was fearfully looking up at the corn patch.

Invisible in the darkening light, Robert looked down the hill at her, feeling a momentary pang of sorrow for her tiny, bird-frightened figure outlined against the yellow rectangle of the open doorway. Around her, the sharp lines of the dark little house stood out. A trail of thin, sickly smoke pushed up from the thin chimney. Circling the cottage, a parched blanket of mown fields lay in every direction and sloped steeply up to Robert's feet.

Come see me.

The rattling whisper sounded behind him again.

He turned quickly toward it, staring into the line of cornstalks. A mixture of fear and awe kept him silent. It had taken him much of his ten years to get this close to this forbidden territory.

A slap of icy wind pushed into the rows, making them hiss.

"Robert!" his mother cried frantically, and the boy suddenly realized that she was making her way up the hillside and would see him.

He turned away, beginning to wind his way silently down the slope, circling away from his mother toward the road leading from town.

Behind him, the whisper sounded a last time.

Later, lad.

Above, the silver goblet moon dipped into a cloud.

With soup and bread came boldness.

His mother circled him like a hawk for an hour, probing with the talons of her questions. He told her he had been delayed in town with his friends; they had been playing late, watching the young women make the corn dollys for the Festival.

"Why don't we ever have a corn dolly in the house, momma?" Robert asked. It had not been the first time he had asked.

There was ice in her voice.

"Stay away from the corn, Robert. Stay away from those women, and everything to do with the Festival."

"But why? All my friends always go, and they call me names—"

"Because it's evil! We want nothing to do with the village and their pagan holidays." Robert saw that the hand that held her beads was trembling.

"But I *want* to go this year. Just to see what it's like, all my friends, to make a wish with a corn dolly—"

"Enough!" She was nearly shrieking now, and Robert was suddenly frightened of her.

For a moment she seemed to be staring into some unnamable pit where fires burned; but then her eyes shifted toward him, and the vision that had made her so frightening seemed to melt away. She abruptly reached out and brought Robert to her, pulling him tightly to her breast and rocking him back and forth. He could feel one of her tears drop onto his neck and then suddenly he was crying too, sorry for the way he had acted that had made her this way. He threw his arms around her.

"Oh, momma, I'm sorry...."

"Hush, Robert, it's all right." Her voice was soothing now. "I'm sorry, too."

"I would never do what you don't want me to. It's just that I was curious—"

"I know, I know. Perhaps someday you can see—" she shuddered as she said this "—but for now please do what I say. Please be a good boy." She held him away, looked down into his brown eyes. "It's very important, Robert. Please promise me you won't go near the corn. And that you'll forget about the corn dollys and the Festival."

He almost told her about the voice then, the crackly whisper that had called to him. He almost asked her if that was an evil thing.

"Yes, momma," he said.

She hugged him again. "You're a good boy, Robert."

Later, in bed, with his mother moving restlessly in the room next door, Robert opened his window a crack to feel the frosty breeze wash over him. The moon was low and large now, resting like an eerie white face on the crest of the corn patch. Tendrils of ghostly light played around the shifting stalks, and once again the image of a flank of sharp, thin soldiers formed: standing restlessly in place, feet rigid, their thin, ghoulish heads bobbing from side to side.

There was a rush of wind, and Robert thought he heard his name carried above it in a breath from the top of the hill; but then the wind was gone.

Corn!

The day before the Corn Festival, the village was made of string and wire. Wires flew across streets, into and out of windows, into dark alleyways where only the town drunks congregated, and out again. Up and down flagpoles, making Maypoles of them. Where there wasn't wire there was string. Spools of corn silk laced out above doorways, around house lamps and out across windowsills. Inside, the same. Some kitchens looked like spiderwebs, meshed fine with cornsilk. Where there wasn't cornsilk there were ribbons: green and yellow, especially yellow. A corsage of harvest corn hung on every doorway and on every lamppost. The meanest miser hung out a clutch of dried corn on his thickly paneled door. The meanest house sported an often grander version of the same— with want of plenty came pride. Girls played tag, thinking of the games they would play the next day festooned in corn garments. The Corn King and Corn Queen, chosen by lot the month before, but inevitably a handsome young man and comely young girl, readied their own raiments: rich, bright costumes adorned top to toe with givings of the corn plant: a necklace of corn buds for the Queen; earrings the same; her dainty crown of tiny interlaced corn dollys, her robes of woven cornsilk festooned with ribbons (again, yellow and green); corn slippers, corn dress, corn blouse; corn rings for her thin, regal fingers, corn bracelets for her slim wrists, one wispy bracelet for her ankle. The King dressed similarly, though everything in huskier scale: and for him, a thick woven staff to prove his royalty.

As the day wore on, activity only increased. Cider was pulled from casks and tested, then tested again by one of the town drunkards inching forth from his shadowy alley named above. The streets were swept clean; every house, hovel and manse alike, made spotless. Dogs were bathed, dressed in collars of corn; cats, mostly black, retreated warily to high shelves and pantry tops and coolly watched the preparations. A huge, full, artificial moon made of the finest carved woods and painted in colored paints made of corn meal a hundred years before, was dusted, waxed and hoisted noisily over the town clock in the square: the hands were remounted on its front and would tell time for the next day around the perimeter, crossing as they made their way over the inscrutable cutout eyes and slyly grinning cutout mouth of the Moonman. Children would try to loft corncakes up and into that mouth; those that did would be greeted not with scoldings but with gifts. Corn, dried and just picked, sprouted everywhere: from windows, from every available opening. In a matter of hours the town grew and ripened, waiting for the harvest of the next day which would assure the harvest of the next year.

The village sang with activity, and all day long Robert listened to the song from his room. His friends, all of them, were in the middle of those bright festivities; in his mind he was with them, watching their every move and step. They ran from house to house, trailing cornsilk streamers, and he imagined he was at their lead; they practiced on the Moon-clock's mouth, using rocks as missiles, and Robert ran away laughing with them when the constable chased them off. He hid with them in the mouths of dark alleyways, watching the drunkards with feigned contempt masking fascination. He led them past the bakery to try to steal an early bit of corn bread, fragrant and hot from the ovens. He tried, with them, to peek into the parlor where the Corn Queen tried on her robes, and argued with them later over whether or not they had seen anything—and, if they had, what it was they had seen. He played tag with them; danced in circles with them: sang with them; wrestled with them. Robert imagined all of this; and knew, as he heard the fainter sounds coming to him from his open window as twilight descended, that they were doing all this without him and that they were also making fun of him. There was always that distance between he and them at this time of year, a faint sense of accomplishment shared among themselves of which he was no part. They called his mother names, he knew. They called him names behind his back. They were his friends, and then again they were not.

His mother called him to supper, and there was silence.

"What is it, Robert?"

She knew.

He said nothing, only stared into his soup. His knuckles were white around his spoon and fork.

"Robert," she said in a fearful whisper, "I want to hear no more of it. After tomorrow it will be over."

"It will be over," he said sullenly, almost viciously, "and again we'll be laughed at. I'll be laughed at."

"Robert—"

"No, momma, it's true. They all laugh at me. Because you lock me in here all day long like an animal. There's only one day the whole year when the whole town is together, and we miss it. All the fun, and you lock me away. I never get to dance, or make a wish—"

"Stop it!"

"I won't!" The words shot out of him. He had never done this before; there was a new strength in him. He knew he was passing a signpost, and that he would never be a little boy again. "There's no reason for it, momma."

"It's evil."

"It's *not* evil! How could it be?"

"Pagan rites, Robert—there's nothing sacred about it. They act like animals, with their Festival, and their *wishing*."

She was shaking.

"*We* act like animals, momma. They only do it for tradition. It's all in fun."

"It's not all in fun!" She was hysterical. "You don't know! It goes back thousands of years; they've twisted it around so that it looks innocent. But it's not, Robert. They dress their town up, and make it all look like a game. It should have ended long ago." She was clutching her rosary as if it would be torn out of her hand.

"I'm going to the Festival tomorrow, momma."

It was a statement of fact, not a question.

"I forbid it." His mother's voice was trembling.

"I'm going." The strength of his words, the sureness of his conviction behind them, almost frightened him.

"Robert—"

"They call me bastard! Because you set us apart, because I have no father, they call me names! And you make it worse by not letting me be with them on the most important day of the year. I will go to the Festival tomorrow."

Suddenly her shoulders sagged. The rage was gone from her voice, and only desperation, and a growing resignation, remained. Robert saw with triumph, mixed with a kind of fear, that he had beaten her.

"We will go to the Corn Festival tomorrow, you and I, Robert." Her voice was nearly a whisper. "For a little while. Just for you to see. For your friends to see you. But you can't have a corn dolly, and we will not take part in their pagan wishing rite. Do you promise?"

Robert's heart leapt at the prospect of going to the Festival at all. "Yes, momma. I promise."

A ghost of a smile crawled onto her face for a moment, then quickly dissipated. "We'll show them that your mother is not such an ogre after all." The smile was replaced by a hardness: the rage was returning, held in check. Robert nearly pulled back under her eyes, nearly began to cry and ask for forgiveness for the things he had already said and gained.

"Only for a little while," his mother said, "and no corn dolly. Then we will come home, and you will stay in your room." She sighed heavily. "You've been bad, Robert. But I understand. I hope that...after tomorrow you will understand, too. We'll go just for a little while." That ghostly smile again. "We'll show them your mother isn't so bad. All right?"

"Yes, momma."

She turned away then, and Robert saw that she had pulled so hard at her rosary that it had broken.

A corn dolly for everyone.

The sun came up yellow, lighting a yellow town. Corn dollys were everywhere. Before dawn the children, Robert's friends, some of them, had risen to do their task. Creeping like so many spiders out of so many doorways, yawning with nightsleep and pull on sweaters as mothers looked on, tasting last spoonfuls of oatmeal and porridge and last slurps of wake-up tea, they came together in the town square. They were quiet at first, until sleep let them go, and then excitement began. They moved off, one giant clump of sweatered dust motes, to beneath the clock where the barrels waited. In the barrels, sacks, one sack for each to strap on.

No sack was opened, waiting for a signal. Silence reigned in the square. The moon clock moved its hands, too slowly to bear, toward six o'clock. Hands gripped the sides of sacks, waiting to tear them open. The hands moved a tick. Almost up and down but not quite. Another minute. Six o'clock! The moon face lit up as the first sunrays hit it.

A cheer went up from the children.

Sacks were ripped open.

Corn dollys spilled out.

In a flash, children were everywhere. And with them, yellow corn dollys. Each wire strung across each archway was hung with dollys; each door found one tacked to its knocker. They seemed to fly up into the air, they were hung so fast. The town was nearly drowned in them. Windows, carts, lamps, trees—nothing escaped ornamentation. Children became real spiders, climbed up the sides of buildings it seemed (though they actually stood on each other's backs), found their way into corners a cat couldn't reach.

In ten minutes the job was done.

The Corn Festival had started.

Dancing began at seven. There would be no stopping this day until the sun went down. There were no clouds in the sky; the air was so blue and chilled you could bite into it like an apple. Some tried, but found better luck with red apples, which were everywhere. Everything, the best of everything, was everywhere. The town had become a corn town, a Festival town.

Robert, up at dawn, had heard the distant shout in the village as the corn dollys went out. He ached to be with them, but satisfied himself with the knowledge that he would be with them later. There would be no laughing at him tomorrow. His mother, he knew, was in the next room, praying. He had heard her crying in the night, and had almost gone to her, almost told her that it was all right, he would listen to her and they did not have to go to the Festival in the morning. But something had held him back.

The hours wore away. He sat glued to the windowsill, his arms becoming numb from being propped up on it. The sun was high overhead now. He could hear his mother moving around in the next room. After making breakfast she had gone back in there, and he knew that when she came out they would go. The waiting was unbearable. Each shout that went up behind the hill, each cheer and cry, meant that something else was lost to him. That much more of the day and the Festival had dropped away from him; there would be that much less to talk about tomorrow and forever.

"I'm ready, Robert."

He turned, and saw that she had dressed in her finest dress. She was smiling, but Robert knew that the smile, behind her lipstick, had been painted on and that her eyes were wild with bright.

"We'll have a good time, momma."

She held his hand tightly, though he wanted to leap ahead shouting. As the hill curved away to reveal the town a shout went up in his throat. "Momma, it's beautiful!" He tried to pull away, but she held him tight.

The next hour flashed by in an instant. Robert saw a group of his friends and begged his mother to let him go to them. She did, after making him promise not to leave the square. But there was no need to leave the square. With a leap Robert was in the midst of them, their leader. They showed him everything. He sailed a corncake through the moon clock's mouth on the first try. He did the same on the second and third try. His friends agreed that he was the best they'd ever seen. They played Johnny-ride-the-pony, and Robert won. They played corn soccer, and he scored the first goal. They played trace-the-wire, trying to find the origin of a particularly tortuously-wound thread of corn silk, and Robert got there first.

They were beginning to play hide and seek when Robert heard his mother call.

He tried at first to ignore her; he knew her eyes had been on him every moment. But when she called again he turned to go. As he did so one of his friends called out to him, throwing something at him.

"Robert, your corn dolly!"

He caught something stiff and crackly, and looked down to see the little mass of dried cornstalk and corn silk staring up at him.

"See you tonight!" his friend called.

Robert held up his corn dolly in farewell, and as he did so he felt it pulled from his hand.

"Time to go, Robert."

"But Momma—"

"We talked about it yesterday," she said. "We've come to the Festival, as I promised, and now we must go home." She had tossed the corn dolly on the ground, trampling it with her foot, and was dragging him, with amazing strength, by the arm from the square.

"Momma, you're hurting me!"

"Robert, we must go home." Her eyes were the eyes of a wild person, and her grip tightened. Some of the revelers around them had stopped to watch silently.

"Momma, my corn dolly!"

At this her grip tightened even more, and she turned to look at him.

"Leave it!" she hissed. Once again, Robert saw fear behind her eyes. "I will not let you have it in the house. It is evil. And I'll hear no more of it!" Her voice had risen to a hysterical whine, only tempered by the looks of those around them.

Robert saw with shame that his friends had followed them and were standing, horrified, in a line, watching as he was pulled away.

"Momma, *please*—"

She struck him then, once across the mouth, and he gasped in pain. They had nearly reached the edge of the village, and Robert could see through the tears in his eyes the curve of the hill leading back to their house. At the top of the hill the corn patch, a tall yellow crewcut, sat in the lowering sun.

All at once Robert felt something pressed into his hand, and looked down to see a small corn dolly. The little girl who had passed it to him was already running, barefoot, to hide in the crowd of people that watched them from a short distance away; she looked back at him coyly from under her golden, dirty locks before disappearing behind two of his friends.

He quickly hid the dolly under his shirt and gave a short wave of thanks before his mother pulled him around the hill and the town was lost to view.

When they returned home she locked him in his room. For an hour he heard her crying and praying aloud, moving around the outer room and bumping into things as if she were mad. Then there was a short silence, before she knocked on the door to his room. For a quick moment Robert was frightened, thinking that perhaps she had lost her mind and would beat him; but when she came in her tears had been dried and she came to him, holding him tighter than she ever had before.

"Robert," she said, "I love you so much it hurts me. I didn't mean to hit you. Please believe me." She sobbed over him then, after a few moments pulling him back and looking into his face to see if the resentment and defiance he had shown was there again. But he had no heart to hurt her then, seeing the look of abject terror and loss in her face, and so he said that no, he was all right.

"I just wanted to see what it was like today, momma," he said quietly.

"I know, I know," she said, and then she pulled him to her again, and then went away, locking him in again.

"I still must punish you," she explained softly from behind the door, and then she was gone.

The moon had risen now, fat and white, over the cornfield. Through the crack in the window, Robert heard the festivities continuing in the village behind it.

Come to me, lad.

It came as a whisper.

The voice again, from the corn patch.

Corn is ripe, lad.

With effort, Robert edged the window up a little higher. Wind-chilled corn silk caught his face. In the village, behind the hill, a sudden bright light went on, and a sudden cheer erupted, and Robert knew that the Corn King and Queen had been officially crowned. The torches had been lit and the procession up to the cornfield had begun.

Corn is ripe, lad.

In a moment, the whisper was drowned by the singing of the procession.

And then, in the gray-blue moonlight, the procession wound around and up the hill and climbed into view.

In every hand a corn dolly was held aloft. Robert felt under his shirt for his own. There were songs, and Robert mouthed the words along with the singers. There was the beating of drums, and Robert beat time on the windowsill.

Without knowing completely what he was doing, he forced open the windowsill and found himself making his way up the hill.

He danced. A fever seemed to have shot into him, a Festival fever. He twirled as he ran, and his mouth sang high and loud. A light not altogether moonlight seemed to radiate on him. He held his corn dolly aloft, and a white mass of light beams seemed to emanate from it.

Come to me, lad.

The voice crooned quietly in his ear.

At the top of the hill, above him, the revelers had stopped, unaware of Robert but waiting silently as the Corn King and Queen approached the cornfield. Each held a dolly high, and then each tossed it into the air into the center of the patch. A cheer went up.

The procession, in a straight line, moved slowly along now, each processioner stopping momentarily before the corn to toss his dolly in. Under each breath a silent wish was made. And suddenly at the end, unseen, came Robert.

An energy filled his bones; he grasped his corn dolly so tight it nearly burst in his hand. It crackled in his grip. The line moved slowly, so slowly—a hundred corn dollys, a hundred wishes—and Robert wanted to be there *now*.

Suddenly, he knew what his wish would be.

Down below, at the bottom of the hill, a cry rang out. The procession stopped, and all, including Robert, looked down to see Robert's mother, her hand to her breast, darkly outlined in the doorway of the cottage. She began to make her way frantically up the hill. There was a terrible urgency in her movement but she seemed, perversely, to be moving through water of her own making, clutching at her skirts to keep from falling.

"Robert!" she screamed out.

The line of processioners now was beginning to turn toward him. He knew that this moment would be lost. They were beginning to move away from him—but he realized that they were not making a path for his mother to get to him, but rather for him to run to the front of the line.

"Robert! No!"

With a rise of feeling he leaped toward the corn patch. He jumped, and at the high point of his arc the dolly left his hand and sailed into the center of the field. The dried stalks, that line of stick soldiers, almost seemed to stretch upward to catch and caress it.

He made his wish.

"My father!" Robert shouted; "I want to see my father!"

"Robert!"

All eyes turned to the hysterical mother, and then back again.

Robert was gone.

In the corn patch, there was a rustle. A sigh.

"I only wished for him to be mine!" Robert's mother cried. "I only wanted a son!"

Another sigh.

Somewhere in the center of the cornfield, propped up where the dark rains of coming November would turn it to wet straw and dark mold, sat a ten-year-old corn dolly.

And somewhere, far off under the moon, carried away on the edge of the wind, the word *Lad*.

And, farther away yet, the answering word *Yes*.

. . . a robot, a dusting of snow, a length of noosed rope . . .

The Electric Fat Boy

"Fat, Fat, go away,
"Don't come back on any day.
"If we want to, then we will
"Roll old Chubby down the hill...."

The chorus died away. Twenty linked hands fell to ten young sides.

Within the circle, at the hub of twenty round, stinging eyes above ten sharp, cruel mouths, Chubby sobbed.

His body was huge. He cried with his full weight, pushed great wet tears out of his eyes from a deep and bottomless well lodged somewhere in his heart.

His sobbing pleased them. In ones and twos, they drifted off to corners of the schoolyard, content in their first chore of the lunch period. Now they wanted other things—games of tag, baby gossip, a game of ball-against-the-wall.

When they were gone a voice, a tiny squeaky voice, spoke up, sounding like nothing so much as a gnat against Chubby's ear.

"I'm sorry," it whispered.

"It's all right, Roy," Chubby managed to sob out. His soft fists were balled tight into his eyes, and when he pulled them away he saw that his cotton madras shirt, out at the waist, was wet with tears.

Roy spoke again, edging closer from out of the shade of the elm he had been pushed under. Chubby saw that his glasses were broken, their black frames peaked at the bridge. A grass stain bleached one knee of Roy's baggy chinos.

"At least I got them to leave *you* alone," Chubby said, grinning tepidly through a long sniffle. He attempted to push his shirttail into his pants but quickly gave up.

"You're my friend." Roy pushed his glasses up on his nose, and they fell off in two pieces. He picked them up and put them into his pocket, and then suddenly, timidly, he put his hand on his friend's shoulder.

"Chubby," he said, "I'm going to make it up to you. If it takes me the rest of my life, I'm going to do something for you."

School days passed into summer days. The bullies bullied; on the last day of school they took Chubby's belt, and the gold star Roy had gotten for being a good speller. But then, miraculously, they disappeared. The schoolyard emptied and soon was padlocked against the heat and summer boys doing mischief. The battlefield was quiet.

June passed quietly into July, July leaped out of the frying pan into August. Deep green turned to light green which turned to brown. Thundershowers played lightning fiddles against the clouds, danced on to make loud music elsewhere. It was time for baseball and horseshoes, the era of saltwater and hot dogs.

Chubby and Roy, the best of friends, made summer together. They caught lightning bugs when the sun went away. When the sun came back they climbed down into cellars, yanked out chemistry sets and model racing cars, built plastic airplanes and plastic monsters. They flipped baseball cards and always ended up even. Roy's mother had a pool in the backyard, and they spent hours squirting water at each other from their mouths and playing dive bomber off the ladder. They looked at the moon through Chubby's telescope by night, by day rigged it to project sunspots onto a white sheet of paper. They went to the movies, and they read magazines in the shade that Chubby's house made in the afternoon.

One day, when August had turned from mean to mild and when the stores were beginning to stock high with black and white marbled note books and Bic pens, Roy suddenly jumped up from his stack of *Mad* and *Cracked* and *Archie* and *Popular Mechanics* and gave a yell. "I've found it, Chubby! I've been looking all summer and I've finally found it!"

He pressed a folded magazine under Chubby's eyes. It was a back page of a science magazine, filled with block ads for mini-bikes and do-it-yourself helicopter kits. But there in one corner, lined by a thin black border under a badly drawn picture of a fat person with his arms over his face as another boy, thin, pushed him aside, was something else:

Tired of being pushed around just because you're fat?
Tired of people laughing, and calling you names?
Tired of taking all the guff?
Try
ELECTRIC FAT BOY
Not a puppet or robot, but a REAL device
Send $18.95 to Electric Enterprises, Box L, Electric City
Electric Enterprises
Makers of Electric Fat Boy and other fine Electrics

"Don't be foolish," Chubby said, pushing the magazine away.

"But it's what I want to do!" Roy insisted in his timid, squeaky voice.

"It's dumb. And it wouldn't help."

"I've got $18.95."

"Give me the money," Chubby said. "We'll go to the movies."

Roy was silent as a mouse.

That night, after dinner, they caught more lightning bugs than ever before.

August came to the brink, sighed, and fell over into September.

Chubby didn't see Roy for the last two weeks of summer vacation. The butterflies moved faster, out of Chubby's reach; the lightning bugs became dimmer and dimmer, dots in the night. The magazines all started to look the same. But on the first day of school, when the playground was un-padlocked and the new black tar that had been spread on it waited eagerly for the dusty scuffmarks of brand new sneakers, Roy was there, new glasses, wire-rimmed, and all.

So were the bullies.

Roy and Chubby saw their circle through the chainfence gate, waiting to knock their uncracked schoolbooks, their new yellow pencils with ends sharp as hummingbird heads, from their hands and kick them out of the way. They would pull Chubby's new shirt out of his pants. They would circle Roy and when they retreated Roy would stand with his new glasses twisted on the ground.

"They're going to hurt us," Chubby said.

"No they aren't." There was a new kind of smile on Roy's face. His voice didn't squeak, but was even and sure. He pulled Chubby into the bushes outside the schoolyard fence, made him close his eyes and count to ten.

"Open your eyes," Roy said.

Chubby yelped. For a moment there before him was a fat body with a silver football for a face; then, suddenly, the face and body was his own. Chubby looked into the eyes of an exact duplicate of himself, down to the untucked blue and red checked shirt and uncombed hair.

Chubby gasped: "Electric Fat Boy."

"Try to push him around," Roy said.

Chubby shrugged, stepped forward to muss up the Fat Boy's hair.

The Fat Boy growled, pushed Chubby to the ground and stood over him. "Leave off," he said in a no-nonsense voice.

Roy said, "You wait here and let the Fat Boy take care of them, and I'll come back later for you."

"Wow," Chubby said, and then he said it again as the circle formed as always at the entrance to the yard and then suddenly there were shouts and parts of the circle were flying off everywhere.

TOYBOX

● ● ●

When Roy came out from school Chubby was not in the bushes, and couldn't be found anywhere. The Electric Fat Boy was in the schoolyard the next morning, taking money from everyone who came in the gate. Roy tried to sneak up behind him, but the Fat Boy caught him, and took all *his* money.

Roy was scared.

Chubby didn't show up at school or at home the next day, or the next. It was then, in the night, that Roy left home behind, left the models and the card flips and the swimming pool and magazines in the shade. The weather had turned cool. He knew that soon it would be time to carve pumpkins and talk about Santa Claus. The world was turning its back on summer.

The train was crowded at first. After hours of green and yellow countryside, countryside putting on its fall clothes and covering its makeshift baseball diamonds with tarps of grown grass and end-of-summer neglect, all of the passengers had been spit out like seeds and Electric City loomed ahead. It was big and small—big to Roy who had never seen a city but just a baby to other cities. Big with a cab stand and a news shanty at the train station, small enough so that Roy had no trouble finding Box L or what it led to.

As noon struck in an old bell in an old belltower, Roy stood before the Electric Fat Boy warehouse. An ancient building, old with time and seeming disuse. The front was flaking, but there was evidence that part of it had just been painted with fresh green paint; and the white letters of THE ELECTRIC FAT BOY COMPANY stood out sharply. The front was quiet, but Roy heard noises around back—banging and shouting and loading sounds, a lot of men at work. He had his hand on the front doorknob but removed it, moving to an alleyway thick with trucks three, four, five deep. Roy edged past them, snaking his body along the wall till he rounded a sharp corner, nearly falling into the back yard.

There were Electric Fat Boys everywhere. Forty in a row they were, with fat silver footballs for faces and huge, round silver globes for bodies. One after another, a long line of Electric Fat Boys rolled out of a conveyor belt from the bowels of the factory. Each lined up to be packed in a box and packed in a truck and packed into someone's life.

"What the hell you doing?"

Roy turned around to see a man, not at all fat, but grizzled and sweaty with a cigar in the middle of his teeth, glaring at him.

"I bought one of these...."

"You ain't fat," the man said suspiciously.

"For my friend. Something went wrong; it went amok."

"Read your warranty; go away," the man said, taking Roy's arm and pulling him toward the street.

"I want to see the president of Electric Enterprises."

The man barked a laugh. "Won't be here for weeks. Out at one of the other plants—Electric Ugly Boy, Electric Stumble Boy, Electric Four-Eye Boy. New plant opens every day. Electric Club Foot Boy, Electric Stutter Boy, Electric No-Sports Boy. Electric Fat Girl and Electric Ugly Girl." He suddenly realized he was talking to Roy. "And don't come back," he said around his cigar, pointing to the mouth of the alley.

That afternoon Roy spent in Electric City, in every corner of Electric City. Box M, Box N, Boxes O and P. Every street had an Electric Enterprise on it. Trucks filled the streets like salmon in a stream, jammed the highways leading out and filled the roads leading to the highways.

At each factory it was the same. Electric Shy Boy, Electric Unglamorous Girl, Electric Minority Boy. Then, as the work bell at the Electric Bad-Breath Boy plant poised at five to five, Roy told the foreman, another man with a cigar in his teeth, "I'm supposed to deliver the new Electric plans to the president, for Electric Horsey Girl an Electric Unfunny Boy."

"Hadn't heard of those. Things have been jumping, though." The foreman pointed up. At first Roy thought he was pointing directly overhead but then he saw that the finger pointed up and over the rim of the factory. "Take your nose to the edge of Electric City. Climb the steps, keep climbing the steps." He looked at his watch as the bell rang loud. "Might be a good time to see him. Might be home." And then the foreman was gone.

Steps. There were nothing but steps. The steps went on forever. Winding up from a cracked granite base, they suddenly lurched into a limestone cave, came out into bright sunshine, wound over through a trellised garden and into sunlight again. Roy found himself on a little porch and looked down to see Electric City below him, gray and smoky in the twilight—the smokestacks which dotted the Electric plants in even rows over the plain that was Electric City were billowing brown smoke yet, as another shift came on to work the busy night. The town had grown smog; the trucks were rolling so thick together they formed unbroken tentacles out of the roads leading north south east west and made the City look a huge octopus. Roy turned and saw nothing but more steps leading up to the clouds. But now there was a scent that came close, touched his nose and moved on, a scent of late summer flowers or early autumn ones, fresh, alive. Roy followed his nose.

More steps. The height of the steps lengthened and shortened, as if the builder had run out of one material, used whatever was at hand—or been blind. Roy's legs ached. The stairs notched into the cliffs again, burst out onto another porch which only made the City below look like a smaller octopus, climbed up and in again.

The stairway ended so abruptly Roy nearly fell down. Suddenly he stepped onto even green grass. The grass smelled like perfume—it was so rich and dark and wet it caressed his feet right through his shoes.

The lawn rolled out from his feet like a carpet leading to the whitest and biggest house in the world. Though the sun had nearly set there was light enough falling on it to make it shine like midday. A porch spread across its bottom long enough for forty wicker chairs with leg room between.

A screen door banged somewhere, out behind. Roy heard the

tiny sounds of faraway movement and then saw a light tick on in an upstairs room. A profile set itself against the yellow rectangle of the window, a profile at once fat and sad and ugly and awkward. The profile moved back and forth, back and forth, teetering in a rocking chair.

Roy's sneaker made the front steps creak; after waiting a frozen minute he moved to the screen door which creaked even louder. The waxed-bright boards of the entryroom floor groaned as he headed for the mahogany staircase warmly nestled against a far wall behind acres of furniture.

"Rimbaud, is that you?" came a call from upstairs, in a voice high and mousy. Roy imitated a rabbit in a car headlight. There was no further sound for a moment until the voice said, "Whoever you are, come on up."

At least there was a carpet at the top, wet and green as the outside lawn. There were gas lamps. There was delicate red flowered wallpaper, and much furniture that looked as though it had just been dusted. There was a stack of white set stacked neatly beside a polished hunting board.

"Come, come," the voice said impatiently, as Roy stepped into the shadow of the open doorway.

In the room, under the amber light of an overhead petal lamp, sat the oddest boy Roy had ever seen.

He was fat, to be sure; and ugly. He wore black rimmed glasses, with thick bottle lenses that made his eyes look round and wet. His pants were baggy and unstylish; his shoes black with thick laces, the kind people with foot problems wear. He looked as though he had a club foot. He turned his limpid eyes on Roy, looked away toward the window, tried to heave himself out of his chair. He failed, and sat back with a grunt. He tried to fold his hands in front of him but, finding that uncomfortable, let them wander uneasily over the arms of his rocker.

"You're the one asking about me," he said in his voice, high-pitched and breathy.

"You're the president of Electric Enterprises."

"True," the fat boy said, as if he didn't quite believe it himself.

"One of your machines ran amok. My friend Chubby—"

"It's been a long time, this time," the fat boy broke in, seeming to ignore Roy. He was staring out the window at the puffing sprawl of the various Electric Enterprises below him. He suddenly put out his white, pudgy hand to Roy. "Come, look."

Reluctantly, Roy edged closer to the window. The fat boy did not touch him; his hand fell once more to the arm of the rocking chair where it crawled, fat, spiderlike, slowly up and sown the length of the arm.

"This was a sleeping city less than a month ago, " the fat boy said. His voice held something—regret? Longing for sleep? —that Roy couldn't fathom. His hand waved at the scene below the cliffs. "All those chimneys were white with bird droppings. Sleeping...."

"My friend—" Roy attempted to say.

"'The meek shall inherit the Earth,'" the fat boy went on. "That was the quotation that started it all."

"I—"

The fat boy turned his eyes on Roy, away from the window. "'And the meek shall inherit the Earth.' The magazine advertisements always run, you know," the fat boy went on. "Always. They're the originals, and they still work. The idea was so simple: there's so much meanness in the world, so many *little* meannesses that eventually add up to the big ones that start wars and bring death. If you diffuse the little meannesses, make them go away before they grow monstrous, wouldn't that help prevent the big ones from ever happening? Little bullies become big bullies. What if you struck a balance, met the little bully with an equal force that told him that you can't push the little fellow around after all? Then, just maybe, the little bully would go on to other things and lose interest in being a bully. Sometimes—a *lot* of times—it works. Push four-eyes around in the schoolyard day after day—but then one day four-eyes fights back. Next day he fights back again. Pretty soon you leave four-eyes, and the kid with the big nose, and the skinny little runt, and the fat kid, alone."

The fat boy rested his hand on Roy's shoulder for the briefest instant before dropping it again. "So, Electric Fat Boy, Electric Ugly Boy, Electric Every Boy Who Needs A Little Help Because He Gets Picked On For Something He Has No Control Over."

Roy tried again. "But—"

"There are a lot of little meannesses out there this time," the fat boy went on, turning again to the window. A bumper crop. If these electrics don't cut it off right now, at the start, well...BIG meanness. War. The end. Who knows." He sighed, a high, mousy, unpleasant sound. "So once again the meek shall inherit the Earth for a little while."

"My friend Chubby—"

"There's nothing wrong," the fat boy said, seeing the anxiousness on Roy's face, "with your friend. It's a little failing—meanness, perhaps—of mine, that I put just a little too much spunk into the Electric Fat Boy. The real Chubby has no doubt taken over again by now." He smiled, and Roy saw that he also had bad teeth. "I wonder where Rimbaud is? There are things he hasn't set up yet at my little retreat here, and it looks as though I may be here a while this time. My fine things are another little failing of mine—the only one I'm really allowed now...."

"You started all of this."

"Me? In a way...."

"But you said it's been a long time—"

"Tell me," the fat boy said. "Why did you come here? What made you so bold as to ride all the way to Electric City to do something about your *amok* friend Chubby?"

"It was the right thing to do."

"Yes. But would the old Roy have left home, taken money, gone off by himself, get mad enough to do something like that for himself—or even for his friend!" He broke off his train of thought, lifting the index and middle fingers on his right hand and examining them under the light, rubbing them one against the other. "Rimbaud was supposed to dust all of this," he said, shaking his head. "Later....

"Come, I want you to look at something."

The fat boy pushed up the arm of his ill-fitting jacket, rolled up the too-long-sleeved blue shirt underneath to expose white skin.

Holding out his arm directly under the amber light from the petal-lamp, he took a pinch of skin from the middle, fleshy part of his arm and tore downward.

There was a deep metal well there, filled with batteries and wires.

Roy gasped, "You're electric...."

"How else to continue? It's the price I paid." He tapped his skull. "It's still me, in this metal bowl. I could trust the electric enterprises to no one else. It's my responsibility. So...."

"You wake whenever all this is needed, start all the factories."

"Then close it all down tenderly when the job is finished. And wait for the next time." He suddenly grabbed Roy tight by the hand, and, before Roy could pull away, ripped a fold of skin down on the forearm, exposing a copper well of electric machinery similar to his own.

Roy cried out.

"Of course you're electric," the fat boy said. "Electric Shy Boy. The same time the real Roy ordered his friend Chubby's fat boy. How else would you be here? The real Roy wouldn't. Although maybe when he sees what the Electric Roy has done in his name he'll do it himself the next time."

"Is that really all I am?" Electric Roy said, horrified.

"*No*. Much more. Underneath you're just a couple of metal spheres glued together. That's underneath. You're Roy, only you're the part of him needs working on."

"I'll disappear when he's through with me?"

"No again! You'll be part of him, that stronger part that will stay with him. Remember, you *are* him. Your electric body will sleep. You won't. You're lucky; you're flesh and blood while I'm trapped in this metal casket. My body of flesh is long gone...."

A figure appeared in the doorway, short and stooped, with thin, steel-gray hair in wisps about his head and with round clear spectacles. His hands were as thin and gray as the hair on his head.

"*Rimbaud*," the Electric Fat Boy announced. He turned once more to face Roy.

"What will I do now?" Electric Roy asked.

"Go back to him, of course. Your battle is won already. Let's hope the others are as lucky."

"Chubby?"

The Electric Fat Boy laughed. "A resounding success." In a confidential whisper he added, "The fat ones always win a little sooner than the rest."

He pushed Roy gently toward the door. The little gray man passed into the room, and Roy heard the Electric Fat Boy say, "Rimbaud, my human friend...."

Roy descended the long mile of steps one at a time. Below him the orange dawn was beginning to break, turning the thin clouds of smoke over Electric City the color of persimmon. The trucks rolled, an unending line of electric life streaming out and off into the world. Roy counted the eight roads out, deliberately, as if on a string of beads, and stopped strongly and gently on the one that led home.

Snow

On the day before Christmas, a few rogue snowflakes fell. They drifted like unsure intruders; dropped, reluctant parachutists, from a sky still clear and blue-cold with autumn. They fell on Eva's nose and melted, fell onto Charles' outstretched tongue and were warmed into water.

"I wish it would snow forever!" Eva said.

"And ever!" Charles said.

"We'd build forts and go sledding!"

"Have snowball fights and dig tunnels!"

"Forever!" Eva said.

"And ever!" said Charles.

"We'd never have to go to school again!"

"Hurrah!"

And, in other places, other Charleses and other Evas said the same things.

The skies darkened.

It began to snow.

It snowed on Christmas—all twelve days of it. It snowed, inch upon inch of white, falling in flat layers from an always-gray sky.

Eva and Charles sledded, drank hot chocolate, and cheered. They had snowball fights, and built forts.

And still it snowed.

It snowed for twenty days, then twenty days more. Each day it snowed. Drifts sat on snow drifts. There were layers of snow, geologic demarcations, that traced the storm's history.

School was canceled again and again.

Eva and Charles cheered, played Monopoly inside as snow layers climbed up the sliding glass door of the family room, topped Mother's bushes, made their tiny twig fingers wave goodbye as they went under.

It snowed.

And snowed.

And....

Snowed.

"It's never going to stop," Mother said, staring out at the snow with her haggard face, a cold cup of tea nestled forgotten in her hands. "It's going to snow forever."

"And ever!" Charles laughed, and then he and Eva went out to build another snow fort as Father, in the driveway, cursed his snowblower, which coughed and then died.

It snowed.

And snowed.

And snowed some more.

There was no school, and then there was no mail. There were no packages. The stores, the malls, the 7-Elevens, winked out one by one. People drew into their homes like ticks, battling their walks and driveways before finally giving up. Snowplows roared, then died like dinosaurs at the end of their reign. They plowed sideways into curbs and then sputtered out, their drivers hopping out as if afraid, tramping hurriedly home through the disappearing streets.

It snowed.

And snowed.

Eva and Charles played, built walls of snow that were eaten, threw snowballs that were swallowed. Soon they could almost reach the house's gutters with their mittens. They ran huffing in to drink the last of the hot chocolate, topped by the last of the marshmallows. It continued to snow.

And snow.

And snow.

And then:

"I'm sick of snow," Charles said.

"Me too," said Eva.

They stood looking from their family room at the mountains of snow, the layers of snow, the valleys of snow, the plateaus of snow. Snow made the windows white, the earth white, filled every nook, each cranny; sifted into every corner and crack and edge of the world. They had done all the sledding they could stand; all the snow forts they could build had been built: the first ten buried like Pompeii, the last five in degrees of backyard burial even as they watched. A thousand snowballs lay entombed: lumps of white coal waiting to be turned into diamonds by the crushing, building weight of snow.

Through the sliding glass door, only a thin line of gray sky could be seen at the top, above the geologic layers of snow.

And, in the gray sky, it snowed.

"I'm sick of snow," Eva said.

"So am I," said Charles.

They were weary of snow boots, of gloves and mittens; tired of tasseled hats and long johns and layers of socks; disgusted with dressing like astronauts each time they went out.

In the kitchen, where Mother and Father sat all but lifeless staring at their teacups, the radio called for more snow, crackled, went silent.

At the top of the sliding glass door, the last line of sky was filled in by snow, enclosing the world, making it go away.

"I'm *afraid* of snow," Charles said.

"Me too," Eva said.

And, in other places, other Charleses and other Evas said the same things.

Eva said: "Then we'll tunnel our way out."
"Yes!" said Charles.

They mounted their expedition like professionals.

Whistling, smiling, Charles rummaged through his room, through the cellar, through the attic. Eva organized. Charles loaded his arms with layers of socks and his book on Admiral Byrd. Eva piled up digging tools from the garage, the camping stove, Sterno cans for heat and cooking, and whatever was left to cook. She stuffed their school backpacks full with flashlight batteries and candy bars, comic books and automobile flares, boxes of matches, pots and pans. In the pockets she put sunglasses against the glare, and her Walkman with tapes and Charles' lucky baseball card. She zipped the backpacks closed, afraid the straining seams would burst.

They dressed in their best clothes: ski parkas stuffed with goose feathers, snow pants with elastic straps to keep them in place. They had gloves with leatherette palms and fingers for gripping, crisp blue jeans, flannel lined. They wore two pairs of wool socks, gray and thick, and thermal underwear, and turtlenecks under sweatshirts that said 'GO ARMY!'

Outfitted and backpacked, they stood before the sliding glass door in the family room.

Eva looked at Charles, and Charles nodded.

Slowly, Eva unlocked the door, slid it back on its rails.

A wall of snow, smooth and white, high and wide, confronted them.

"Ready?" Eva said.

Charles said, "Ready."

They began to dig.

They dug.

And dug.

Scoop by scoop, handful by handful, Eva pushed snow back at Charles, who pushed it back into the room behind. A depression in the wall formed, kid-high and wide; the depression deepened and deepened until there was a little room made of snow, with snow walls, snow ceiling and snow floor, which they moved deeper into as they dug.

And dug.

And dug.

Charles looked back through their deepening tunnel. He saw the room they had left, the house they had left, far behind them, a shrinking cave opening.

And there—Mother and Father just glimpsed, beyond the family room piled with snow, heads lowered to the kitchen table, unmoving.

"Dig!" Eva ordered, and Charles turned away, taking Eva's handfuls of snow, packing them tight into the walls and ceiling and floor as they inched forward, onward.

Darkness deepened in their tunnel. Eva, panting in her snowsuit, stopped to hand Charles the big flashlight. Charles clicked it on. The walls gleamed blue-white. But already Eva was digging again, throwing snow back at Charles to pack away.

He lay the flashlight on the tunnel floor and went to work, inching the light forward.

Forward.

In the snow, on the floor under Eva's hand, something solid struck her fingers.

She brushed away snow, pushed away snow, packed away snow— and there beneath her lay a line of chicken wire across their path.

"Wha—?" Charles began.

"The fence!" Eva shouted. "It's the top of our backyard fence!"

And now Charles could imagine it, there beneath them in the far reaches of their yard, the line of wire tacked to posts.

Charles began, "That means—"

"We're four feet up!" Eva said.

They sat still, hushing their breathing.

Above them, far above, they heard the swishing of snow, the falling of snow.

"Keep digging!" Eva said.

"I'm tired!" Charles said. He lifted the flashlight, heavy in his hands, and shined it back behind them, where the light was lost in the far reaches of blue-white tunnel.

"We'll rest later!" Eva said, her own breath panting steam in the air.

Charles put the flashlight back down, pointed it at the wall of snow in front of them.

They dug.

And dug.

"Stop!" Eva said, breathing hard.

Charles dropped to the floor, leaned his back against the wall, let his arms drop like weights to his side.

"Tired...." he said.

Eva, still panting, brushed her heavy gloves one against the other, clearing them of snow. She reached into her pack and brought out candy bars and juice packs, potato chips and cookies.

Charles, gaining strength, began to eat, then drank. He ate everything she gave him.

"We don't have much more," Eva said, frowning.

Charles took the pack from her and dug in, finding more cookies.

"I'm hungry!" he said, ripping them open, letting Lorna Doones drop to the floor before he scooped them up.

Above them, snow swished and fell, brushed and fell, piled and fell.

After they began to dig again, the flashlight began to dim.

Almost at once, Eva's hand found something else solid in the floor.

She and Charles brushed and pushed snow away.

The edge of something square revealed itself.

"What—" Charles said.

Eva pushed more snow away, dug down and around, threw snow away with her fingers.

The corner of a box, steel with glass underneath.

"A phone booth!" Eva said.

She brushed more snow away, uncovered a sign with a bell on it, more glass below.

Charles shined the light down, saw the curve of a man's hat, the man slumped down, hand frozen to the dangling receiver, the man's face turned up toward him, *frozen*—

"Yahhhhh!" Charles said, scrambling back.

Eva took the flashlight, looked down into the booth herself.

"He's dead. Nothing we can do," she said, and immediately put the flashlight down again, aiming it ahead. "We're getting close to town."

She began to dig again, in the dimming light.

They left the phone booth behind. Soon they uncovered a telephone pole. They dug around it, leaving it standing straight and brown through the middle of their tunnel, creosote-smelling, with one steel footrest angled up like a pointing finger. They dug, and Eva's arms ached. Her fingers were numb with cold and work—but still she pushed and brushed and pulled at snow, raked it back at Charles who packed and pounded and beat and smoothed it into the walls and ceiling and floor. They felt the afternoon wear on, could feel the cold night coming, feel the snow falling, and sighing, and drifting, and soughing above them.

They dug.

And dug, and then Eva's nearly frozen fingers touched something solid beneath her, and she excavated around it.

She gasped, pulled her hand back.

The top of a head.

Black hair.

The flashlight was nearly out, a barely glowing bulb. She pulled it close, and Charles crawled up next to her.

Pushing more snow away, she uncovered a curve of feathers surrounding the head, rising in front to a war bonnet.

"Mr. Gray's wooden Indian!" she exclaimed.

Charles said, "We're in town! Next to the drugstore!"

Shaking the flashlight to make it brighten, they pushed the wall farther on. They dug and scraped and packed and bored, and soon hit the front of a store window, a wide plate of glass etched with Mr. Gray's name in large, arching letters.

Pressing their cold faces to the glass, they looked down into the store.

There was blackness within.

"Darn!" Eva said, shaking the flashlight viciously, startled to find it go bright for her.

"Shine it inside!" Charles urged.

She directed the beam inside the drugstore. She played it over the soda fountain, over the glass cases, the prescription counter, the floor.

The beam fell on the dead figures of Mr. Gray, Mrs. Gray.

Eva turned the flashlight off. She and Charles lay in the dark, in the cold, listening to their own deep breaths and their own caught sobs.

Charles began to cry outright.

Eva smacked him with her gloved hand.

"Quiet!" she said.

"But I saw Mom, and Dad—"

"Yes!" Eva said.

"We might as well stay right here," Charles sniffled. "We might as well let it happen here...."

Eva said nothing, listened to the snow above them, the snow falling.

Drifting.

Murmuring....

"No!" she said. "I won't give up!"

"We have no food, no light—nothing!"

"Dig!" Eva ordered, shaking the flashlight again and turning it on.

This time it only fluttered, a weak orange glow, making the tunnel around them look like Halloween.

Charles sobbed, "I...can't...."

"Well I can!"

Eva began to bore up, angling away from the side of the drugstore.

She dropped handfuls of snow on Charles in the pumpkin light until he stopped crying and once more began to push and pack and pound.

They dug up.

Up.

Eva sensed the snow waiting for them. As she climbed she felt and heard it: the wash of snow, the gentle fall, the dusting and breathy blowing of snow. It reached out to her ears and heart, pulled her up toward its inevitable self. Behind her Charles sniffled and worked, inching the dying flashlight up with one hand while he pounded and smoothed with the other.

The flashlight went out; Halloween went away, leaving them with night.

Charles dropped the flashlight, listened to it slide down the steep tunnel like a sled until it was gone.

In the dark, they dug.

And dug.

And dug.

And then: the wall of snow in front of Eva suddenly went away: fell down around her in a shower leaving a hole.

The tunnel opened into dim light.

Eva and Charles climbed out onto the world.

It was snowing.

The planet was white. Snow drifted, twirled, and fell.

And fell; dropped in whispering breaths from the gray-white sky; shimmered pure and crystalline; fell fluffy and piled and moved like dust over the surface of the earth. From north to south, east to west, the world was white.

It snowed.

And snowed.

"Oh, Eva, what are we going to do!" said Charles, his eyes once more welling to tears.

Above them, the gray-white clouds darkened to gray.

Darkened still more.

Night was coming.

And it snowed.

"What—" Charles began, sobbing, but his sister took his arm and pointed.

"Look!"

There, through the drifting, swirling, gently lashing snow, was a dim point of light in the near distance.

"A star!" Charles said.

Eva took Charles' arm.

They tramped through the snow.

But now, the light began to stutter and die. Snow occluded it, and suddenly it was gone.

"No!" Charles cried.

The star blinked back on.

They hurried, and then they reached it: a star on the ground, a five-pointed lamp dimming, half buried by snow.

"Is it—" Charles said, but he knew what it was even as Eva began to brush snow away from it. She uncovered the top of the town Christmas tree, taller than any building.

Down there, under all the packed and piled and layered snow, was a huge branching evergreen tree with red bulbs and strings of fat lights and thick silver strands of tinsel.

The star flickered.

Went out.

Eva stood, and she and Charles watched as the snow drifted and accumulated and covered the top of the last point of the star.

To every horizon was snow; mountains and hills and valleys of snow. Only snow.

"Oh, Eva!" What are we going to do?" Charles said.

Eva looked at Charles and said, "I don't know."

Darkness fell.

It snowed.

And snowed.

Snow covered their tracks, drifting and sighing, swirling and filling. Eva and Charles wandered, flashlightless, freezing. Snow drifted and moved and mounted and fell in the dark blue-white, the air was a curtain of dark white.

It snowed.

On hands and knees, exhausted, they crawled until they could crawl no more.

"I...can't," Charles whispered, and stopped, turning over to sit in the snow.

Eva sat down beside him.

"Neither," she whispered, "can I."

She looked up, felt soft snow caress her cheeks, dance across her eyebrows, melt on her warm-cold nose.

"I wish it would stop snowing," Charles said.

Eva closed her eyes, felt snow tap on her face like fingers, slide down her cheeks, mingling with tears, which crystallized into snow.

"Me, too," she said. "I wish it would stop snowing."

There came a hush in the air.

Above, in the sky, Charles saw something that was not snow. A tiny light appeared in a tiny split of clouds. A swirl of falling snow blew aside and more tiny lights appeared.

"Stars!" Charles cried. "*Real* stars!"

Beside Charles and Eva there was a sound in the snow. A sudden tunnel appeared. A bright stab of light shot out, followed by a mufflered boy bearing a flashlight.

Behind him came a snowsuited girl and another boy, all hat and scarf and ski jacket.

Other tunnels opened—a thousand tunnels, with other stabbing beams of light followed by other boys and girls.

"Look!" Charles shouted, pointing at the sky.

All over, flashlights were turned off and eyes were turned upward.

The night was full of stars and vanishing clouds.

It had stopped snowing.

In the night, by the light of the friendly moon, they brought up the world from below.

Through the tunnels, they carried up food and light and shelter. They brought up candy and juice packs and cookies and cake. They tunneled into empty Kmarts, carried up batteries by the boxful, chairs and tents and sleds and blankets. They brought up propane stoves and heaters, they brought up comic books and tape players and toys. They brought up more toys.

The starry night drained into rose dawn, and gave them day. They stood staring open-mouthed at the stranger sun. They cheered as it climbed high into a cloudless firmament, cheered as it warmed their faces, made them throw off watch caps and ski masks and ear muffs and scarves. They cheered and sang and continued their work, toting up an entire new world from below.

In the golden afternoon Charles stood smiling, Eva beside him. He laughed at the sight of a forming puddle of melted snow.

"Maybe it'll all melt, right back down to the earth!"

"I hope," Eva shouted loud, *"it never snows again!"*

A cheer went up, everywhere.

In the sky, behind the sun, like a shy and peeking visitor, a thin cloud appeared, joined soon by others.

The skies darkened.

It began to snow.

Garden of Eden

"Come on, Chump!" Griffey called.

Griffey was ready and so were the others. Mug and Brudder and Chaz were all out there in the alley, decked out in backward baseball caps and old sweatshirts and dirty jeans and sneakers that used to be white.

Chump, sweatshirt caught halfway over his head, ambled to the window and shouted, "I'll be right down, fatheads!"

"Fathead yourself!" Mug shouted up angrily. "Move it, you dope!"

"Yeah!" Brudder shouted, extending his vocabulary with the utterance. "Yeah, move it, you...dope!"

"Ahhhhh, shaddup!" Chump shouted back down at them, sweatshirt now in place as he searched his dresser frantically not for his comb but for his cap, which he finally found in the most unlikely place—on his bedpost, where it belonged.

"Dat muddah of mine," he said, shaking his head even as his mother's voice rose up from the depths of the house below.

"Chauncey, are you up there? I think some boys are here for you—but remember, you're being punished!"

Quickly, Chump turned to the window.

"Cheese it, youse guys!"

The gang below scattered.

"Chauncey, do you hear me?"

"Sure I do!" he shouted down.

There was a pause and then his mother said, "All right, just remember you can't come out of there till dinner! It was very careless of you to break Mr. Carlson's window with that baseball!"

"Sure, Ma! Sure! Very careless!" he shouted, even as he was climbing out the window, taking hold of the rain spout to lower himself to the ground two stories below.

As he reached the lower window he paused, holding his breath.

There inside sat his mother with her bridge cronies, playing cards.

"Chauncey is really such a *good* boy at heart...." his mother was saying.

Chump shook his head as he slid the rest of the way down, into the alley.

"Muddahs," he said.

"Hey Chauncey!" a voice whispered fiercely from behind a nearby garbage bin.

A moment later Griffey stepped out, grinning, followed by the others.

Chump stood tall, marched up to Griffey and took him by the collar.

"I told you not to call me dat, you mug," Chump said. "Call me dat again and I'll wipe the alley wit ya."

The color drained from Griffey's face.

"Sorry, Chump," he said.

Chump let him go.

"All right, boys," Chump said, hitching up his pants, giving a big smile to his gang. "Let's go."

They strutted out into the afternoon like they owned it. With Chump at the lead, the others ranging out behind him, they made a quick left at the corner, passing a close line of houses, all identical.

A little kid riding his bike in front of one of the houses looked up as they passed.

"Hey, Chump!" he grinned. "How ya doin'?"

"Just fine, Bertie," Chump grinned back.

"Hey!" Bertie said. "Ain't you bein' punished?"

Without breaking stride, shoulders thrown back proudly, Chump nodded.

"Yep."

"I'm gonna tell!" Bertie said, jumping off his bike to run back toward Chump's house.

"Hey!" Chump shouted, and when he snapped his finger Mug ran after Bertie, catching him in mid stride and dragging him complaining to stand in front of Chump.

"You was saying, Bertie?" Chump said.

"Lemme go! Lemme go, Mug!"

Chump said, "Still gonna rat on me, Bertie?"

Bertie shook his head emphatically.

"'Course not, Chump! I was just kiddin' is all! Lemme go!"

Chump made a motion with his hand, and Mug dropped Bertie to the ground.

"Sure I'm gonna tell!" Bertie said, backing away from the gang. "Unless you takes me with ya!"

Chump looked at Mug, who made a motion to grab Bertie again.

"Go ahead!" Bertie said. "Do whatcha want! Beat me up if ya like! But as soon as you leave I'll still rat on ya!"

Defiantly, Bertie clenched his little fists and added, "Unless you takes me with ya!"

"Know where we're going, Bertie?" Chump said mildly.

"Where?" Bertie said.

"We're going to see the bodies, Bertie," Chump said in a low voice. "The dancing dead bodies."

The color dropped out of Bertie's face.

"Hey, you ain't supposed to go there! Nobody's supposed to go there! It's da rules!"

Chump laughed. "And I bet you believes all that other bunk they feeds you in school and church, about dis town bein' the Garden of Eden, and dat anyone who messes wit da rules gets taken care of, right?"

"Well...."

"Still wanna come, Bertie?" Griffey said, grinning.

"Uhhh...yeah!" Bertie said, suddenly defiant again. "Yeah, sure I wants to come!"

Chump turned and said, "Then come on, ya punk," and walked on, the others following.

Bertie stayed behind for a few seconds, then, screwing up his courage, he quickly wheeled his bike onto his front lawn, dropped it, and ran after.

At the end of the row of houses they made a left, crossed over two blocks of houses, then crossed the street until they suddenly found themselves at the wooded lot that led to their destination.

On either side of the lot the houses looked like they had pulled themselves back, avoiding the site. There were high weeds at the borders, as if the owners had hoped to forget the place was even there. At one time a house just like all the others in the neighborhood had stood here, but it had burned to the ground. Only the weed-choked and blackened foundation remained.

"The bad lot...." Bertie whispered, mouth open.

"You believe that crud?" Griffey said, smiling widely at Bertie.

But the others were silent, too, and nobody had taken a step onto the lot.

"They says the ground's haunted, the grass, too," Chump said. "They says dis is da place where da first fatheads who didn't play by da rules lived. So they took 'em out back, through da woods, and turned 'em into dancing dead bodies."

He waited a moment, then blurted out a laugh.

"I says it's the bunk," Chump said, and without a moment of hesitation he stepped over the curb and onto the lot.

He looked back at the line of unsure faces behind him.

"Well, ya bums? Either youse is with me or you ain't—which is it?"

Bertie turned and ran, yelling out behind him, "See you guys! My muddah wants me to clean my room!"

The others watched him scoot around a corner, gone, then turned to face Chump again.

"Well?" Chump said. "I stepped onto it, and I'm still alive, ain't I?"

Griffey threw his shoulders back and stepped over the curb to stand next to Chump.

"Anyone who don't come is chicken," Griffey said ominously. "Anyone who don't follow Chump ain't nothing but the chicken's egg itself."

"It ain't like we's afraid of the lot itself," Chaz said, and Mug and then Brudder nodded.

"What is it, then?" Griffey asked.

"Well, it's...."

"Spit it out," Chump ordered, suddenly angry.

"It's da *rules*," Mug said.

"Yeah," Chaz continued, "you know, about the dancing bodies."

"What about da rules?"

"You know, the part about nobody being allowed to go see da bodies, unless they're allowed to. Unless they's *old* enough. It's one of da rules, and all."

"So?" Chump said. "Didn't we take a vote? And wasn't the vote that we'd go and see for ourselves, 'cause it's all the bunk?"

"Yeah, but...." Chaz said, looking at his own feet.

"Well?"

"They said Johnny Devo and his boys went to see it, and they never come back."

"That's bunk and you know it!" Chump said. "Everybody knows Johnny and his boys run away and joined the Navy."

"That ain't what I heard...." Chaz mumbled.

"Well, we took a vote, like I said," Chump snapped.

"And I voted against it," Chaz mumbled.

"And I wanted to," Mug said. "Only I was afraid to."

Chump turned, red-faced, to Brudder.

"And what about you?"

Brudder, overwhelmed with the prospect of having to think for himself, turned to his brother, Mug.

"He don't like it neither," Mug said.

"Go on, then," Chump said. "Go on and run home to your muddahs, just like Bertie. But remember this, that when we comes out of that forest, after we see what there is to see, you bums is out of the club for good. Get me?"

The three of them seemed to consider the point for a moment, and then Chaz suddenly turned and bolted away.

"Chicken-crud!" Griffey yelled, and then he and Chump held the other two with their stares.

Chump said, "What about you two? You chicken-cruds, too?"

Mug fought with himself, then, head down, stepped forward, gulping, to stand by Chump and Griffey.

"And you, Brudder?"

Brudder just shrugged again, and, after giving a look behind him, stepped over the curb, too.

"Just what I thought!" Chump said, slapping Brudder on the back. "With us, like always! Buddies to the end!"

Brudder smiled sheepishly.

"Sure," he said.

"I always knew Chaz was a chicken-crud," Griffey said.

"Yeah," Chump said.

"Me, too," said Mug, but as they marched into the lot, Mug gave a furtive look back the way that Chaz had run, and gulped again.

The sky had turned from bright, high blue to slate gray. The summer afternoon seemed to drain away into the tall weeds, leaving the air thick and sweaty, gray as the sky.

They passed the burned-out foundation, stopping to look in at the puddles of dirty water and scatters of charred timber within.

"Looks like the perfect place for a picnic!" Griffey laughed.

"Hey Brudder!" Chump said, "Why don't you and Mug come and live here? Then dat old man of yours can't crack you on the head no more, heh?"

Brudder seemed to consider the offer, furrowing his brow, then shook his head.

Chump slapped him on the back again, laughing.

"Just joking! I wouldn't want you to miss getting that Friday night beatin'!"

"Sure," Brudder said.

"Come on!" Chump said, swaggering ahead of them, toward the thickening row of trees ahead.

They followed.

The afternoon darkened.

As they stepped into the tree line, it was as if someone had thrown a switch. Chump looked up, expecting the sky to be blotted out, but there were generous gaps between the tree tops, showing a blackening, cloud-roiled sky. From somewhere distant a tentative rumble of thunder sounded, a mournful drum beating a faint warning. The sky brightened momentarily, the first jolt of lightning bulbing the black clouds.

Mug swallowed hard before saying, "Maybe we better wait for better weather."

"Baloney," Chump said, leading them ever deeper into the trees.

"But if it rains—"

"—Den we gets wet," Griffey snapped, though he too had started to study the rumbling clouds, a look of worry clouding his face as another, closer shot of thunder rolled overhead. It was followed by a bright burst of lightning that crackled off in the deep woods to their right, sending a wash of ozone across their nostrils.

Chump said, "We keep going, and dat's dat."

"Hey, Chump—" Griffey began but then they heard another far-off rumble, this one not thunder, which grew and grew to a roar and then dopplered gently away from their ears.

"Hear dat?" Chump said. "Know what dat is?"

The three blank faces of his companions were briefly lit by new lightning.

Chump laughed as following thunder sounded. "Don't you bums get it? We're on the right track—*dat's the railroad trestle!*"

"A train!" Griffey said, doubts suddenly drowned.

Above them in the trees there was the sudden slap of fat rain drops hitting leaves. A few drops fell like rifle shots around them.

"Keep goin'," Chump said, and they moved on deeper into the woods, following the barest of paths, while thunder came again following lightning, and water fell from the low angry clouds, building.

Soon the rain stopped them completely. The forest became more than trees and leaves and pine needles. It was now a thing of water, too. Rain fell in broken sheets, splashing high against trunks and boles, washing down in irregular waterfalls. They were soaked in no time, and, in the midst of lightning and the instantaneous booms of thunder, could not make their way forward.

"Stop!" Chump shouted above the din, and they huddled, wet to the skin, hair plastered to their skulls, against the fragrant sap-ridden thin bark of a tall pine.

Chump pushed the water out of his face, his hand like a windshield wiper.

"Maybe it's a warning to us!" Griffey said, his doubts returning in a rush, shivering partly with the coldness of the thunderstorm against his sopping wet clothes, which clung like a second skin.

"Listen, you rat!" Chump said, grabbing Griffey by his wet collar. "I'm tired of your bellyaching! You think I got rocks in my head? You think I don't know you's wanted to take over as leader for the longest time? You think I ain't seen the way you strut around and act big? The way you orders the boys around when I ain't there? Yeah, Mug told me all about you, Griffey, how you's been talking behind my back." Chump pulled back his free hand, balling it into a fist. "I oughtta pop you right here—"

Griffey's face colored itself with fear. "It ain't that, Chump!" he pleaded. "It ain't that at all! I know you's da boss and all! I know it! It's just that...well, maybe we shouldn't be here, is all! Maybe somebody's giving us one last chance, with the rain and all! You know Johnny Devo didn't run away with his gang and join the Navy—we all knows it! You think a guy like dat, wearing a big ruby ring and hat like he wore, the way he wore it on his head jaunty and all, you think he run away? You think a guy like dat'd wear a Navy uniform? You seen his muddah, how she walks around in black all the time, how she cries in the market and all? She knows it and everybody knows he came in here and didn't come out!"

Chump's face flushed with anger, and now his ready fist wheeled around, striking Griffey flush on the face.

Griffey went down, making a splash when he hit the ground, and he lay there, holding his nose, which began to bleed.

"Go on then, you chicken-crud!" Chump shouted, standing over Griffey with both hands tightened to fists. "Go on and run home to your own muddah, if you's so scared!"

Griffey lay propped on one elbow, a hand cupping his nose.

Chump prodded him with toe. "Go on, then, chicken-crud! Beat it!"

A wash of emotion passed across Griffey's face. He opened his mouth as if to say something, then pushed himself back away from Chump, scrambled to his feet and ran off, back the way they had come. A bolt of lightning momentarily lit his retreat.

"You'll be sorry, Chump!" he shouted back. "Your own muddah'll be wearing black before you knows it!"

"In a pig's eye!" Chump laughed, and then he turned quickly to his two remaining gang members.

"And youse guys?" he said. "Are you wit me—or are you gonna run with your tails between your butt cheeks like Griffey?"

Mug was staring at the spot between the trees where he had last seen Griffey.

"Well?" Chump said, shoving Mug with the flat of his hand and bringing his face up close so the other boy would have to look into his eyes.

"I'm wit ya, Chump," Mug mumbled.

"Sure," Brudder said, nodding.

"Real men," Chump said proudly, punching them both lightly on the arm.

"Sure," Brudder said again.

As quickly as it had come, the storm retreated. The pounding sheets of rain reduced to a trickle, then stopped altogether, leaving a false shower in the woods of water falling from high leaves. Thunder and lightning were separated by time again, and pulled away overhead into the back distance. The black clouds softened to muggy gray and then, in widening holes, showed the former blue of the summer day through in bright, eye-squinting patches.

The other rumble they had heard before returned, closer now, before roaring off away.

"Another train!" Chump said.

They left their shelter and pushed their way through wet leaves and water-lined branches, which dropped new showers on them as they passed.

Suddenly, a line of something cutting from left to right, a high, man-made thing, became visible through a thin gap in the woods ahead.

Chump pushed on, put his head down to force his way through a wall of pine branches, Brudder and Mug behind him.

The wall gave way, and the three stood abruptly, startlingly, out in the open.

"Jeez!" said Mug.

And there it was.

They were now in a wide open cut in the woods, a right-of-way neatly trimmed from where they stood to a spot about a half a football field away. The grass at their feet was freshly mown, sloping gently down to a shallow gravel-filled bank that led to a creek. Water from the recent storm was draining into the stream, which chuckled with vitality.

Straddling the water, spaced as far as the eye could see from right to left, were the high, strong, inverted v's of a railroad trestle, holding a double line of track some thirty feet over the water.

And there, hanging from the span between the two trestles in front of them, were hung four rotting corpses.

"*Jeez!*" Mug repeated.

The hair on the back of Chump's head rose as if alive. Brudder stood beside him, mouth open, dull eyes fixed on the four things which dangled straight and unmoving in front of them, neatly separated, dead.

"They ain't dancin'," Brudder said dully, the most words he had ever strung together.

"No, they ain't," Chump said soberly.

He recognized the bodies, the clothes; he recognized the ruby ring on a finger of the half bone, half flesh hand of Johnny Devo, and the cap with pins on it that stood at a jaunty angle on Johnny's skull, stuck to bits of peeled skin.

"They ain't dancin'," Brudder said again, and now, as they had in the woods, they heard the far off rumble of not-thunder.

"A train!" Mug said.

There to the distant left was a tiny black line pushing smoke at the horizon. Then it was barreling toward them, looking like ebony lightning, sounding like thunder that would never end. The distant trestles trembled with the mighty iron weight overhead, a shower of latent rain dropping from beneath the tracks following the engine's path.

The bodies on their ropes twitches and began to swing, and now the train roared by, punching clouds of steam at the sky, screaming iron wheels against iron tracks, the dark engine and tender tearing past like an earth-bound rocket with a line of sooted, dull-colored gondolas and hoppers filled with coal, box cars shut tight with their secrets. The trestles shook and rattled with the terrific pressure, a spray of water washed down, and the ropes were yanked like marionette strings, the boys hanging from them dancing like puppets, arms flapping, legs kicking like Rockettes, feet tapping at naked air.

"*Now* they's dancing," Brudder said, mouth still open, unintelligent eyes filled with inert satisfaction.

The train flew past and onward, its dull red caboose rattling behind, taking the roar with it. The boys on the ropes settled to a gentle swing. The gash-mouth in Johnny Devo's skull regarded Chump with secret satisfaction, as the head shook mildly back and forth before settling to rest once more.

"I've had enough of this crud, I'm gettin' outta here," Mug said. He turned to run, stopping dead in his tracks as the color drained from his face.

"Hey, Chump...." he gulped, as Chump and then Brudder turned to look.

The tree line was no longer lined with just trees. At the border of the woods, where the neatly trimmed grass began, stood a line of people stretching as far to either side of the train trestle. They were leather-hooded to their waists, with holes only for their eyes.

The three closest to Chump and his gang each held a coil of strong new rope.

Others, appearing overhead on the trestle, were already cutting down Johnny Devo and his boys, brushing the remnants of the old rope knots away as the bodies fell thumping to the ground.

And a little later, Chump, as the world dropped away, heard his nearest executioner say, one dressed in black below her hood, in a sweet, sighing voice, "And I thought he was such a *good* boy."

The afternoon sun grew suddenly orange, dropped toward evening.

"Are you tired, Selene?" the Toyman said. "Do you want to nap?"

Selene shook her head emphatically no. Clutching the rim of the toybox, she peered in, her eyes ranging over the rows of toys. She looked deeper, deeper....

And then....

In the farthest depths of the toybox Selene found a darker place, where amber light barely reached. The toys here were hidden in shadow, furtive, twisted, sharp-angled.

"Are they broken?" Selene asked.

"They're dangerous," the Toyman answered.

Selene caught a glimpse—a piggybank with red eyes, a ball of trembling fluff, a misshapen head, other things—

She looked up at the Toyman, who only stared back down at her.

"It's your decision," he said.

She reached down....

THE DUST

There was more of the dust.

The house was kept clean; Mother had cleaned it herself for a long time and then, when she had begun to get old and tired and Father had finally agreed with her that she was indeed old and tired, they had retained someone to come up the hill twice a week to clean immaculately; but no matter how much cleaning was done, the dust remained. Seven of the eight floor and ceiling corners in any room might be spotless, but the eighth would have the dust, tucked neatly in and watching him. Ronnie knew why it watched him, and he hated the dust.

When Mother and Father went out, which they did four or five or sometimes—lately—even six times a week, Ronnie was left with the old lonely house to himself. In fact, Mother and Father locked him in. They went to town, Ronnie knew, to be away from him, and from the memory of the things that had happened with the dust when they lived in another town in another place thirty full years ago. When he had been called Slow Ronnie instead of just Ronnie, and had hated it. When he had begun to hate the dust because of what it did to him.

He had tried to tell Mother and Father about the dust, had been trying to tell them how the house was never really clean for thirty years, but they wouldn't listen to him. Or didn't want to. Mother just looked at him sadly out of her moon eyes, or sometimes shook her head or hid her face in her hands, and Father merely mumbled about the "problems of this boy." Ronnie knew Mother and Father argued about him, about putting him somewhere else away from people and away from them; sometimes he heard Mother's wailings in the night and Father's muffled arguments of "Better this way" or "Cheaper in the long run for us" and he knew that someday, perhaps someday soon, they would come to him with their tearful or blank faces and tell him that they could no longer keep him, that they were too old for it. But he understood all this. He only longed to make them understand about the dust, and about how it must be cleaned away before it consumed them all.

The house was high and dark, set in the side of a wooded hill up away from the town. It was what some might call dreary, but Ronnie loved every bit of it. And knew every bit of, from the cold deep cellar to the musty gables at each end of the attic, including the Room in the Attic and the Secret Room. He knew where every shadow was, except for the shadows of the dust which kept changing, and he knew every sharp corner and hideyhole and how many steps there were in each of the stairways. He liked the house even better at night, when the shadows were thicker, and you could hide anything, even the dust, in them, and the sixty-watt bulbs that Father preferred (because they were cheaper) barely illuminated the large spaces between them. When it was cold in the winter, and nighttime dark, like it was this night, and when Mother and Father were out, which they were, it was his favorite time because he could almost lose himself in those dark spaces and make believe that even the dust didn't exist; that nothing existed but Ronnie—not Slow Ronnie—and that the night and the sharp clear cold belonged to him alone and that whatever happened thirty years ago never happened and that he had only started existing here and now in this blackness. It was wonderful because he was here all alone.

Except for the dust.

The dust was out there, he could see it, even on this perfect night. He could not even shut the dust out now. And that made him angry and frightened, because on other nights like this, of which there were only four or five each year, he had been able to do it, to get rid of the dust, push it out beyond his circle of darkness and back away from the illumination of sixty-watt bulbs to a sulking corner deep across the room, or away and into another room entirely, where it would gather and brood and wait for the daylight to see and follow him again. But this night he could feel it within the circle, clinging to itself and knowing that it had won a new battle and followed him nearly to the heart of his most secret places. There was nowhere he could go now to be alone, except the Room in the Attic and the Secret Room (which even Mother and Father didn't know about), his special rooms where even the dust never followed.

"Go away," he said to the space inside the circle, where the dust lurked.

There was a silent shifting.

"Go away," he said again.

There was another shifting, a sound like many threads being drawn across wood, behind him.

"I said go away! You can't come here!"

Suddenly, there were memories. It was thirty years ago, and the dust was all around him. Pressing him in dryly, more dust than he had ever seen before, covering him, blocking his vision, making him cough and his eyes begin to water.

There was laughter.

More than one voice. A lot of voices. Out beyond the dust, not laughter like when Spike or Pauly stood on their heads and sang "I'm Popeye the Sailor Man," but mean laughter, laughter that had been waiting below the surface to spring on him, and had only needed a bit of running away to get out at him. He was fighting at the dust with his fingers and hands, coughing and beginning to cry, trying to get out of the dust to see where he was, where the laughter was coming from, where the dust was coming from.

There was more and more dust, blinding him now, and then he was pushing at it crazily and it was going away, finally pulling back and away from him and he could see and breathe again.

That was when they called him Slow Ronnie.

There were five or six of them, almost all his friends, the ones who had let him follow them around and carry their baseball equipment and, because he was so big, play touch football as a substitute in the fall after school. They had been waiting for him around the corner from Woolworth's, waiting for him to meet them, to come around the corner so they could drop the sacks of dirt and dust that Pauly had rigged up above the wrought-iron sign that hung on the corner with an orange firebox light on it, and they had pulled the string and were still laughing at him.

"Slow Ronnie," they were screeching. "Slooooooow Ronnie!" Waving their hands and taunting him while they said it. Almost all of them his friends, except for a new one he had never seen before, taller and sharp-faced.

"*Sloooooow* Ronnie," they kept saying as he wheezed and cried and brushed trembling at the dust.

Then he looked through his tears at the new one, the tall one with the bright sharp eyes, and a rage seized him.

"I'm not slow!" he screamed, and then he remembered the muscles in his arms going tight and hard and the breaking of a glass window and sharp red pieces of glass. Then no more. When he was awake again he was in a hospital tied down to a white bed and Mother and Father, their faces also white, looked down from above him. Father's face was whiter, and blanker.

The memories went away.

"Go away!" he screamed at the dust again.

He was within his cold circle, and the dust was trying to come at him again. He was not Slow Ronnie, he knew that; he would never be Slow Ronnie again and as long as he could keep the dust away, and the boy with the sharp hard eyes and smile, he would never be Slow Ronnie again. The boy was a long way away, in time and distance, but the dust was here and he had to keep it away or he would be Slow Ronnie again.

"I am not Slow Ronnie!"

The dust gathered, making a hissing noise, on either side of him. A small ball of it slid by, brushing at his shoe.

"No!"

He stood, making swimming motions with his arms, threatening the dust to stay back. He had told Mother and Father about the dust, and they hadn't listened to him, and now this was happening. He could see into the circle of weak amber light in front of him, and he saw that the dust, all of the dust, was forming. It was covering the floor, like whispering gray snow, clumps and bunches moving here and there across it, and it was pushing toward him. It was into the circle now, and he knew that finally, after growing in separate strength all these years, the dust was coming for him again, coming to make him gasp and scream helplessly, to fill his mouth and nose with absolute and terrible dryness, to make him into Slow Ronnie once more. He could not accept that, he would not let the dust do that to him again.

He shouted "Keep back!" and ran from the room, out into the shadows of the hallway, his shadows, toward the stairway. The dust, as his feet touched it, rose up in wavy fingers and tried to clutch at him, but he screamed and swatted down at it, and ran on. There was dust in the hallway too, flowing out of every doorway to meet in a splash at the center of the hall; Ronnie leaped over it and onto the stairs, taking them two steps at a time. Below him, the dust rose and drew together, flowing up the stairs after him.

Ronnie ran to the attic ladder, climbing it and dropping the door behind him and then frantically pulling at the door to the inner attic room, moving his arm this way and that in the darkness, searching for the overhead light cord. He found it, and the weak bulb clicked on. The room was empty, and Ronnie let out a long and shuddering breath. The Room in the Attic was still safe, and closing and bolting the door behind him, he sat down in the center.

He listened.

There were sounds, soft clicks and rustlings, but these were the sounds that were always in his room. These were the sounds of his house moving and sighing and settling contentedly about itself, and there was nothing of the dust about them. The dust did not come here, to this room; it did not belong and never had and all the sounds of the house, and the house itself, had always kept it out. This was the room that Ronnie went to when he was feeling sad, or when the dust in the other rooms began to bother him too much, or when the weather wasn't cold and shadowy like it was tonight. It was almost his favorite room in the house. There was hardly any furniture, and what furniture and storage there was was oddly shaped and threw long, deep and special shadows. Special shadows that blended with the creaking sounds and made the room always seem cold and dark. The dust never came in here.

The dust was coming in now.

Ronnie jumped up as he saw that the dust was sliding slowly but inexorably under the door. There was a great weight of dust behind the door, the lock was rattling heavily with the pressure of it, and there was a steady, roiling portion of it squeezing into the room and building inside.

Building to engulf him.

There was only one place for him to go, one place where the dust would never go because it didn't even know about it—no one knew about it, not Mother nor Father nor anyone else—and therefore couldn't follow. His Secret Room. The one that only he and the house were alive to, where he could think about anything, and the house would soothe him and the dust would not be there to watch.

He would go to that room and be safe.

There was a place under an old table in the Room in the Attic where the wall was not solid. Behind this was the Secret Room. On the outside of the house it showed as a tiny gable with no window, an obvious mistake of architecture. It was not even high enough to stand in, and was nearly airtight and completely dustless; one had to crouch low to get through its door, and step down into it as its floor was almost two feet below that of the Room in the Attic. There was not even a light in it, and Ronnie kept a flashlight hidden on a hook under the table by the door. The door itself was a paneled section of wood which fit snugly and undoorlike into the rest of the paneled wall.

It was a dark and secret and dustless place.

Ronnie crawled under the table and lifted his flashlight from its hook. He looked behind to see the dust building massively high, roiling and blocklike, and pushing toward him. If he didn't go into the secret place, give the dust the chance of seeing where it was, it would press over him and suffocate him. It would choke him until he couldn't think and he became Slow Ronnie again. He began to cough just thinking about it.

He turned, shaking, to the secret door to the Secret Room and pulled at the latch.

Crouching low, his flashlight snapped on, he pulled open the door and began to step down.

The dust was waiting for him.

Heaving, gray, and shadowless, it filled the entire Secret Room.

And the dust was pressing at him from behind, as it overflowed the Room in the Attic.

A sudden peace came over him, a silent raging peace, as the dust pressed down and upon him, holding him to itself, and the house murmured to him, and the boy with the sharp eyes and face was there before him in the dust, embracing him.

Outside, he heard the muffled hum of Mother and Father's returning car.

He knew who they would find.

Father Dear

He never beat me, but told me stories about what would happen to me if I did certain things.

"The crusts of bread," he told me, cutting the crusts off his own bread instructively and throwing them into the waste bin, "gather inside you. If you eat bread with the crusts still on, you will digest the bread but your body will not digest the crusts. They will build up inside you until...." Here he made an exploding gesture with his hands, close by my face. He smiled. I smiled. I was four years old, and cut the crusts off of my bread.

"The yellow pulpy material left after an orange is peeled," he told me another day, a bright sunny one as I remember, with thick slats of sunshine falling on the white kitchen table between us; I recall the sound of a cockatoo which flitted by outside, and the vague visual hint of green and the smell of spring that came in through the bottom of the window which he had opened a crack (I believe now that he opened that crack for effect, to accentuate the brightness of spring outside with the stuffy dreariness of our indoor habitation—he told me other things about dust and about the indoors), "will make your teeth yellow if you ingest it. With the eating of oranges which, by the way, you must eat, Alfred, for your condition, any specks of this pulp will be caught in a receptacle just to the back of your throat, just out of sight, and will creep up like an army of ants at night to stain your teeth. In time, your teeth will become the deep shade of a ripe banana; perhaps, someday, that of a bright lemon just picked." How I remember the hours I spent whisking those orange fruits clean of pulp, examining my fingernails afterward to make sure no bits had adhered to them; O, how many other hours did I lay awake at night in my bedroom, hating him and at the same time believing him (no, that's not right; the hate came later, much later; there was only love then, and if not that at least a respect for his knowledge, for the things he was so gently trying to save me from—no, it was Love after all) and waiting, with a parched ticking at the back of my tongue where the saliva had dried as I lay fearfully waiting for those tiny insect bits of pulp to march up my mouth, dousing my gums and teeth with yellow spray from their bucketlike tails; O! How many hours did I spend in front of a mirror, trying to see, my mouth as wide as my jaw would allow it, that "receptacle" where those lemon-ants waited!

I hate him now; came to hate him slowly, inexorably, and, in time, I have come to love that hate, to relish and enjoy it since it is the only thing I have in this world that I am not afraid of.

He taught me nothing of value. He taught me to hate books, to hate what was in them and the men who wrote them; taught me to, above all, hate the world, everyone in it; everything it stood for. "It is a corrupt place, Alfred," he lectured endlessly, "filled with useless people possessed of artificial sensibilities, people who respect and cherish nothing. They live like animals, all of them, huddled into cities chockablock one on top of the other; they are of different colors, and speak different languages until all their words mix in one jumbled whirr and none of them understand what any of the others are saying.

"I know, I come from that world, Alfred. They don't know what life is. They don't know what's *safe*. But you know what's safe, don't you?"

I remember grinning eagerly up at him at times like this, like a puppy; he always bent down over me, his hands behind his straight tall back, and I remember at times reaching up to him with my tiny hands, begging him, "Pick me up, pick me up, swing me, please!"

"Swinging you will make your stomach move in your body," he answered, smiling wanly, "and once moved, at your delicate age, it will stay in that new spot, perhaps where your lungs or pancreas should be, and will make you sick for the rest of your life. It may even turn you into a hunchback, or make you slur your words if it moves, on the high arc of your swing, into your vocal cavity. You *do* understand, don't you?"

My arms lowered slowly, tentatively, to my sides.

I was not allowed to play on the swings on the grounds, either, but would stare at them for hours through my bedroom window.

The grounds, naturally, were beautiful, wooded and sprawling. No one, I heard it whispered among the servants, had grounds like this anymore; no one, I once heard a Chinese servant say, *deserved* to have such grounds. The world, he whispered to mute Mandy, my sometimes guardian (when He was away), was still far too crowded for this type of thing to crop up again; there were too many other problems to be solved without one man shutting himself up in such a way. I am sure that Mandy went straight to my father after this bit of sacrilege had been imparted, and the man, if I remember correctly, was gone the following day. Another servant, of course, was in place instantly.

The grounds, as I say, were sprawling, but I was not allowed to make use of that sprawl. There were too many opportunities to be "hurt." The swinging motion I have already described could, of course, be accomplished to dire effect by the swing set just beyond the Italian-tiled patio; there was also at that spot a set of monkey bars which "would upset the balance of your hormones if you were to use it, since hanging upside down by a boy of your delicate constitution would only lead your body to hormone imbalance. The features of your face would begin to move about by the action of the blood rushing to your head, and you would end up looking something like this." He made an extremely grotesque—and terribly funny—face then, and I laughed along with him until I abruptly began to cry. If my memory serves me correctly, I ran and threw my arms around him, thanking him for saving me and asking him to promise never to leave or send me away; and, yes, I remember pointedly and now as clearly as if the moment were again occurring that my teary eyes were staring at his hands, still behind his back, and I was willing them to move around toward me, to show me anything parental and physical. I believe that may be the moment when I thought something was not right between us; for a fleeting second I entertained the thought that maybe he didn't love me after all but then quickly dismissed it, knowing that it must have been me, that I may already have been in danger of contracting some vile disease, something transmitted by a touch of the hands to the head, something transmitted by a loving hold, and that he was merely, as lovingly as he could, trying to avoid exposing me to it. He was saving me from himself. I threw myself from him, aching with apology for what I had almost accomplished. I don't remember if the thanked me or just went away.

"If you gaze at the sky too long," he said, after catching me leaning out of an upper story window, peering at the moon, "your head is very liable to fall off or stay locked in that position at least. Never look up in the daytime."

"Not even to watch a bird fly overhead?"

"Never. How old are you?"

"Seven."

"Never look up again, Alfred. Until now you have been lucky, but with the age of reason comes a severity of life that you will only too soon realize."

I never looked up.

"If you sit in a chair for more than five minutes, your feet will begin to lose their circulation and may never get it back. If you stand for more than five minutes, too much blood will rush to the bottom of your body and your feet will become heavy, as if filled with lead." I crouched when I walked.

"Meat will cause you to turn red."

I did not eat meat.

"Vegetables will cause you to turn their own color—yellow, green orange."

I only ate vegetables when desperate.

"Chocolate will cause you to turn black. Wheat you may take, and potatoes, and you may drink water in moderation after boiling, cooling and then boiling again. Do not drink milk: it will make you white as paper."

He showed me a book with these things in it, or rather read to me from one. The book, I later discovered, was *Moby Dick*. Such a thick book, such thick lies.

And yet I followed his instructions and thanked him for it.

I grew. I grew fat. Wheat and potatoes were my diet, and teenagehood found me stout and ugly. I wore glasses thick with mottled glass, because he told me a lucid pair would cause my eyes to change color and shape. My teeth hurt, and he scolded, saying that I had eaten something, possibly so long ago I could not remember, something that had gone against his wishes and was now catching up with me.

I will kill him when I find him.

He left abruptly; abandoned that massive estate in the dead of night when I was fifteen years old. There was only one hint that this would happen. Late in December of the winter he left, during the coldest part of a cold month, Mandy, the ghostly mute, took to her bed believing she would die. She was attended to by other of the staff, and even my father occasionally visited her. I was told never to go into her bedroom. I had once had a peek into that room—enormous and cluttered, with a high sculpted ceiling (there were paintings on it, clouds and blue sky which made me fearful lest my eyes and neck lock on it) and deep brown carved wooden walls. A huge bed, with high spikes at the four corners. A green-and-yellow coverlet. This was all I remembered. In the very last days of December, when it was made known with the usual whispering (whispers were what filled that manse, whispers and lies) that she would die before the night was gone, I went in to see her.

I knew she was alone. There were statues on that floor, as on every floor, behind which I had often hidden and which I had no neuroses about since my father did not know or had never caught me at it. There was one particular statue, a golden, tiny wood goddess with bow, set prominently high on a pedestal just to the left of the wide winding staircase (I used to occasionally slide down that staircase railing also, until He found me at it one day and told me that my genitals would be forced back into my body by the pressure of the railing if I continued) which gave an excellent view of Mandy's sickroom entrance. Shortly after supper I secreted myself there, watching the comings and goings of the servants, the dour doctor who came from somewhere and departed again to it, and, finally and surprisingly, my father, who came quietly out of the door somewhere just before midnight. He had no reason to check on my whereabouts, since he had made sure I was tucked solidly into my bedchamber just after dinner and had no reason to believe I would be anywhere else (he told me as a baby of the "things that were abroad after dark") but this was one of the few of his lies that I had managed to outgrow, even though at times on my nightly sojourns I thought I spied one of his "beasties of the night"—more likely optical illusions of the night. It occurs to me that he was neglectful in this, but why quibble; I seem to recall he was getting a little old by this time and had forgotten to reinforce some of the foul walls he had built, brick by blood red brick, around me for my fifteen years. Anyway, here I was when he hobbled off (he *was* getting old, and I remember him making use of a cane just before he left the next month) to his own voluptuous quarters somewhere on the other side of the building and one flight up (I had seen those quarters once, too, and they made Mandy's into a tent) and, probably, to one of his live-in paramours, servant-man or woman or possibly someone from outside who was occasionally flown in, usually around the holiday season (which was not, naturally, celebrated in this household).

I waited a full ten minutes, crouched in my hiding spot and beginning to balance the two fears—fear of discovery by leaving the shadow of that statue too soon and fear of my legs being lost to me since I could feel numbness setting into them—before slowly moving out toward the door in a rabbit's crouch.

The lock ticked open easily. The room was not as big as I had remembered, but the bed seemed even bigger. Grey moonlight suffused the room, throwing a pale line of light across the bottom half of the bed; there was also a low-wattage bulb set into the wall over the bedstead, illuminating the upper half.

All I could see was a pile of pillows and that same green-and-yellow comforter which looked as flat as if no one were under it. At first I thought that this might be the case; perhaps they had moved her without my seeing; perhaps she had died and they had lowered her from the window into the waiting arms of the dour doctor to be carted off for burial or burning; perhaps this had all been a setup to lure me to this spot so that my hiding place behind that wood goddess could be uncovered and I could be mind-tortured further. I whirled quickly around but saw no one at the doorway behind me and no one, seemingly, in the corners of the room ready to jump out.

By this time I had moved close enough to see that, yes, she was in bed after all. Barely there, what was left of her. There was a head above the line of the quilt that looked like the head of a monkey, shriveled and nut brown; and below that the coverlet stretched as flat as I had imagined it did, scarcely revealing the outline of an evaporated body.

I leaned down over her, wanting very badly to peel up her eyelids as I had seen once on television (before He had decided that this pleasure, too, should be denied me for my own good) when her eyes opened of their own and she stared straight into my face.

She tried to scream, but nothing came out. Her features contorted, her lips pulling back over her teeth, making her look even more like a monkey. It was now that I saw why she was mute; her tongue ended in a surgically sharp line at the back of her throat, giving her nothing to articulate with. Or so I thought.

After a moment she ceased trying to scream, and a curious calm descended on her. She looked at me for a few moments, apparently recognizing me now. Why had she tried to scream? Possibly she had thought I was someone else. But now, recognizing me as she did, her eyes brightened and she tried desperately to say something.

"What?" I asked, leaning down close with my ear to her mouth, wanting to draw back because of the disease she might impart to me but overcome with a violent compulsion, for the first time in my life, to explore a mystery on my own.

"I can't hear you."

She was muttering something, so far under her breath and with such obvious effort that I hushed my own breathing, concentrating doubly hard to pick up her faint, insect's voice.

"Mo...." she was saying. "Mot...."

"What?" I rasped her, impatient and now with one eye on the door lest someone hear the faint struggle going on in here.

"Mot...."

"Mot? What do you mean, mot?"

"Mot...Mother," she said, so far in the back of her throat that it was like listening to an echo off somewhere in a cave.

My body became ice. I nearly grabbed her by the mouth to make her repeat that word; but her eyes had filmed over and her lips were slack. For a moment I thought she had died there before me, but as I watched her eyes cleared again and once more she looked straight into me, through me.

I said nothing, and then I whispered, "You are my mother?"

Her mouth said nothing, but it formed the word, yes.

"*Oh,*" I said, my throat gagging. I threw myself from the bed, instinctively going for the window and then pushing myself away from it when I looked up to see the full moon staring down at me from above. I fell to the floor. My throat would not work; I lay gasping for air like a reefed fish. My head was on fire, too; I thought for a moment that one of the terrible things my father had warned me about for so many years had come true, that the moon, or my disobedience in being out of my room, or my visit to this chamber, or the sight of this woman, or what she had said, had triggered one of those ugly reactions which had for so long hung above me like a sword. I had eaten too many crusts when a baby, I thought desperately; possibly it was lemons; or bananas, or my brains had blown up to balloon size from hanging upside down, or not hanging upside down, or from bumping into a doorjamb, or not—

With a Herculean effort I staggered to my feet, to the door, into the hallway past the Hunter Goddess (her bow for a moment as I came out of the room pointed straight at my head) and into my own room, clawing my way into bed and so far under the covers that everything—the light, the evening, myself—was extinguished and a sudden darkness dropped upon me....

Only to rise again into dim light later, much later, when the first tepid hints of spring were manifesting themselves, and when my father was long departed, my mother long dead. My father brought most of the staff (at least those he had comported with) with him, leaving only a skeleton klatch of indifferent menials to attend to me, supplemented by his own horrid ghost, hanging in the air, usually in dusty corners, wherever I went in that house, reminding me of what I was and what he had made me and, in his absence, daring me to be anything else.

For the next twenty years I listened to that ghost.

Haunted, bloated by shame, starch and nightmares, I lurched from room to room (save one, of course) in that mansion, trying once again to be an infant by following my father's twisted directions on life. I was not rational; I was nothing but a bundle of neuroses held together by muscle and bone matter. I shouted much, screamed much, cried much except when I remembered what he had told me about crying: "If you weep, Alfred, the water reserves in your body will never be filled again. Recall that you were born with a certain amount of tear-water in you; that all other water which you take in is used for other purposes or expelled; and recall that once that tear-matter is depleted it can never be restored and you will never be able to cry again. Your body will try, throwing you into horrid convulsions, but nothing will come out of your eyes. Eventually your tear ducts will take the liquid they so crave from your eyeballs themselves, turning them into dry, paperlike orbs. Needless to say, you will go blind."

I tried to go blind. I cried incessantly, half-waiting for (and not caring about) the coming moment when there would be a cracking sound from deep within my eyesockets signaling the end of vision and the beginning of physical darkness. It never came, and after many months (years?—there is much about those twenty summers, winters, springs and falls that memory does not serve) I came slowly to realize that here was one of His major lessons that turned out not to be history but fiction. Might there be others? I began to explore. Carefully, of course. The litany of my fears was a long one, and there were some areas where I would not tread—those fears were so deep-rooted. But there were many—"You must *always*, Alfred, walk with a measured step, throwing one foot out in front of the other, pausing before letting it touch the ground, and then letting it down in two phases, heel and then toe, *two separate stages*, heel then toe, or the feet will become flat and useless and hurt you incessantly"—that I was able, with patient years of self-imposed physical and mental therapy, to be rid of. I never, when speaking, doubled the letter "a" when using it as an article anymore (He had assured me it would prevent further stuttering, an offering to the Stutter Gods, I suppose). I didn't knock my knees together when standing up anymore. I didn't blink consciously before looking at something close up (to adapt the eyes to closeness).

And so, at age thirty-five, I was ready to find and kill Him.

It must have appeared quite comical, this fat (though by now not so bloated since I had learned that my diet could be expanded to include a healthier assortment of food; I had also discovered vitamins, something He had never spoken of), squinting (I had done away with the glasses, learning that they were not needed, were actually destroying my eyesight; I would squint with or without them now), white-haired (is it any wonder my hair had turned snow white—actually it was that way after I came to my senses after my mother's death) middle-aged man with enough tics, bad habits and eccentricities to fill two thick volumes, fumbling his way into the world beyond his little castle (I made it a point to pass by those monkey-bars, even swinging once upon them, pulling myself upside down and screaming my father's name at the deepest of blue skies that was evident that day) and out onto the Road of Vengeance, a road I, this abnormal specimen of man, knew nothing about, cared to know nothing about, begging only that it lead him through the maze of the terrible big world to the front door of the man-monster who had caused him to hate not only it (the world) but also his father and himself. Curiously, I had come to love one thing; the image of my mother on her deathbed: a deep and mysterious totem she became for me since I really knew so little about her; any of the servants who were left after my father's abandonment knew nothing of her, and my own recollections were so dim—she took care of me, I seemed to recall, in those odd periods when my father was ill in bed or occupied with one of his paramours. Never saying anything, she was hardly noticed. She had become safe; become, in fact, much larger than life. She was my mother; she had nurtured me, brought me into the world, possibly even loved me secretly, had certainly done nothing to harm me directly; and so, she became Sacred. She became the image I could hold up to Him; and when I found him I fully intended to flay him alive—peeling the flesh from his now ancient bones, as many strips for Her as for myself.

I found him easily.

Almost too easily; I admitted a little disappointment that the chase did not go on longer because the scent was so strong. The City was a strange place but not all so horrible; I had heard him speak about it to me for so long in revulsive tones ("You must *never*, Alfred, I repeat *never* go into the outside world, the vile City waiting out there, for it would be your end"); I found it somewhat less than my imagination had made it out to be. It seemed merely too many people pressed into too small a space; but they were, after all, people, and did not frighten me or revolt me as I had expected they would.

I had fully expected the Hunt to go on for some time, and so found myself immensely surprised when the most discreet inquiries as to my father's whereabouts led to his discovery. He seemed to be someone of import; I had never had doubt as to his monetary worth since the very fact that we had resided on such a vast expanse of land, at a time (you'll remember the comments of the servants as to this) when no one seemed to live this way, but I was duly shocked to find him so readily known *outside* of our isolated manse.

I was careful in approaching him. He resided in the most well-to-do building in the most well-to-do part of the City (naturally), holding an entire floor in a dreamlike blue metal and glass monstrosity; it overlooked the river, which, in its flowing blueness, hurt the eyes with all that visual concentration at one far end of the spectrum (he had once told me the color blue would hurt me; would make me, he said, "see nothing but blue until you are driven mad and want to tear your eyes out"). I had also been told, by one overly cautious individual who had easily succumbed to bribery for information (he insisted that we meet in a series of brief encounters in a park, where he imparted, on a bench by an ice cream custard stand—once, even, in the bushes by a children's zoo—tiny snatches of information that, when added together, gave a picture of a man of immense power in the last throes of life. This hurt me terribly, because if He were already dying he would be that much less horrified by my appearance, never mind my actions, and would probably already be faced toward the last dark precipice which I would gleefully tumble him over. I didn't want him to die. I wanted to kill him.

I made my way to Him with the utmost caution. Ironically, and to my delight, there was in the entrance to his entire 14th floor a statue remarkably like that wood goddess in our manse which I remembered with so much fondness and which, in a way, was the catalyst to my new life; with her arrow she had pointed me in the direction of Salvation and Revenge and had, in her smooth and godlike way, brought me to this delicious point.

I hid behind this statue, distinct from that other only in that this one was clothed, and I methodically, patiently mapped the comings and goings to His suite. I did this for days, managing to hide myself from the watchful (or half-watchful—he was not very attentive to his job) orbs of the guard who seemed always to be present. There were visitors, all during the day—men with briefcases, dull brown suits always buttoned, grim gray faces; but I noticed that in the evening there were never any visitors, and that somewhere around nine o'clock the bored guard usually slipped off for a cigarette, no doubt shared with other bored guards on other floors of the building. He invariably stayed away a half-hour, and no one ever checked on him, so after a week of this surveillance I quietly slipped from behind my lair (knocking my knees together once as I rose—damn Him!) and stole my way into his metal manse.

If possible, this abode of his was even more regally attired than the other; the richness of the furnishings—velvet-covered furniture in blacks, reds and greens, tapestries, oiled wood walls and floors and antique ceramics—not to mention the other artworks, paintings and, yes, sculpture everywhere—that I began to gag in reaction to it. He had been a Pig before; but the realization that he was now an even greater one, a *public* one—this was all too much. I fingered the blade in my overcoat pocket—I had searched long and hard through the manse for just the right instrument, finally settling on one that, if the little blurbs often found in museums next to art treasures are to be believed, was once used for ritual sacrifice in Celtic Ireland. Oh, yes, I would use it again for just such a purpose, reviving a custom....

Room after room of nauseating ostentation passed before me, until the hairs on the back of my head ("Don't ever let the hairs on the back of your head rise in fright, Alfred: it will cause you, in time, to lose your hairs as they are pulled into the back of your skull by the action of forced straightening") (!!!) stood on end and I knew that the richly carved, heavy-hinged door (hares and hunters on that door, how delightfully appropriate!) before which I stood was the last in the apartment and would lead to his bedroom. And indeed it did, for as I edged it open I heard a faint but unmistakable voice call out questioningly, "Grace? Grace?"

I was going to answer that no, it was not Grace and that the state of grace was what I hoped he possessed for the journey he would soon take, but when I saw that the room was so completely black dark that he would not see me until I stood just over his bed I decided to slip through that oily darkness and do just that. He called out again, very faintly, and then lapsed into a ragged, even breathing that told me he had slipped into sleep.

In a stealthy moment I was at his bedside, and leaning over him to turn on the Tiffany lamp by his bed.

At the instant I turned on that lamp he awoke.

"No!" was all he said, hoarsely. He tried to mouth my name, but I knew at that moment that he had suffered a stroke at this very instant of nirvana and would have trouble saying anything at all. I drew my blade out slowly, running it over my nails in front of his straining red face; he was gulping for air like a blowfish out of water.

"Alfred," I said slowly, quietly, completing for him what he was trying so hard to say. He shook his head from side to side, his eyes never leaving my face.

"Yes, Father, it is I. Are you surprised?"

He was puffing hard, and I lowered my ear (as I had done so long ago for my dear mute mother!) to hear him say, "Go...back."

I laughed. I pulled my head back and spat laughter, and then I put my face close to his.

"I don't think so, Father."

Again he was straining.

"Must," he said.

"Why? To keep me away from you? Don't you want me by your living side?" I lowered my wide eyes just inches from his, and brought the blade up close to his straining, yellow nostrils. "Would you rather I didn't speak? Would you rather I cut my own tongue out, make myself mute like my mother?"

His eyes went very wide and he shook his head violently from side to side.

"What, Father? What is it you want to say?"

I pulled him up by the shoulders, a little frightened by how light and frail he was, and pressed his lips to my ear.

"No . . ." he said.

"Speak, damn you!"

"Did it...herself...."

"Did what?"

"Cut her...own...tongue out...."

I pushed him back down into his pile of silken pillows. *"Liar!"* I said, raising my fist to strike him.

"No!" he said, suddenly finding his voice from somewhere down deep before it cracked off into a whisper again. "True...."

Calming abruptly, or rather moving off beyond rage to a calmer, more clear, more vicious place, I once again lowered my ear to his lips.

"Why did you leave, Father?"

There was a gurgle in his throat, and then, "...her...house...."

"What do you mean, 'Her house'?"

"...kept me there. Gave me everything to keep me silent. Made me...."

"Made you what?" My voice was regaining its edge.

"Made me...." He was breathing very unevenly, and said with great effort, with what a fool could have taken to be pleading in his eyes, "You."

My voice was very calm now, and I made sure he could see me drawing the blade through my fingers, letting it glint off the weak light from the amber reading lamp.

"You're lying," I said. "You're lying like you always have to me. Your life is a lie from beginning to this, the end. You twisted my mind from as early as I can remember. It's a sewer now, Father. It always will be. I am scared to death just to be outside that mansion. Just coming here made me tremble and sweat. My life is a catalog of unnamable things, sick things, tics and neuroses that I can't escape. I fear everything. Except you." I brought the blade down slowly, delicately toward his old man's chicken neck.

"Did it for you, go back," he croaked, looking at my eyes, not at the blade. "Hybrid. She...hated you. Only way to keep you alive. Statue," he said, his face suddenly getting very red, blood pumping into it from the ruptured machine in his chest and making his eyes nearly pop out of his face. His voice became, for a moment, very loud and clear. "Alfred! She was from the woods, not like us! Go back, save your life!" He grabbed at me with his spindly arms, his twiglike fingers. He tried to pull himself up, tried to clasp his vile body to mine. "...back...."

His grasp loosened then, and he slipped, like a flat rock into a pool of water, down into death.

I sat up, panting, and looked down at him; the blade felt sharp in my hand and I entertained for a moment the notion of carving him up anyway, of taking the pound of flesh I had come for and at least giving to my mother the sacrifice I had vowed. But instead I lowered it into my coat and stood up. He was pitifully dead, and in death he appeared much less the object of hate; the soul had left, leaving only meat behind.

It was then, when I was leaving his bedroom and passing the massive, gilded mirror over the dresser by the doorway, that I saw something that made me stop.

My skin had turned red. I thought immediately of the meat I had eaten in the past months, of the bounteous meat I had eaten in the past days in the City. I shook my head to clear it, turned on the bright lamp on the dresser and once again my color was correct. I smiled knowingly at myself: for a chilly moment my teeth looked yellow and I thought of all the oranges I had eaten—the back of my throat became uncontrollably dry and it felt as though something tiny was ticking around back there—but then this passed too.

"Fool," I said, and left the apartment in haste, throwing a fleeting glance at the statue in the foyer before passing on.

Everything outside was blue.

Overhead, there was a fat full moon, and as I looked up at it it turned indigo and my head began to ache, giving me trouble in lowering it.

I sat down on a bus and then a train, and my feet went numb.

I now felt, inside me, the movement of my organs and the gathering of bread crusts as they pressed out through my ribs, hernialike.

Somehow, I made it back to the grounds of the manse. I think a servant found me outside the front gates in the morning, curled up like a gnarled root, my face pointed at the killing sky. I don't know how he recognized me, since as they carried me in I passed a looking glass and saw that the features of my face had rearranged themselves, grotesquely mimicking that funny face my father had made at me so long ago.

They placed me in my father's old bedroom; the dour doctor came and went, and from the look on his dour face I knew that he would not return from the woods from which he was summoned.

I don't know what color I am now—red, black, blue, green, bone white. I do know that the pulp-ants are active this morning and that therefore my teeth must be a particular shade of yellow. Lemon yellow, perhaps. My genitals have retracted into my body. My head feels as though it will shortly fall off my shoulders.

I have had the statue of my mother moved into my new bedroom and placed in my line of sight. The arrow in her bow points directly at my forehead and I now see a look of lust and self-loathing on her features that I didn't see before. I want to look at that statue; I want to look at it hard and long.

I think often of my father.

I know that soon my tear ducts will rob the liquid they need so desperately from my eyeballs, turning them into crackly paper orbs, and that, naturally, I will go blind.

CHILDREN OF CAIN

Tonight I killed my mother in her bed.
Because:

Hank and I hit it off right away when he started school. It was late in the second semester, but they let him into the sixth grade anyway. He was a foster kid. I'd never met anyone like him before—he was always smiling and he always had good ideas for things to do. After classes we'd play wiffle ball, or check out the magazines at the drug store, or sit under the drooping umbrella of the weeping willow in my backyard and make believe we were trapped in a force field. We did everything together. He said I was like a brother to him.

"I've always wanted a brother," he smiled.

"You've got one," I smiled back.

One day near the end of April, a kid name Porky Kolhausen brought a one-pound bullfrog into school in his lunchbox and shoved it so far into our faces that we had to all but eat it. "Got it out of Cooper's Pond," he bragged, knowing we'd be impressed with the feat. "Bet you guys couldn't do that."

I said, "Bet there's bigger frogs than that in Cooper's Pond."

"Bet we could catch one of 'em," Hank quickly added.

"Bet you couldn't," Porky challenged, and that same afternoon after school found Hank and I outside the Cooper property.

We found the hole in Cooper's fence, and crawled along the concrete foundation of his tool shed. We stopped at the edge. Forty yards away was the pond, a cool oval of blue reflective water dotted with lily pads, water-flowers, banked by moss and close-cut grass. There was supposed to be bass in that pond, and Porky had bragged he had caught a bluegill but had no evidence since he claimed Cooper had started yelling at him from the house and he'd had to drop his net and run. That one we were allowed to doubt.

"Think we can make it?" Hank smiled.

I was more nervous. "I don't know—"

"Come on." And then he was gone ahead of me, crouched like a commando, moving past a green enameled metal table and chairs and into the open.

I followed, and swore I heard Cooper yell after us. But I looked back to see the flat white face of the back of his house, and no one in sight. The screened porch was empty. A hammock blew lazily between the two elms shading the porch.

"Come on!"

I hurried to catch up. Hank was already nearing the edge of the pond, squatting on a rock speckled with duck crap that jutted out boldly into the water.

"The old man's going to catch us, I know it."

"Don't worry about it," Hank said, stretching out to look into the water. The calmness in his face was reflected back at us.

There was nothing to see, just water and weeds, the drift of silt and last autumn's caught leaves at the bottom of the pond—and then I saw vague movement. "There," Hank said, pointing to a spot a yard out to our right. I saw nothing, then Hank added, "Keep watching." Something separated itself from the drift of pure water: a lashing tail, the lazy wave of tiny fins.

"A bluegill!" I said.

"It's a small bass," Hank corrected. His eyes were wide with concentrated pleasure. I saw him lower his hand like a snake charmer toward the water, then suddenly his arm dived in and he came up with the fish. It tried to slide out of his grip, throwing its small head from side to side, but Hank quickly backed off the rock and laid fish out on the mossy lawn. It began to flop toward the water, drawn like a magnet. Hank dug the toe of his sneaker under it and flipped it away from the water another yard.

"Great. Let's see what else we've got."

I eyed the bass, which curled tentatively and then lay still, and followed Hank around the bank toward the treed side of the pond.

"Where are you going?" I asked anxiously, my mind still on the house and Cooper.

"This is where the bullfrogs would be."

He dipped into the deep shade, back away from the water. For a moment I lost sight of him.

"Here."

He had reemerged in a tiny clearing surrounded by tightly wound branches close to the lapping shore. There seemed barely enough room for two. I kneeled close by.

My hand fell on something long and machined and I pulled it up from the tangle of weeds.

"Hey, Hank, it's Porky's net!"

Hank stood staring at the water. "We don't need it."

"But—"

"Be quiet," he whispered.

This time his hand shot sideways, on the bank, and he brought up something green and fat with long legs. I hadn't even seen it.

Hank smiled. "They hide in with the grass and water weeds," he explained. "He was there all the time, watching us." He lowered the frog into Porky's net and took the handle from me. "Let's go back."

He turned into the woods and wound toward the spot where we had left the bass. "Happy?" he smiled, and I nodded. He presented me with the fish, which seemed to pant in my hand and tried once to flip away from my grasp. Soon we were back at the hole in Cooper's fence and making our way to the back of the rubbled lot next door.

"Now comes the fun part," Hank said.

"Aren't we going to take them home?"

Hank smiled at me, his head tilted a little sideways. "Nah."

"But we've got Porky's net for evidence—"

"Screw Porky," Hank said, continuing to look at me that way. I had never seen him look like that before.

I was going to argue, but he turned away from me to the tall concrete wall at the back of the lot. The wall was topped by a ragged stretch of rusted barbed wire; behind it was a junked car lot and the barbed wire kept nobody out because there was a hole in the concrete wall, a chipped circle two foot high gouged out over many years by kids with crowbars and screwdrivers and old hammers.

"Come on."

Hank wormed through the hole and waited for me. On the other side, surrounded by the cool shadows cast by rusted semis, he took the frog out of the webbing and tossed the net back among the truck parts.

"Hey."

"Never mind the net. Watch this," he said.

I watched the bullfrog. It had been quiet till now, quiescent in its captivity. Hank held it before him with both hands, like a barbarian holding a sword, and felt down with his fingers to a place on the frog's belly. "Now." He squeezed, and the frog began to croak, a low, belching sound. I laughed.

"Now keep watching," Hank said.

He pressed harder on the frog's belly. It emitted another croak, lower and huskier than the first, and then its mouth opened wide and its eyes widened and its tongue drew out as if it had been blown up like a tiny balloon.

Hank kept pressing as he turreted toward the concrete wall. The entire front of the frog now looked like an inflated balloon.

"What—" I started to say but Hank shrugged me off with a laugh as his hands closed suddenly around the frog's middle. There was a squishing sound and the frog's eyes exploded outward and its head split wide. Its tongue, along with much of its gut, flew out of its mouth and hit the wall like a projectile.

"Jesus!" I said and turned away from the red raw splotch of frog guts on the wall. "How could you do that?"

I looked at Hank. I thought he would have a retching look on his face, or would start laughing like some kids do when they see gross stuff, but his face was flushed red. When he dropped the remains of the frog he looked perfectly happy.

"Now you," he said.

"Are you crazy?"

I looked at the bass in my hand. It was nearly dead; already I could feel the scales around its middle where I'd been holding it beginning to dry out and peel away. Even if I had rushed it back to the pond or to other fresh water it would die. But that wasn't the point.

"I don't want to do that," I said.

Hank didn't do what I thought he would. He didn't say, "Are you chicken?" or laugh the whole thing off. He just kept staring at me expectantly.

"I don't want to," I repeated.

And then I did. Convulsively, I turned to the wall and choked the bass just behind the head, feeling its brain and upper guts fly out like a squeezed pimple. The head split off from the body and hit the cement wall whole, falling to the ground.

I stood watching it, and then I dropped the rest of the bass and ran, shimmying through the hole in the wall and running through the empty lot to the street. My legs pumped and tears filled my eyes as I jumped the curb and crossed the lawn of my house and ran into the garage and up to my room. I closed the door behind me and blocked it with a chair.

I threw myself on the bed and cried. When my mother came to call me for dinner I was still crying because I knew that I had killed that bass because I wanted to.

I didn't see Hank for awhile after that. There were a hundred excuses, but he didn't push me. We were in the same homeroom, and the same Math class, but I managed to not even pass him in the hallway. Once when we did bump into each other I looked at his face but didn't look into his eyes.

I spent a lot of time in my room. My Mom began to ask me if I was all right, so I had to fake her out, tell her I was going to the library, then go out to the garage to be by myself, or tell her I was going to play ball in the park and then sit behind the grandstand with my knees up and my head down.

I kept seeing Hank's expectant smile. It was as if he'd known I would do what I did to that fish, as if he'd known that, suddenly, a door had opened in my mind that had nothing to do with fish or frogs but something much more horrible. All the frogs and fish that had ever died were just the first grains at the beginning of a beach leading to the largest ocean in the world.

I *hadn't* wanted to kill that fish. I *had*.

I was afraid of Hank, and of myself.

It was four weeks after the day at Cooper's Pond that Hank came for me again. I had begun to think that he had forgotten about me, that maybe he had found someone else to hang around with, or perhaps had decided to leave me alone. I had dreamed about some of the things that Hank might do, and always the dreams ended with Hank's smile, his happy, knowing smile, hovering over me, detached, like a scythe.

But after a month even the dreams had started to go away. It was the end of spring, the beginning of summer, and soon school would be over. I would be going away to camp, I had projects to finish before classes ended, and I had begun to forget, at least as much as I would, that day and what Hank and I had done.

I was up in my room. I remember the late spring breeze blowing in the curtains, bringing into the room the particular odor that late spring flowers have, a heavy pollen scent that smells like living things themselves. I was putting the last of my British Museum dinosaur models into a diorama I was building for the Science Fair at school, lowering a stegosaurus into its spot in the midst of HO model vegetation at the base of a papier mache volcano, and when I heard the doorbell downstairs ring and then heard my mother call up to me I knew that it was Hank.

I dropped the model. I wanted to cry all of a sudden. I sat rocking myself, my eyes blurring with tears, my face growing hot, and then I clutched my hands into fists and buried my face in my lap and began to hit myself on the sides of the legs hard.

"No! No!" I sobbed, muffling my angry voice so my mother wouldn't hear.

"Rudy, you hear me?" my mother called. "I said Hank is here. Should I send him up?"

I must have made a noise in answer, because a moment later I heard a shuffle on the stairs and the door to my room opened and he was there.

"Hi, Rudy." The smile hadn't changed. Nothing about him had. He was still the same Hank I had known for two months, hit fungoes to, flipped baseball cards with, hunted for frogs—

"Whatcha doing?" he asked. It was as if he had seen me yesterday. He put his hands in his pockets and bent down to look at the diorama. "Neat." He uprighted the stegosaurus, set it down exactly where I would have, brushed some HO lichen from the spiked tail. He bent lower, bringing his eyes in line with the front view, sweeping them across the Jurassic landscape, up the slope of the volcano to the lava-rimmed caldera. "Good stuff."

He stood up, tucked his hands deeper into his pockets, smiled. "So whatcha been doing?"

"Not much," I answered, looking at the floor. "Been real busy."

"I bet." His eyes roamed away from me, around the room, over the baseball trophies, the autographed Mets baseball, the posters. "Oh, *neat!*"

he said, going to a new model I had finished the week before, a red '56 Chevy convertible. "Where'd you get it?"

"My mother bought it for me," I answered quietly. "Good report card."

"Want to go somewhere?" he said suddenly, turning to look at me.

"No."

"You sure? Be a lot of fun."

"I've got too much to do. Got to finish this project."

"It's *Saturday*, for Pete's sake. You can do it tomorrow. Want me to ask your Mom if it's all right?" He made as if to go out into the hallway.

"No. Don't. I...don't want to go with you."

I looked at him then, expecting to see feigned surprise, or hurt, on his face, but instead there was only his smile.

"Come on," he said.

"Jesus, Hank, I don't want to!"

We looked at each other for a few moments, and then my mother called up, "You boys behave, or I'll make you go outside!"

Hank's smile didn't waver. His eyes held the smile and expanded it, expanded it like the ocean that leads to the horizon that never finds land—

"Sure," I said, my voice barely a whisper. "Okay."

"*Awright!*" Hank said, taking two long steps toward me, hugging his arm around me like a brother.

We avoided my mother, going out through the garage. "Need your bike," Hank said. I pulled my ten-speed from the wall and mounted it, riding out the open garage door into the full spring afternoon, waiting while Hank trotted up to the front porch to get his ten-speed and gear down beside me.

The day outside was like that breath of flower-life had been in my room. The world was burst open with flowers, green lawns and leaves—the trees so laden they looked wet. I breathed it in, feeling the lushness fill my lungs, breathing out the scent of chlorophyll and freshly spread fertilizer and mowed lawn. I wanted to feel life around me, forget the ocean that rolled and swelled in my head.

"Nice day," Hank said.

I just looked at him.

I followed him in low gear up the hill away from my house, then coasted down the long hill into town. We timed the lights so that we didn't have to brake. Hank took his hand from the handlebars and sat up, letting the wind blow across his face. We went straight through town and out, toward the farmstands and woods.

"Where are we going?" I asked.

"Follow, Bwana," he said, grinning.

I knew then where we were going. When Hank had first moved in I had showed him a special place—a hollow of woods at the end of a trail in an old Boy Scout camp which had been abandoned twenty years before after a forest fire. What had grown back was small and stunted between the burnout. I had cleared out the hollow with a couple of other kids the summer before. We had made plans to sleep out overnight when our parents gave us permission.

My mother never had.

I had taken Hank there once, making plans to camp out with him the coming summer. The place had been overgrown with a year's worth of weeds then, but as we rounded off the road into the woods I saw that the trail had been cleared, the bushes pushed back, even cut in some spots where they were thick outcroppings. We passed the burned-out jamboree hall, a charred square of water-rotted timbers, and veered back into the forest.

"Almost there!" Hank called back, and the same sob that had assaulted me back in my room rose once again to my throat and threatened to break out.

We skirted a huddle of moss-grown picnic benches, then abruptly shot out into the mottled sunshine of the hollow.

The dale had been brushed clean.

It looked as if an overnight Boy Scout campout had taken place, followed by a good cleanup, grass raked almost to the dirt, old leaves, branches and twigs swept away.

"Like it?" Hank said, dismounting his bike, leaning it in a smooth motion against the thick trunk of an oak. "Been working like a dog out here."

I got off my bike slowly and rested it on its kickstand.

He looked at me and laughed. "What's the matter? You look like you've seen the boogeyman."

I lowered myself to the ground, holding my stomach. I suddenly wanted to vomit. I closed my eyes, the ocean appearing before me, an ocean of thick red, thin clusters of veins, the bob of a gray organ in the swell, a hand reaching up out of the sickly-sweet-smelling sea to turn over and fall, disattached—

"Whoa, buster," I heard close-by. I looked up to see Hank standing over me. His face was blank. I smelled vomit, looked down to see my pants covered, my sneakers, my hands.

"You okay, pard?" Hank said.

"No."

"Take a minute. Clean yourself up." He stepped back away from me, from the smell. He'd left a handkerchief at my feet. I mopped myself, feeling my stomach turn over again, then keel to steadiness.

"Feel better?" he asked.

"A little."

"Good."

He began to whistle, thinly, through his teeth, as he worked something away from the backpack at the rear of his bicycle seat. It was a crinkled paper bag. Inside was a sandwich. He sat down Indian fashion next to his bicycle and began to eat. The vague smell of bologna and mustard came to me.

"Didn't get to eat lunch," he said. "Let me know when you're ready, bub."

He ate one half of the sandwich and then the other, watching the trees around us. Dappled sunlight brushed his face, making him squint.

Suddenly, he pointed excitedly into the underbrush, his words muffled by food. "Look, a fox!"

My stomach tightened. I waited for him to jump up and chase after it, draw a knife from his belt and hack at the fox's face until all resemblance with nature was gone. But Hank didn't move. The fox was there, a red flash of tail with a white tip, and then it was gone.

"Neat-o!"

My stomach churned again, steadied.

"Tummy okay?" Hank said, giving his attention to me again.

I nodded weakly.

He put the remaining crust of his sandwich into the paper bag, crumpled it up, stood, dusted crumbs from his pants and put the paper bag into his bike's knapsack. "Good," he said. "Then let's get to it."

To the right of his bicycle was a thin trail, and Hank abruptly slipped into it. I heard him thrashing around in the bushes. I heard his voice, low. At first I thought he was talking to himself, but with repetition his words became audible. "Here, fellas," he coaxed, over and over.

Movement stopped in the underbrush, and Hank stopped talking. Then I heard him say, *"Shit! Oh, shit!"* He moved through the woods again, reappearing with a large, high cardboard box in his arms, his face reddened with anger.

He set the box down in the middle of the clearing. "I thought it was high enough," he said, anger receding with embarrassment. "But one of them got out. Sorry." He looked at me with genuine contrition spread across his features.

I said nothing.

"Well," he expanded, "we'll just have to wing it."

He turned his attention to the box, lifting back the flaps. His features lit up.

"Hey, boy!" he said brightly to something down inside. He put his hands down into the depth of the box and brought something small, soft and brown up.

A puppy. A mutt, mostly cocker spaniel, with ears hung flat down and huge brown eyes. Its paws were overlarge. Its tongue panted out expectantly, its attention riveted to Hank.

Hank laughed. "All right, boy, okay." He cradled the dog tightly with one hand, reaching into his jacket pocket to dig out a dog biscuit. The puppy snapped at it, taking it into its mouth with a grunt of pleasure, holding it with its paws over the top of the box.

"Good fella," Hank said, putting the dog down and spreading a few more biscuits at its feet. "You won't run away, huh? Nah, you'll stay, right?"

The dog looked up at him adoringly. Hank laughed again. "Good boy."

Hank looked at me. "There were two," he said, "the other was bigger. He must have got his paws over the top of the box."

We both looked at the brown puppy, whose tail wagged happily as he growled away at the dog biscuits.

Hank suddenly rubbed his hands together and said, "It's showtime."

With a short laugh at the dog, he scooped it up and handed it to me.

My hands felt heavy as stones. The dog must have sensed my feelings, because it began to whine, trying to squirm its way out of my loose grip. Hank put his hands on top of it and held it down. "Whoa, boy, whoa, take it easy." He dipped back into his pocket and came up with a biscuit that had broken in half. He gave the half to the dog and rubbed its head. The dog whined, then began to pant and growl playfully, working at the food.

"You can't freak 'em out," Hank said to me. He grinned down at the dog, rubbed the slick fur on its head. "Right, fella?"

The dog whined excitedly, looking for another biscuit.

"Sorry, no more food," Hank said, and then he took his hands away from the dog, leaving it in my grip.

"Go ahead," he said, turning his smile to me.

"I can't," I got out. I held the dog close to my body; it had warmed my hands, but my fingers trembled and threatened to pull apart, throwing the dog into the woods to join its escaped sibling.

"Wish that other sucker hadn't gotten away," Hank said ruefully. "It would have made things a lot easier." He rubbed the puppy's head then stepped back. "Sorry, but you have to do it yourself."

"But I *can't*."

"No?"

And then I did it. I turned the dog in my hands, belly up, cupping it so that I could see its face. I took its tiny head between my palms, its huge brown eyes looking up at me, and I squeezed, letting my mind be a vise that spread down my arms and into my hands. The puppy gasped once and then opened its mouth wide, trying to turn and bite me, but my grip was too tight. Its eyes grew wider, staring into my eyes, and then a bright light, the end of life, filled the eyes and then they blinked out as if a shade had been drawn down them as the dog's head imploded in my hands. My palms nearly met, and the dog's head spread out away from my hands, colors of red mingling with brown fur and bone. I kept squeezing. My hands nearly met. I wanted to feel my own live flesh against itself.

I heard a buzzing sound from far off that grew like a swarm of hornets and threatened to overwhelm me. Then I realized that it was my own mouth, screaming. I screamed and screamed and then someone's hands were upon me. A voice was trying to cut through the screams. The hands shook me and I let go of the dog, my arms flying wide, my eyes burning like hot coals. I threw the hands that held me away and screamed. The hands took hold of me again. My burning eyes saw Hank looking at me, smiling happily, and I reached out to take his face in my hands, but instead I put my hands to my own head, screaming *"I don't want to! I don't want to!"* and then I sank to the ground and the hornets went away and I cried and cried and finally slept....

When I woke up the sun was going down. Hank was gone. He'd taken his bike, but not before he had cleaned up. The hollow was antiseptically brushed and raked as it had been when we arrived.

I sat up. I looked at my hands. Only when I looked under the nails could I see dried blood. Hank had cleaned me, too. My pants and shirt had been rubbed with soil. Most of the stains were gone. Those that remained were pale and indistinguishable.

I crawled to a tree and sat with my back against it for a few minutes. Then I got up and rode my bike slowly out of the camp, through town and back to my house. When I got home it was suppertime. My mother didn't say anything to me about where I'd been. I ate dinner and then I went up to my room and closed the door. I put on my pajamas and got into bed, and slept.

I dreamed about the extinguishing light in the puppy's eyes, and about Hank's expectant, happy smile.

All night I dreamed.

The next day I woke up and didn't get out of bed, and my mother didn't notice because it was Sunday and she got up late. When it was time for breakfast she came to my room, and I told her I didn't feel well and stayed in bed. I stayed in bed all day. The next day my science project was due, but I stayed in bed the whole day, the dinosaur diorama passing through morning light and afternoon shadow to night again. At suppertime my mother came in with her worried look on.

"I don't like the way you look," she said. "Are you sure it's just a cold?"

I nodded; I'd been warming the thermometer up to 102° all day with a match and drinking all the orange juice and chicken broth she'd brought. The Panadol she'd given me I'd flushed down the toilet.

She continued to study me. "If you don't get better by tomorrow I'm calling the doctor. There's a lot of mononucleosis around. If you've got that you could miss the last month of school. And you wouldn't be able to see Hank for weeks. You don't want that, do you?"

I shook my head.

She produced another glass of orange juice. "Try to rest now. I'll be back in later to see if you need anything."

I drank the juice, and feigned rest, and thought about mononucleosis, and when she came in later to check on me I feigned sleep. After she was gone I stared at the ceiling as long as I could keep sleep away, and when it finally came the dreams came with it and hounded me till morning.

The next day I didn't use the match, lowering my temperature to normal. My mother pronounced me cured. As she bore away the last of my orange juice she stopped in the doorway. "I forgot to tell you, Rudy. Your friend Hank called. He said he'll either see you in school tomorrow, or come by in the afternoon. He said he had something 'neat-o,' as he put it, to show you." She looked at me, shaking her head as she closed the door behind her. "Still don't like the way you look...."

The rest of that day and all night, the dreams came with my eyes open.

The next day I went to school. Hank was late for homeroom, but he passed me a note during Math class that read, 'See you after school?' I wrote back, 'Yes.' He didn't try to talk to me after class, and I didn't see him the rest of the school day.

After the last bell he appeared, falling into step beside me as I headed for home. "Can you come now?" he asked.

"I don't have my bike."

His grin widened. "You don't need it."

"I should tell my Mom."

"Are you kidding?" he laughed. "Come on."

We walked two blocks to the county bus depot. Hank motioned me onto a bench while he went to the window. I saw him pull a wad of bills from his pocket and count them out, sliding them under the glass cutout. He came back with two tickets, handing me one. "Here," he said, "it's a round trip."

I looked at the ticket, and it had the name of a town forty miles away on it. "What the—"

"Trust me," he grinned. He pointed to an open garbage bin next to the bench. "Throw your schoolbooks in there," he said. "You won't need them anymore."

I did as he said, and then we boarded our bus. The doors hissed closed, and the bus groaned away from the station.

From our seats behind the driver we watched the scenery. It was quickly dominated by farmland. We passed through a few small towns, the bus braking to a halt in front of a dusty station before pulling out onto the road again. Soon it was all farmland we watched.

In an hour and fifteen minutes we had reached our stop, a mere sign on the highway. Hank urged me off the bus ahead of him. As he stepped off, he turned to the driver. "Last bus through at eight?" he asked. The driver nodded with boredom. Hank jumped off beside me.

We walked for two miles. It was a warm afternoon, the kind we would have played baseball on, but today we walked through a rutted farm field, ranked with cut feed-corn stalks, toward a near line of hills. "My foster parents built a summer house up there," Hank explained. "There's a cabin, a lake nearby." Smiling, he said, "no fish or frogs."

We climbed, the hill quickly shading itself with pine and spruce. There was no trail, but Hank used the sun, and soon we broke out onto a dirt road.

"Won't be long," Hank announced.

In another fifteen minutes we stood before the summer cabin, an A-frame with a wrap-around deck. It looked brand new. In confirmation, Hank said, "They finished it a month ago. My foster parents said we'd spend all of August up here."

He bounded up the steps onto the deck. He produced a key from his pocket and opened the front door. He held it open for me like a bellhop, letting me pass through first.

I entered a sparsely furnished room with sawdust still wedged in the corners, sunlight streaming through the glass-walled A of the front. The back of the A was high stone with an unused fireplace cut into the bottom.

"Neat, eh?"

I looked around at Hank.

He had settled into one of two bean bag chairs in the center of the room. He crossed his outstretched legs at the ankles. "Hungry?" he asked. "I brought up some stuff yesterday, bologna and mustard and bread; some devil dogs, too."

"I'm not hungry."

He shrugged, settling his hands behind his head.

"Suit yourself."

"Why are we here?"

I had begun to get that nauseous feeling again, a fever-like roiling that burned up from my stomach into the back of my eyes.

"Sit down," Hank suggested.

"I don't want to."

"Are you sure?"

My stomach was boiling, pushing bile into the back of my throat. I swallowed it down. I did want to sit down all of a sudden, and dropped into the second bean bag chair across from Hank.

"Tell me why we're here, Hank."

"Soon." I looked at him through the blur of my sickened stomach and hot vision, and he smiled at me broadly.

"I don't want to be here," I said.

He bounded suddenly out of his chair. "Think I'll make a sandwich."

"Don't...."

I had trouble speaking. The ocean in my mind rolled me like a ship in a gale. I knew what the ocean was and wanted it to go away; wanted the limbs in the sea of blood to stop cresting the waves, reaching out to me, then sinking again to mingle with the screaming, dying fish below.

He stopped his retreat to the kitchen, walked slowly back to his chair, sat down.

"You okay?" he asked.

"No."

"There's nothing I can do for you," he said.

His smile was gone. In its place was not the dropped mask I had anticipated, the long-fanged, crazy, lustful visage of a murderer. He looked suddenly tired, and old.

"I can't help you, Rudy," he said, and, briefly, he touched my knee with his hand.

I must have screamed, then. I saw him lean toward me, and then fire filled my eyes, boiling back into my head. The sea not only was inside me but was everywhere. I was the sea, I was an ocean of blood myself, the limbs were my limbs and I possessed all of death, possessed it because it was me. I was death itself and my own screams were the screams of all the dead, swimming in and through me.

"What have you done to me?" I screamed, and I forced my flaming eyes to see through their fire and found Hank kneeling close to me, peering into me as if I was a mirror. "WHAT HAVE YOU DONE?"

"I'm sorry," I heard him say. His face was so close I could feel his breath, and then he tilted his head back, giving me his throat.

Fire and blood filled me, was me, and I took his throat in my teeth and screamed. The world became red. There was another scream in my ocean of blood which was not my own, and at the end of the scream, as it became a wave of blood in my sea, I heard Hank say, in crying relief, *"Thank you...."*

I awoke in twilight. The sun burned weakly into my eyes through the huge A of the front window, a dying ember about to fall into the night.

I arose from the floor. There was a lamp silhouetted in the twilight, and I stumbled to it and turned it on. Its weak wattage subsumed the sun and made weak day for me in the room.

Where I had been there was blood. Hank lay with his throat torn wide open. His face was disfigured, his severed limbs scattered about, chest and bowels ripped open, pulled from the body like stuffing from a mattress. Near his shredded trousers, I saw the receipt half of the one-way ticket he had bought at the bus depot.

There was wood next to the fireplace, neatly stacked. I added kindling from a filled brass bucket and started a fire.

When I had the fire stoked to big hot logs, I put the pieces of Hank into it, feeding him to the flames as if he was wood himself. It took time, but the fire was hot enough and in the end there was just bones and ash left. The blood I cleaned up. Then I showered, scrubbing my hands and face until they were clean as a baby. Under my fingernails was blood, and I could do nothing about that.

In the bedroom I found the change of clothes Hank had left for me. There was even a golf jacket in my size. He had known it would be chilly when I left the summer house.

I had a sandwich, bologna with mustard, and a devil dog, and then I turned off the light and left. I hiked back down the hill and across the fallow field to the bus stop. It was almost eight o'clock when I arrived. The bus found me ten minutes later.

When I got home my mother was waiting frantically for me. "Oh, God, Rudy, I've been so worried about you! Have you been with Hank today?"

I told her no; that I was off hunting Indian arrow heads by myself and had forgotten what time it was.

"Thank God! It's so awful—the police found Hank's foster parents in their house today, murdered. They're sure Hank had something to do with it." She looked at me as if she was afraid of hurting me, as if I was made of porcelain. "Oh, poor Rudy! They say he murdered his best friend and his real parents in Maine two months ago, and has been killing people ever since." She held me close. "Oh, God! You don't know where he is, do you?"

"No."

She continued to embrace me. "I want you to have some dinner and then go to bed."

"I'm not hungry."

"Poor baby."

I went to bed, and I lay staring at the ceiling, practicing my smile, and the dreams were real and they wouldn't go away. I heard my mother go to bed, and I went into her bedroom and killed her. Then I packed a bag and left the house.

I'll wander until I find my brother.

Red Eve

It was Red Eve. Red balloons rose. In the glass city, between the glass houses, beside the glass walkways, from the glass towers and glass highways—red balloons rose. Darkness was falling—fell. Below, through the darkening thick clouds, the earth could not be seen; in the clear high air above, the stars were sharp and cold. It was Red Eve, and winter was coming, and the children pushed their red balloons into the air to mingle with glass and stars, singing, as they always sang:

> *Red Eve, Red Eve,*
> *The night of blood,*
> *No blood we see,*
> *Balloons release,*
> *The earth below is dead.*

It was Red Eve.

In Eidolan's Palace, red balloons rose.
Red balloons bounced playfully against crystal ceilings, tapped along glass walls like soft fingers, bumped into one another. The dining hall was filled with them, rising together from some secret compartment in

the floor—light-gas filled, coming to rest like a bobbing blanket against the high glass dome, blotting out the knife-sharp darkness, and the sight of thousands of other red balloons outside, all lifting to hide the burning-bright diamonds of the stars themselves.

"Where is our teacher?" Mondranie asked languidly, as he painted above the rest of them. For a moment the rising balloons obliterated his spectacle—but then secret windows in the clear palace dome swung up and open and the balloons were gone into the night air, as Mondranie's painting flowed and burst into even greater combinations, under a ceiling of ascending red.

"Yes," said Verdigris, yawning, pausing with the thought in the middle of playing his newest composition: a thing of electric body waves with notes dancing from his fingers. "Where is she? I'm beginning to get bored." He continued his music, his hands spitting quarter notes into the air to mix with the color beads of Mondranie's paints, forming a swirling mix of sound and color.

Darnella, courtesan supreme, darkly beautiful, only nodded her head while lifting another choice, rare meat to her red-lipsticked mouth.

They ate; they drank; Mondranie and Verdigris, finished with their pursuits, along with LaFortina, poet, who had been amusing himself by running a hand over Darnella's breasts while reciting in a whisper into her uninterested ear, joined the table.

"This year," said Calumon, political leader, fat and hearty as a Roman," she promised her finest lesson." He paused to dip his thick fingers into the plate before him, lifting another bloated shrimp into his mouth.

"Yes," said LaFortina, taking his lips from Darnella's ear, "and I can't believe she would disappoint us!"

"I don't know," Mondranie sniffed. "The last year or two, I've found Eidolan to be a bit...." he waved a hand searchingly in the air.

"Pedantic? Tedious?" Verdigris offered, stifling another yawn.

Mondranie nodded, and Calumon, ever the diplomat, began to say, "Now, now."

But at that moment the room darkened.

"I hope," came Eidolan's soothing, silky voice, "you won't find me boring."

In the darkness, great vistas rose around them: mountains and rivers, the roar of crashing water, a great round moon rising magically slow over the ceiling above.

"Wonderful holos!" cried Mondranie, and from the table came other cries, "Yes! Yes!"

The holographs vanished, the room lightened, and someone cried, "Eidolan!"

She appeared from nowhere, from the floor or walls (from the same hidden box that had held the balloons?), becoming emplaced near Mondranie at the head of the table. She was slim and long, hidden only by thin shifts of red silk. Her face and hands were white and unblemished, her hair deep black, her voice soft as her skin.

"Eat!" she cried. "Drink!" Her robes shifted, slitting to show perfect white breasts slimming down to a perfect flat belly. Her hands closed over her robes. "I pray," she said, "you won't be bored."

"Hurrah!" shouted Mondranie. He rose unsteadily to his feet, one hand with a red-wine glass. "To Eidolan—teacher par excellence—hurrah!"

"Hurrah!" from the assembly.

At the head of the table, Eidolan's red mouth smiled slightly, her perfect head bowed in thanks.

They ate and drank; drank; ate. The fifth course was passed and belched, the sixth devoured (tongue of bird, wing of bird, head of bird), the seventh and eight not so much eaten as absorbed through greasily wet fingers and hands. Mouths were slicked with blood and fat, wine and liquors.

Calumon leaned back into his pillows and cried, "Ah!" as the desserts arrived. There were airy whipped froth things, red-cherry topped, crimson chocolates delicate as bone china, confections so light they melted reaching the mouth. Second dessert came and went; third dessert—parfaits, red creme with redder creme, redberry tarts—came and went, and then there was more—apple, red apple, essenced, milled, liquored.

"This is by far the finest meal—" Calumon began, but he was interrupted.

"Now!" LaFortina said, lifting himself unsteadily to his feet with the unsteady help of his neighbors. He spoke in a blur. "Give us your finest lesson—now!"

"Hurrah!" came a slurred chorus behind him. Others tried to rise from their cushions, hampered by drunkenness and gluttony.

"As you wish."

Eidolan's fingers fluttered, and the hologram moon overhead brightened to almost painful intensity. It was brown and white, artistically cratered; not the gray, pale, distant, bomb-blasted circle they knew, outshone by some of the stars, night-silent, dead. This moon tugged at them, at their eyes, their hearts—made rhythms in their blood.

"This," said Eidolan, "is my lesson." Her voice was the voice of this moon, pulling at them, making them hers. For a moment the moon blinked out, leaving them with a gasping view of the red balloons still playing out through the clear-glass walls from the other palaces surrounding them—a black-night sky waltzing with rising balloons.

The moon blinked back on; the ceiling, the night, disappeared. "This," Eidolan said in a gentle hush, "is my story—"

LaFortina pushed himself up, pointed a finger at Eidolan, at the moon. "Your *finest*," he insisted. "You promised!" Swaying slightly, he turned his finger downward, pointed through the crystal table, the glass floor, to the roiling, dark, sickly yellow clouds that hid the Earth. "This year you promised your best—better than this moon! We're tired of the same old Red Eve lessons! We're sick of the Vampire Wars, of dead Earth below, poison gas, proton bombs, stakes through hearts, screaming men! We're tired of bogeymen with fangs, reflectionless images, children hung like beef for living blood, the battles for the moon—it doesn't entertain us! We're bored with the thousand-year-old histories, the slaughter in

Asia, the Night of a Thousand Impalements, the building of the Crystal Sphere, the Deadly Climb to Life, the story of the Last Stake! It's old! And tired! Children's stories, for a children's holiday! We're tired of this tedium and we want better! We want—your finest lesson!"

"Yes," Mondranie demanded. "Your finest!"

"Here! Bravo!" added Verdigris.

Eidolan regarded them with a hurt look. "My friends," she said, spreading her hands, smiling slightly, "did I not promise?"

"Hurrah!" Calumon shouted. "I told you she would please us!"

"Please us, now!" LaFortina demanded.

"Yes!" Mondranie added, and he was joined in chorus by the others. "Now! Tell us!"

Even Calumon's fat face flushed with demand: "Tell us!"

Eidolan bowed.

"Of course."

The world went dark.

The moon returned, young as a baby. It pulled at their limbs, at the very earth. They were in a valley at the base of a black, cave-mouthed hill. Green, wet forest carpeted away from them to fanglike mountains in the distance. The air clung like hot, wet skin. Wolf shapes crawled close to the land, watching with guarded eyes.

There came a chanting in the air—it was their own music, all of them: Mondranie and Calumon and LaFortina, the damsel Darnella bare breasted at their lead, face blackened, arms rising and dropping hypnotically in time with Verdigris's drum.

A bonfire roared up before a cave mouth. Its heat lashed out; by its light they regarded one another's savage faces.

They were possessed. They followed as the wild Darnella circled the bonfire once, twice again. A wolf howl skipped toward them over the craggy line of mountains. The woods shimmered like stick men dancing, throwing shadows, orange and black.

Darnella halted.

The music ceased.

The drums became silent.

Even the fire did not dance.

Darnella's hands went high—her nipples stood out like pointing fingers.

"The last beast," Darnella sang.

The bonfire leapt, licked at the air once more. They rose, bearing torches, and Verdigris began to beat his drum.

Tam. Tam.

They entered the cave.

Rock walls narrowed, widened. Their shadows danced.

"Follow," Darnella whispered, and they moved deeper.

Verdigris's drum: *Tam. Tam.*

At the rear of the cave, marked with bones and the head of an animal stripped bare, its horns pointing at them, was the path they followed. Warmth assaulted them. The walls were alive with drawings—headless men and animals, dancing bones, bodiless fanged mouths devouring children and women, dark, winged shapes. They angled down. There were symbols on the path, bones stacked one atop the other, crossed branches. As the path sloped steeply, the walls became infested: every inch drenched with etched bloody eyes and claws, genitals, severed limbs, hands and fingers, heads with stiff, bulging tongues. The floor was sanded white with bone dust, splinters of bone. Faint sounds—low laughter, the cries of birds—echoed, flew away.

The earth swallowed; they went down.

Down.

Tam. Tam.

"Stop," Darnella hissed.

A sudden opening pushed them into a low, wide room. There were rough, sagging rock walls, black with age and gravity, a ponderous ceiling heavy as the moon outside, a floor bleached and rough as ash bark, covered with grinning skull jaws.

Darnella whispered in awe, "The...last beast."

Tam—

Verdigris stopped hitting his drum.

In the center of the room, within a circle of guttering torches, sat a pallet holding a bound figure. Twig-thin arms strained fiercely against the leather thongs binding it. Long, naked legs were thin almost to the bone; the toes on the feet showed rubs of bone at the ends. The waist and chest were sunk into its body, giving a hoarse bellow of breathing. The bare, hairless skull head showed the permanent wild hollow stare, rictal grin, of starvation.

They approached. The thing on the pallet whipped its head around, hissed, opened its foul-smelling mouth, showed its thin forked tongue, two frighteningly long and white upper incisors.

"The last...beast," Darnella whispered.

The others, gathered close behind like children, repeated her chant.

Verdigris beat weakly at his drum; they slowly encircled the body.

The thing on the pallet screeched, beat against its bonds, tore its bone-long fingers at the air. Its eyes bulged from its head.

"The last," Darnella said, bending down close.

The thing snapped at her, hissed, cried.

"Now," Darnella said, reaching behind.

Mondranie stuffed the head of his torch in the floor, broke it in half, handed it to Darnella, who gripped it in both hands, raised it high.

The thing on the pallet shrieked, tried to move its sunken chest aside.

"Now," Darnella said.

Verdigris beat his drum hard—*tam tam*—as Darnella brought the stake down to the heaving chest of the thing on the pallet.

It sank in, and through.

The body convulsed. The mouth opened impossibly wide, the head arched back. A cry escaped, the eyes straining for something unseen, the fingers clutching at oxygen, bone ends meeting, clicking together.

Tam—

Verdigris stopped beating his drum.

The thing on the pallet expelled breath, sank into itself.

Darnella and Calumon, Mondranie and the rest, reached in to tear at the heart—

Darkness came, covering all around them.

"And then," Eidolan said gently, "a thousand years went by."

Darkness retreated, leaving them elsewhere. The moon was back over them. There were clouds, light and high as blankets, scrolling across it, making it peekaboo.

They were on a street of houses. The night was sharp and cold as a cut apple. Street lamps made trees dance with night color; leaves, brown, gold, apple red, spun down like parachutists, filling the gutters, dervishing the sidewalks, whipping like racers onto porches, circling jack-o'-lanterns before settling with a sigh.

The air was filled with shouts and growls. They were howling, costumed beasts on a sidewalk, their ankles brushed with leaves. They ran, keening, waving paper bags with handles, down the length of the street. Their faces were beast masked.

The moon winked down at them. Something hot was in their veins—a dim memory of fear, a tapped source of the night and season—and they whooped, and jumped, and watched the leaf-shrugging trees and grinning pumpkins.

They ran in the costumed night—and then someone reared up from behind a tree, a tall black shadow with wings. They drew up short and clung to each other, gasping.

The thing spread its cloak; its ghastly white face grinned, red lips parting to show long, tapering, night-hissing incisors—

They screamed—until one of the fangs, soft wax, fell from the play ghoul's mouth. The thing turned and ran, laughing, bearing its candy bag toward the nearest house, porched invitingly in yellow October light.

They laughed, and followed—

"Until," Eidolan spoke gently.

Darkness cloaked and uncloaked them again.

The street, the costumes, the October night—all were changed. They heard real screams approaching. Again the moon blinked on above them, this time bathed in red. The smell of copper pushed into their nostrils. The very clouds seemed to bleed. They were together, running, and everywhere they ran there was suddenly blood, in the gutters running like rainwater, splashed against the trees, bright patches against the sides of houses, on porches, before front doors. The night was copper red, lawns were red, streets were red. They smelled red, touched red, breathed and tasted, heard the sound of dripping red. Blood fell like acid, pumped into the sky from open hearts, open throats. The canvas of the earth was painted red.

The moon arched across their sky like a time machine—crescent, quarter, full, quarter, crescent. Each time it paused it was redder. The years rolled in front of them. And still they ran, unable to banish the taste of blood from their tongues, the sight of blood from their eyes, the sound of dying blood from their ears. Copper, crimson, blood-garnet was the earth.

The moon ran overhead, east to west, again and again, faster, faster, vainly seeking to break free from the awful spectacle of earth below.

High up, the moon froze in place.

They watched its crescent light up in deep red. A booming bright thud felt down to the earth, followed by another, yet another. The moon became sick and distant, gray and dim.

There were more booming crimson thuds, close by, the boots of God slamming craters into the earth.

The earth filled with something more than blood. The yellow clouds came. The cries of men were mixed with other cries, plutonium stakes thrust through irradiated hearts.

The earth began to die.

Verdigris, Mondranie, LaFortina, Darnella, Calumon—they ran on.

But now, a wondrous sight appeared. The sky was filled with spun glass. A billion spiderwebs of crystal pierced the yellow clouds, hardened above, connected, spread, and melted together where the air was thin and clean.

On crystal ladders, Verdigris, Mondranie, LaFortina, Darnella, Calumon, climbed to a new world. Crystal glass waited to succor them, bathe them, nurture them, feed them.

Below, they heard the last screams fade. The yellow earth burned, dying, sealed like a bottle forever, trapping the screaming shells of a billion last beasts, drops of irradiated blood drying on their lips.

Darkness cloaked.

"And," Eidolan's voice said in gentle coda, "another thousand years went by."

The moon snapped on above them. For a moment they blinked at its pale, distant form, thinking it unreal. Then they blinked wide, saw themselves in Eidolan's crystal castle, seated before her crystal banquet table.

A new course of choice delicacies was set before them: red cheeses, vermilion desserts. New liquors rose like the sun from below, scarlet, maroon, ruby, set themselves on the table. Outside, red balloons rose high, a diminishing blanket. The last chant of Red Eve went up, as children sang, making their way home to crystal beds:

> *Red Eve, Red Eve,*
> *The night of blood,*
> *No blood we see,*
> *Balloons release,*
> *The earth below is dead.*

A distant children's cheer went up. The sky filled with a final soft blanket of balloons, lifting, red kisses, to brush the unblinking stars.

The moment ended; the children were gone, the holiday over.

Eidolan stood patiently at the head of the table.

No one spoke; then Mondranie, seated to her left, spoke.

"That story was...." he began—then he yawned.

"Now, now," Calumon said quickly. Impulsively, he reached for a thin goblet of plum liquor, suspending it between two of his plump fingers. "You must admit," he said, as if trying to convince himself, "the timing was exquisite. The holos—"

"The holos were redundant!" LaFortina shouted. He rose unsteadily to his feet. "Nothing new! The same old trees and beasts and moons! The same old Vampire Wars!"

"I must say," Darnella said, baring her breasts to study them drunkenly, "those holo nipples left something to be desired."

"Desired, yes," said Verdigris, reaching across the table at Darnella, who slapped his hand curtly away.

"Boring!" LaFortina pronounced.

He sought opposition. Verdigris merely nodded, Mondranie, more emphatic, cried, "Yes!" Even Calumon, flustered, hid himself in the ruby dessert before him, pretending not to hear.

"Boring!" LaFortina repeated. His face was flushed with anger. He attempted to stand straight, found himself swaying into Darnella, who steadied him until he clutched the table for support. "You've bored us for years with your 'lessons,' and tonight, after promising your finest, you've given us"—he swept his hand overhead, where the last red balloon, high above the crystal palace, the crystal world, dotted itself against the star-speckled night before winking out— *"nothing!* I was not entertained, or enlightened—I was fed and made drunk—but your finest is *nothing!"*

A hush dropped upon the table. Even LaFortina realized the immensity of his insult. He sat, finding the center of his chair with difficulty, and drew the closest goblet containing the closest liquor, a blackly red, almost custardy thing, to his lips.

"Your lesson was...." Calumon began sheepishly, glancing sideways at their hostess, who continued to stand quietly at the head of the table "a...bit...*tired.*"

"But," Eidolan replied, in the lowest, most gentle of whispers, "my dear Calumon, I never said it was finished."

"What!" LaFortina exclaimed.

A general gasp from the table was followed by a shout from Mondranie: "Bravo! Hurrah for Eidolan—that beautiful timing, the holos ending with the end of Red Eve—but the lesson not over! A wonderful ruse! Hurrah!"

There came a round of huzzahs, followed by another round of huzzahs. Somewhere between cheers, and LaFortina's stuttered apologies, Mondranie proposed carrying Eidolan through the streets upon their shoulders, which would have been attempted had they not discovered drunkness tying them to their chairs. Instead, toasts were offered, more liquors swallowed.

Eidolan waited patiently until Mondranie shouted, "So, continue!"

"Yes," cried Verdigris, "go on with the lesson!"

"Your finest!" Mondranie added. "Hurrah!"

"Hurrah!" shouted Calumon, as LaFortina stared sullenly into his half-empty goblet.

"Of course," said Eidolan, bowing.

They waited for the darkening of the crystal palace, the bright sickle of moon, the holos, the trees, the caves. But nothing happened. Instead, Eidolan stood quietly.

"Ha!" cried LaFortina. "Here's your ruse, Mondranie—there is no more lesson!"

Mondranie looked from LaFortina up to Eidolan. "Well?"

"We need no holos," Eidolan said.

"What—?" Mondranie began, but quietly, patiently, Eidolan continued.

"I gave you the lesson in holos, but you didn't learn. So now I will tell it to you simply. Where did we start? A thousand years behind a thousand years. The last beast destroyed, until ten times a hundred years later the memory of it has become a children's holiday. And then the beast returns, in strength, and only the combined force and viciousness of man can wipe it out, along with his own planet. What follows? Another thousand years of tranquility, resulting in memory once again dulled to children's games. What lesson does that teach?"

"You're a fraud!" LaFortina shouted. "There is no more lesson!"

"Have you wondered," Eidolan went on, lifting her hands to embrace the immensity of the space surrounding her—the airy depths of the crystal palace, the glass-enclosed recesses outside, the black, forever depths of night, "why the beasts return? Has it occurred to you that it is because they must, that they are in us, in our genes, waiting to mutate because they are better? Has it occurred to you that there is no last beast?"

"Charlatan!" LaFortina screamed, his face crimson with anger.

"Eidolan," Mondranie said, "I'm afraid we must insist you end the lesson."

"I must agree—" Calumon said timidly, fighting his eyes open against drunken stupor.

"Have you realized," Eidolan continued, looking down lovingly at Mondranie, "that this time there is no technology to battle fate with, that a thousand years of forgetfulness has left you *all* like children? That this time there would be no last beast, because there is nowhere left to run?"

"Liar!" LaFortina screeched, knocking his goblet over, watching a pool of thick ruby spread before him.

"End it, Eidolan!" Mondranie demanded.

"Yes," Eidolan said. She reached down to Mondranie's face, cupping his chin with firm gentleness, turning his head aside to bare his neck.

She smiled wide, to show them.

"This time, children," she said, somewhere in the midst of screams, as the real, distant moon and stars once more became the color of blood, "the lesson is learned forever."

PIGS

The day they took Jan was like any other day. The sky over the Vistula was fat with billowy gray clouds, "thick puffs from God's pipe," as Tadeusz had once said of such smoky formations. He stood on the bank of the river with Jan and with Karol, leaning on the thin rope bridge, the three of them sharing one cigarette as they waited for their solemn friend Jozef, who did not smoke, and did not approve of it. It was November, but felt like late September, cool but muggy. Karol dropped pebbles into the river below, his flat, open face spreading into a grin as his "depth charges" disappeared into the water. "Just like that American Clark Gable, in *Run Silent, Run Deep*," he laughed. "Captain, we've been hit!" Tadeusz had his cap pushed back on his head, which always forecast the weather because Tadeusz would pull it down tight over his ears in cold or wet times. He did not like the cold and complained bitterly when it rained, calling it a punishment from God for some great sinner in the city. "In Warsaw," he once told Jan, as they sat hunched over the smallest table by the smallest window in their tavern, so close together their pints of beer were pressed into their coats. The noise in the café was nearly unbearable. They looked out at the rain pelting the tiny window, at the thick wash it sent across the four panes intermittently, because it was either look at that or into each other's close faces, or into the coats of the standing patrons surrounding them—damp wool that would suffocate their conversation. "In Warsaw, when a great man, some member of the Party, commits a great sin, there is rejoicing in heaven. They laugh loud and long, because another Communist has proved himself weak and human, not equal in purity and character with God himself. You know," Tadeusz continued, poking Jan's nose lightly with his thick finger, an annoying habit, "that this is the great fault of Communism. In seeking to abolish God, it merely replaces him with Man. This is why it's doomed to failure. And God knows this. So, when a Party official commits a great sin, one of greed or lust, God and his angels laugh until they can no longer contain themselves, and God allows his angels to relieve themselves on the city of Warsaw. It is a just and mighty retribution—as well as a great relief for the angels. Unfortunately," he said, shivering at the rain outside, "it's a pain in the ass for those of us who live in Warsaw."

"What about God?" Jan asked him, gently warding off Tadeusz's finger heading toward his nose to make another point. "Doesn't God ever piss?"

"Of course he does," Tadeusz answered, offended. "But he is God, and his bladder is vast. It's as large as the Milky Way galaxy. And if you're going to ask me if he'll ever use it, the answer is yes. He's saving it, though, for a very special occasion." Tadeusz leaned close, pushing Jan's head around so that only his ear would hear his next words. Jan smelled the sourness of Tadeusz's breath, the odor of sausage and beer and stale tobacco, before he felt the rough stubble of Tadeusz's mustache at his ear. "God is waiting until that biggest man of all, the Big Man himself, the one in Moscow, commits the biggest of all sins." He turned Jan's face around, moving his own back. He smiled. "And then—BOOM! The big rain, right on you know where, and then you-know-where won't exist anymore."

"And then?" Jan asked, smiling in a friendly way.

Tadeusz held his hands out in his confined spot, palms upward, indicating what surrounding them. "And then this is ours again."

They looked out through the small window silently, before Tadeusz added, slyly, "There's only one catch. I have it on very good authority that you-know-who in Moscow has already fucked a chicken, and," he sighed, "nothing happened."

They turned to their own thoughts, watching the sliding wet sheets of rain on their tiny window, in their tiny space surrounded by heat and the smell of damp shorn sheep, until Tadeusz added, "And why do you ask about God, Jan? I thought you knew all about him. It's you who was going to be a priest."

At the bridge, leaning lightly on the rope railing, smoking and waiting for Jozef, who now approached them sullenly, the words of his disapproval of their smoking probably already forming on his never smiling mouth, Jan thought of the priesthood and wanted to laugh.

"And what do you find so funny?" Karol said. "Are you thinking of pigs?" Seeing Jan shudder, he quickly changed the subject, nudging him to look at Jozef. "Now *there's* something worthy of laughter. Our friend Jozef was born with a frown on his face." Karol, who almost never frowned, laughed heartily.

"He doesn't even smile when he gets off a good fart," Tadeusz said, throwing the remains of the cigarette which had been passed to him into the river and turning to meet Jozef, who had now reached them.

"Save your breath," Tadeusz said, slapping Jozef on the shoulder. "We've heard all your lectures on smoking. And we're late for work as it is."

The look on Jozef's face made him stop his joking.

"What's wrong?" Karol asked, as a cloud of seriousness descended.

"They're looking for Jan," Jozef said.

"What do you mean?" Tadeusz nearly shouted, and then he barked a laugh. He laid the back of his hand on Jozef's brow. "Are you ill? Have you been drinking? Who is looking for Jan?"

"The police."

"A mistake," Karol spat.

"No," Jozef replied. His dour face was pinched tight. He turned to

Jan. "I saw them come out of your mother's house as I passed. They must have just missed you. I waited until they were gone, and then I went in. Your mother was at the kitchen table, weeping. I asked her if they had hurt her. She said no—but there was a pot of oatmeal broken on the floor, by the stove."

"Bastards," Jan said, angry.

"She might have dropped it herself, when they came in," Jozef continued. "She was very upset, Jan. She said they wanted to speak with you, but she could tell by the way they came in, knocking once and then nearly throwing open the door, that they were there not to talk but to take you away."

"Why?" Karol shouted, indignantly. "What could they possibly want Jan for?"

Jozef shrugged. They saw now how frightened he was, his big-knuckled hands working one over the other, his thick coat pulled tight around him, the collar up as if protecting him from a chill wind.

Jan said quietly, as much to himself as to the others, who now faced him as if waiting for an explanation, "I've done nothing."

"Of course you've done nothing," Tadeusz said, scratching the black stubble on his chin. "But we have to hide you. We can't let them take you. When the storm passes over, it will be like nothing ever happened."

"There is no place to hide," Jozef said, his eyes on the ground.

Karol, in anger, grabbed Jozef by the front of his lapels. "Of course there is."

"I've done nothing," Jan repeated, as if in shock.

Tadeusz said, "We must get him to my house, off the street, then move him to a place that can't be connected to him." He took Jan by the arm. "Quickly."

Jan looked at him. Comprehension of what was happening to him on this fine day, with its cool, late summer breeze and fine gray clouds—on this day when he had smoked a cigarette with his best friends, and leaned on a rope railing overlooking the roiling water of the Vistula—dawned on him. Something out of his control was closing in on him, with his name imprinted on it, and unwavering instructions to bring him to ground. The police would not go away. They had been told to take him, and they would.

"I'll give myself up to them," Jan said.

Karol's face came before his own, flushed and angry. "Come with us," he said. *"They're not going to take you."*

Tadeusz's grip on Jan's arm tightened. Karol took his other arm. For a brief moment he felt as though he was going to faint. But then the world, the gray sky, the billowing gray clouds, the smell of the moving river, came back to him.

They moved briskly away from the bridge, Jozef darting glances behind them, and ascended stone steps to the street above. "Walk casually," Tadeusz ordered. They began to converse, trying to keep the tension out of their voices.

The street was filled with late factory workers hurrying to their jobs. Some wore winter coats, since the last few days had been colder than today, but they were opened at the collar, enjoying the last hint of warmth before the damp winter settled in. Most carried black lunchboxes.

They walked along with the workers. The pace quickened as the clock in the church steeple near the end of the street began to toll the hour, promising reprimands for those not at work by the time it had ceased. Jan and his friends hurried along until Tadeusz said, "This way is quicker," and brought them through a narrow alleyway, lined with discarded boxes, to the next street. "Stay back," he ordered when they reached the end. He went ahead, slipping out onto the street before motioning for them to follow. They crossed the road and mounted a flight of wooden steps to the second floor.

Tadeusz fumbled a huge iron key out of his pocket and turned it in the lock. Below them, on the street, someone rounded a corner, a man in a trench coat and brown hat. "Shit, he's right out of the movies," Karol said as they pushed Jan into the flat. The man in the trench coat was followed by two uniformed policemen, who kept a discreet distance.

They watched through the window as the man in the trench coat stopped and waited for the two uniformed men to catch up with him; there followed a discussion over a piece of paper which the man in the trench coat produced. The discussion escalated in volume, with the uniformed cops arguing and the man in the trench coat waiting for them to stop.

"Are they the ones you saw come out of Jan's house?" Tadeusz asked Jozef.

"I think so." He squinted hard through the window, then pulled his head back. "Yes."

"Jesus," Tadeusz said, "they must have gone right to the factory and found we weren't there. They're looking for this place."

The man in the trench coat suddenly threw his hand up and his companions ceased arguing immediately; the three of them then proceeded down the street away from them.

"They'll be wanting a telephone, and then they'll find the correct address," Tadeusz said. "We can't wait here. There's no time to waste." He reached into his pocket, pulling out a clip of bills, and handed it to Jan. The others did likewise, Karol cursing when he could produce nothing more than one small bill and a handful of coins.

"You must get to a bus," Tadeusz said to Jan. He held him by the shoulders, looking hard into his eyes to make sure that Jan understood what he said. "You must get out of the city. Do you know of a place away from here?"

Jan shook himself from his torpor. "There's a town called Kolno. It's about a hundred kilometers northeast of here. My grandfather had a farm there, once. I remember...." A sharp memory flashed across his mind, was gone. "There was a hotel outside the village, I think. I can't remember the name. It had a pot of flowers by the sign out front."

"Good," Tadeusz said. "On Sunday, two days from now, I'll meet you there. We'll get money together. I'll go to the priest and he'll help. They all will." He squeezed Jan's shoulders tight, bringing him close. Then the three of them, Jozef muttering goodbye, Karol punching Jan on his arm with his fist, looking angry and impotent, were gone, leaving Jan alone in the room.

"They'll all help," Tadeusz had said to him. But even as his friend was saying it, even as their eyes met while he was uttering the words, they both knew that, in the end, the police would find and take him.

Jan stood in the middle of the empty, cold, dark flat. He looked down at the money in his hand. Suddenly, for no real reason except that he refused to give up, a sort of life came into him. *Maybe they won't take me.* Maybe there was escape. Even if there wasn't, he would not let his friends down by not trying. He owed them something. He thought of his mother, in her tiny kitchen, cleaning the remains of his breakfast which he had cavalierly refused because he was anxious to get out of the little stuffy house, to smoke cigarettes with his friends ("No, Mother, I can't eat it, I'm not hungry"), the almost arrogant way he had refused her cooking. He thought of all the little things she did for him, her mending of his boots, the way she had replaced the lining of his coat after he had had it ripped during that brawl in the pub the previous September. She hadn't even scolded him about his fighting—though, later, he had seen her in her bedroom, the faded, colored quilt tucked still under her pillow, the mattress of the bed high and uneven from the old filling it possessed, kneeling with her elbows on the quilt, hands clasped around her rosary, head bowed. When he went to his own room he would find a holy picture tucked under his pillow, just as he had every night since he was a boy, since his father was killed during a worker's strike. Jan though of his mother, and his eyes filled with tears. She would never see him again. She had been in her kitchen, probably scraping the remains of his uneaten breakfast back into the pot, to save for later, perhaps to serve with the potatoes with dinner, and the policemen had come into her house, and had asked her rough questions, and then had left her, not laying a hand on her perhaps, but, just as well, striking into her body, into her heart. He cried not because he would never see her again, but because she would never see him. He was the one thing in her life she truly cared for—Jan, her only son, the image of her husband, the boy who would, perhaps, be a priest. He had told her that once, when he was young, with his tongue connected to a boy's confused heart, mostly because she had wanted to hear it so badly. Yes, he had said, he would become a priest. Later, when he had realized that he was now a man and not a boy, he had almost stopped speaking to her because he realized that he could never be what she wanted of him. He resented her for wanting him to be something he could not be. She had never said anything to him about it, had never mentioned the priesthood again, but still, every night, under his pillow the holy pictures, the image of Christ, the Sacred Heart burning in his open breast....

I'm sorry I couldn't fulfill your dreams, Mother, he thought. *I'm sorry I didn't tell you mine.*

More than anything, he must get away for his mother. If she knew he was safe, she would be all right.

Jan's eyes were dry by the time he opened the door. The street below was empty. But it would not stay so. At any moment the man in the trench coat and his two thugs might reappear, heading with certainty toward the very spot where he stood. That would be the end of it. He would have betrayed his mother. He would have betrayed his friends—and their money, which they had thrust into his hands and which the police would quickly confiscate, would be gone.

He turned his collar up and descended the stairs. As calmly as possible, he crossed the street, heading for the alleyway Tadeusz had taken them through. From the next street he could reach the bus depot by mingling with the shoppers in the marketplace.

"You there, just a minute."

He was turning into the alley when someone called to him. He thought of turning with his fists out. He could use the boxing move Karol had taught him, which they had used to such good purpose during the bar brawl this autumn. But there were three of them. There was no way he could overpower them. The one in the trench coat would be a few steps behind him, his two companions to either side, guns drawn, already aiming at a point between his shoulder blades. There was nothing the cops loved better than a prisoner resisting arrest. It was sometimes a quick road to promotion to add to one's record the shooting of a wanted man attempting to escape.

"I—" he began, turning around. Confusion was replaced by elation. It was one of Tadeusz's friends, a man named Jerzy who had sometimes observed their chess matches. He was a pensioner who lived alone, and, though he never spoke while he watched, Tadeusz claimed that he recorded every move in his head, learning the game voraciously. "One day," Tadeusz said after one of their matches, when the old man had limped down the stairs to his own apartment, giving Tadeusz the chance to bring out his good tea, which he hoarded, "he will beat us all. His eyes are a hawk's eyes."

"I say, Jan," the old pensioner said. The glow of concentrated purpose that Tadeusz had spoken of was in the man's eyes. "Do you think I might have a game of chess with you sometime soon?" He trembled; he must have practiced the speech before approaching Jan. His great shyness, and the great need bursting now from within him, made Jan reach out and put his hand on the man's arm.

"I—"

Behind the old man, Jan saw the man in the trench coat with his two henchmen approaching Tadeusz's flat.

He gripped the old man's arm tenderly.

"I'm sorry, Jerzy, not any time soon."

He turned away, nearly as much in avoidance of the disappointment on the old man's face as in haste.

As he had hoped, the marketplace stalls were busy. He was able to blend with the crowd of haggling women, schoolboys playing hooky and the young marrieds out together to buy vegetables and, perhaps, a little meat for dinner. He mixed with the hagglers, arguing himself over the price of a bag of chestnuts, which he leisurely ate as he strolled.

When he reached the last stall, Jan thought it must be at least noon. But, to his great surprise, the clock over the bus depot showed it to be only twenty minutes past nine. His initial feeling that the bus station would surely be watched by the police was replaced by a conviction that it would not. They had only been looking for him for a little more than an hour. At this point, there would only be the three men he had seen after him. When he was not located, there might be more, and a general alert would be posted, but now it was three against one.

His theory was proven correct when a covert inspection of the station revealed no sign of police activity. Jan's spirits were further lifted when he discovered that a bus heading out of the city in the direction he wanted was preparing to leave. He had no difficulty hiding his features from the ticket seller, who was more intent on his magazine than on studying the faces of bus passengers. He took the same precaution handing his ticket to the driver, using the opportunity to glance out over the driver's shoulder to see if his three pursuers might have shown up. They had not, and a few moments later, as Jan reached an empty seat halfway toward the back of the bus and away from the driver's direct gaze in the rear-view mirror, the bus lurched forward.

Twenty minutes later, they were out of the city and passing into the rural region north and east of Warsaw.

Though Jan never actually closed his eyes, a great feeling of lassitude overcame him. He felt as if he had been detached from himself, floating above the unfolding drama of his life, watching his own plight on a television screen. With some interest, he wondered what would happen next. In the drama, the man had eluded his pursuers, but now what would the script call for? In every television crime show he had ever seen it was easy to plot the destiny of the felon. If he was a good character, he would elude his hunters and ultimately triumph. If he was a villain, he would be caught and brought to justice. But what was Jan? Was he hero or villain? On the television productions, whenever the state wanted a man he was obviously a criminal, to be judged and sentenced. But what had been Jan's crime? Why did the state want him? It didn't matter.

About halfway to Kolno, the bus stopped to let passengers off. Jan waited for them to continue but instead the driver left the bus. Jan nervously waited for his return. After fifteen minutes he was sure that word had somehow spread and that policemen would appear momentarily and drag him from the bus. But as he was rising to leave, the bus driver suddenly reappeared, reclaiming his seat and pulling the door shut behind him.

Jan was filled with anxiety, undecided as to whether he should stay or rush to the front of the bus, throw the door open and flee, until he overheard one of the passengers in the seat in front of him laugh and say to her companion, nodding toward the driver, "There he is with his loose bowels again, it never fails." And the other one replied, knowingly. "Sausage for breakfast as a habit will do that. I tried to tell him that our last trip, but he wouldn't listen."

"Men never do," the other woman answered, and they both laughed and nodded their heads.

Jan settled back into his seat.

The trees thinned, showing dry farmland. Somewhere in the distance he thought he saw the remains of his grandfather's farm, the fire-blackened ruin of the house which had sent him and his mother to Warsaw, his grandfather's burning cries from the cellar mingling with squeals.... But then trees reappeared. And then, suddenly, they had reached Kolno. The two women in front of Jan got out ahead of him, stopping a moment to scold the bus driver on his breakfast habits. The bus driver waved them on impatiently, and Jan hurried out behind them, keeping his face averted from the driver and from the two women, who were nosy enough to remember a face. The bus doors closed with an airy hiss and the bus groaned off. Jan noticed that it leaned slightly to one side in the back, another state vehicle in need of repair it wouldn't receive.

The bus had left him at the edge of the small town square. So as not to draw attention to himself he went to the base of the statue at the other end and sat down on one of two benches there. An old woman occupied the other bench. She was blind, one of her hands rubbing softly at the blue-veined wrist on her other arm. Her black cane rested against one hip. Her eyes calmly stared into blackness.

"Excuse me," Jan said.

"I'll tell you anything you want," the woman said, "if you buy a pear from me." She lifted the corner of her cloak revealing a small wicker basket of pears nestled beside her. "It will cost you five hundred groszy."

"Certainly," Jan answered, drawing out one of the coins Karol had given him and pressing it into her hand. "Can you give me change for this?"

"I don't' have change to give," she answered.

Jan was about to say that she could keep the whole coin, but realized her game. "I'm sorry," he said, reaching to remove the coin from her palm, "I can't buy your fruit, then."

"I'll give you change," she said, smiling mischievously. She pulled a purse from beneath her cloak. She drew out coins, shorting him one to see if he would notice. When he protested she handed him all she owed him.

"I'm looking for the hotel with a pot of flowers out front," he said to her.

"Oh, I can't help you," she said. Her mischievous smile returned.

"You promised to help me. I can tell you you won't get another groszy from me, old woman."

"I was playing with you," the old woman laughed. It was a hoarse, unpleasant sound. "It's just outside of town. There's a horse path behind us, and you take that for about a half kilo. It's on the left side. A man named Edward runs it." She laughed again. "A skin flint like me. Don't let him cheat you. There isn't a room in the place worth more than ten. The best rooms are in the rear, where there's plenty of sun in the morning."

Jan stood up. The woman's sightless eyes followed him. "Are you going to stay long? Perhaps there are other things I could tell you, people you should watch for."

"Thank you for your help," Jan said, not trying to hide the annoyance in his voice. He moved on.

It was a longer walk than the woman had said. After what must have been a kilometer the road narrowed, leaving space for barely a cart, certainly not two horses abreast. The day had grown almost oppressively hot, an anomaly for November. There were thick hedges beside the road, the branching trees getting their brown coats of turning leaves overhead. It was like walking through a close burrow. Jan began to feel claustrophobic. He carried his coat over his arm. He rolled his shirt sleeves up, and loosened his tie. It felt like August, the humidity in the air palpable. He wanted to sit and rest but the hedge was cut so close to the road, there was nowhere to do it. His entire former life seemed like a dream, something he had left behind only a few hours before but which was a lifetime away from him. He tried to conjure up his mother's face, or Tadeusz's, but could not precisely remember what they looked like. If someone had told him a day ago that in twenty-four hours he would be stumbling through a darkling, hot tunnel, hiding from the police, running from a crime that was unknown to him, he would have laughed or executed the fighting move with his fists that Karol had taught him—the quick one-two.

Or maybe he was dreaming. Perhaps he would awaken at any moment, pushed gently on the shoulder by his dear mother, and would look up into her face, and tell her that he had had a dream of guilt, that he loved her more than anything, that he was sorry he had not told her of his feelings for her in such a long time. He would tell her that he was sorry that he had grown arrogant and distant, perhaps embrace her. Hopefully, the breakfast he had left on the table this morning was yet to be faced, waiting for him out of this dreamland on the kitchen table at this moment; and his mother stood over him right now, ready to end this guilt dream, about to give him that gentle nudge, this mother who had awakened him so many times, gotten him off to school, changed the sheets on his beds, seeing the stains he had sometimes left there with his wet dreams—his mother who was closer to him than anyone....

Oh, mother—

He did not wake, because it was not a dream. But suddenly he came up short, nearly walking into a black wrought-iron post curving out above the road to hold a brass basket of white and red roses. Riveted to the pole was a tarnished sign that said, KOLNO INN.

Flanking the sign was a lane, and he turned into it.

The path was lined with rose bushes, trellised up to nearly Jan's height. He could see where some had been clipped for the basket out front, strong green stems covered with thick red thorns, which suddenly ended in sharp, slanting lines. But there were more than enough, in various states of bloom. The largest, in full flower, was wider than his closed fist. He vaguely recalled that roses normally bloomed in June. Wasn't it November? But these vague thoughts, which battled with all of the other fears and anxieties that had been in his mind since the morning, were pushed aside at the sight of the hotel.

It seemed to appear before him out of thin air. One step he was on the rose-enshrouded path and the next step he was in the courtyard. His first thoughts were of a peasant cottage on a monstrous scale. There were three stories. The front was flat, lines of ornamentally shuttered windows set on a dark, chocolate-brown façade of diagonally laid planks of wood. The roof was edged in scrollwork, and at the four corners there were turrets, each with a small, square window.

The front door of the inn was low and wide. Dark flat stones led up to it.

Fearing only what lay behind him more than what lay ahead, Jan walked to the door and used the heavy brass knocker.

The sound echoed once and then was swallowed from within. No one came to let him in. He pulled at the wrought-iron handle, curved against the door in the shape of a long, bristled boar-pig. His fingers drew back; a memory came whole into his mind, was instantly blurred. He remembered this door handle; the image of a pig, large blank swinish eyes staring into his own, his screams, his grandfather lifting him, pulling him away from that bristled face, those blank button eyes ("What, no sausages today, Jan?" Tadeusz always kidded him. "But you're Catholic—not Jewish!").

He put his trembling hand on the door and it opened, letting him in.

At the end of a short hallway, through an entranceway, was a small lobby. It looked as though it might once have been a taproom. The ceiling was oppressively low. The front desk might once have served as the bar. Above it, butting the ceiling, was a thick square beam which ran the length of the desk. On it were intricate carvings of animal grotesques. Jan shivered. There were bloated pigs with the faces of wild men, mouths grinning, sitting on their haunches, bellies sliced open to reveal hanging strings of sausages and bacon slabs immersed in twisting clouds of smoke. There were pigs with the heads of women, sprouting great tufts of hair, open mouths full of sharp teeth. Some were biting themselves; one had its head thrust into the gaping stomach of an adjacent sow. Above these fantastic animals, at the line of the ceiling, had been carved scenes of violent weather: fat thunderclouds with thick jets of rain pelting down, hailstones square as bales of hay, blizzards of snow tacked up in leaning drifts against the unheedful animals below. Jan studied the bizarre scenes, moving along the desk slowly from depiction to depiction. The thick black beam drew him, mesmerized. Again, he knew this place—

"What do you want?"

The rough sound of a human voice startled him. A short man was now facing him from behind the front desk. A door behind him, which had been closed, was now open wide. The man had a shock of white hair like those of the fantastic swine-women above him. But there was no hog body below his neck, only a hard torso sporting a green felt vest. In one sharp-fingered hand he held a piece of bread which had been torn from a loaf and a slice of sausage, which he now pressed together before bringing them to his lips. Half of this meal disappeared into his mouth and he chewed, waiting for Jan to speak, regarding him with his unfriendly eyes.

"Are you Edward?"

The other continued to chew, his hand holding the remaining sausage and bread pressing them together. He started to bring his hand up to his mouth but stopped and said, "You have a reservation?"

"No. Your hotel was recommended to me by a friend."

"Recommended, eh?" For a moment the man's stare softened, but then he put the rest of his meal into his mouth and wiped his hands across the front of his vest. "It will cost you extra if you don't have a reservation."

"How much?"

"Twenty for the room. And ten more for not phoning ahead."

"That's too much," Jan bluffed, remember the old blind woman's warning about the proprietor being a skinflint. "When my friend stayed he said it was ten for the room."

"Twenty." Edward shook his head. "Costs go up."

"I could stay at the other hotel."

"Go on, then," Edward said, but he added, "All right. Ten it is for the room. In advance. And ten more for not reserving."

Remembering the blind woman's other words, Jan said, "I want a room in the rear of the hotel."

"Fine," Edward said, impatiently. "Just pay in advance."

Jan paid him, and was taken to a small room in one of the back corners of the third floor. It was hot. It looked out onto an oppressively close stand of oak trees. What little light reached the room filtered through the sway of branches. Looking out through the small window, he saw that the entire back of the hotel was suffocated by encroaching trees. *Damn old woman.* So much for her advice about morning sun.

When Edward had left him Jan lay on the bed. He found it lumpy and tilted annoyingly to one side. It smelled of old feathers and mildew. He laced his hands behind his head, finding with his fingers a rip in the pillow. He stared at the ceiling, trying to think of nothing, to make this day, what had happened to his life, vanish. But it would not. He saw it all again, as if played on a television screen: the haunted look on Jozef's face as he approached them on the bridge with his news; the smug visage of the man in the trench coat, sure of his job and his prey; and his mother's face, looming over him, telling him to get up for work, then weeping alone in her room after the police had gone, her rosary clutched in her praying hands, kneeling over the quilt, crying and praying to God crucified over her bed on his crucifix—

He pushed himself up on his elbows at a sound of movement, and there at the end of his bed was a girl he had never seen before, holding her hand out to him. She was short, her pale face suffused with freckles, her hair straight and red. She did not look Polish. But when she spoke she spoke Polish to him.

"Don't worry, Jan."

He reached his hand out to her, and she took it in her own. Her touch was gentle but in the fingers he felt a fierce hardness. He sensed that, if she wanted, she could grip him so tight it would feel as though his hand was in a vise. And yet she held his hand now as gently as a lover.

"Come with me," she said, in her beautiful, soft, enigmatic voice, letting his hand go.

He rose from the bed. She walked into the far corner of the room. He thought she had disappeared. But then he saw that the shadows in the corner lengthened, and that the walls did not meet. There was a hallway there.

Jan entered the shadows, leaving all but faint tendrils of light behind. He felt the walls with his hands. Abruptly the hall ended, and there were stairs. He climbed. Above him the stairway ended, and he faintly saw the girl turn away from him. There was only a wall ahead. When he reached it he found himself in another hallway which turned to the left. The girl was ahead of him, opening a door.

"Come on, Jan," she called tenderly to him.

He reached the doorway. Inside was a huge attic. At first he did not see the girl, but then he located her at the far end of the room. She was bending over something in the midst of a forest of stacked boxes.

He hurried to catch up to her. There was dust on the floor, as deep as fallen snow. He had to kick it aside to walk. He covered his mouth to prevent his lungs from being filled with it. He began to cough. He had kicked up so much dust that he could not see.

"Where are you!" he shouted to the girl, but there was no answer.

Suddenly the room was very dark. There was a noise off to his right. He turned toward it but found only darkness and settling dust.

Something ran by him, brushing his leg and kicking up more dust. "Help me!" he yelled in fright. He could not see through the dust and darkness. There was a cold grip on his ankle, and he cried out. The grip released and the thing was gone in a cloud of soot.

"Where are you?" he called to the red-haired girl. "Help me!"

The dust settled to the floor like a cloak. She was very close to him. "Don't worry," she said, soothingly. "Follow me, Jan."

He looked, and saw that there was a stairway at her feet.

He followed.

They went down a steep flight of steps. It was like the one in his grandfather's house that led to the cellar. Another memory washed through him. He had gone down there to see something. He remembered squeals, the sweet red smell of blood, his grandfather's face turning up under the bright overhead bulb to look at him, his spectacles red-spattered, the drawn dripping blade held at the sweeping height of its arc, the limp pink thing held in his other hand making a weakening whooshing sound like air escaping from a gasbag, Jan's own cry mingling with the wheeze of the dying pig, rising past it to reprise its lost squeal, his feet slipping, falling—

Jan felt a movement of cold above him. A sudden, unshakable fear took hold of him. He stopped, head level with the floor of the attic. He saw the girl proceed ahead of him; a moment later she was gone. It became very dark again. He reached down, gingerly, and touched the step he was on; it felt exactly like the steps in his grandfather's cellar, dry wood cracked to splinters.

The air was cold all around the upper part of his body. He became filled with terror. When Jozef told them that the police wanted him he had felt fear, but it had not been like this. This was a formless thing; this was concentrated to a sharp, needlelike point that seared his middle, making him want to scream. He felt on the verge of becoming a mindless thing; he wanted to push the fright from his lungs with his shrieks and thrust it away from him.

In the darkness above him, there was the slightest of movements. He heard a tiny scratching sound, like a fingernail across slate. He thought he heard even breathing, above the sound of his own ragged breaths.

Something touched his head. It was a tap, as of a hard fingertip tapping a blackboard. The carvings in the beam over the bar in the lobby rose into his imagination. A shiver swept over him. He remembered the pigs with the faces of wild men, stomachs happily revealing processed innards. One of those creatures, he was sure, was crouched above him, leaning over the stairwell, a mere inches from his head.

The step he was on sagged. Something moved past him, down the stairway. There was a passing hot breath on his face. A grunt of laughter.

It ran back up the steps; something hard and bristly (a leg?) brushed his face.

He screamed.

The hardness of a nailed foot tapped his head.

Suddenly the coldness left the upper part of his body. The thing crouching above him scuttled into the darkness of the attic.

Below him, the stairway became visible again.

She was waiting for him.

"Don't worry." She smiled.

He descended after her. He found himself back in his small room. The girl stood by the bed, silently smiling at him. Wordlessly, not taking her eyes from him, she removed the shoulder straps of her gown. The gown fell to her feet, revealing her naked to him. She was a mixture of girl and woman. Her face, the perfect white lines of her body, were childlike, yet the rise of her breasts, the V of deep red hair below her belly, the loving smile and the magnetic sexuality of her look and stance aroused him deeply. She lay her hand out. He went to her, and as he took her hand she lay back on the bed, pulling him down above her. She lay very still, looking into his eyes. Her hair was almost the color of cherries. She let his hand go so that he could touch her. He wanted to kiss her. She looked into his eyes. "Someday," she whispered, a moan.

And then her eyes became huge and blank, her skin bristled as she vanished beneath him.

Someone struck Jan roughly, on the back. He was pulled away from the bed and turned around, then pushed back, feeling the lumps of the old mattress under him.

The man who had pushed him now held him with his hand on Jan's chest and sat down next to him on the bed. It was the man in the trench coat. Behind him, to either side of the window, stood the two uniformed policemen. They looked tired; one of them yawned into his hand.

The man in the trench coat took his hand off Jan's chest and flipped open a small notebook.

"You are Jan Pasek?" he asked, matter-of-factly.

Jan said nothing.

The man in the trench coat looked down at him; when he spoke he sounded almost bored. "I can make a phone call from downstairs," he said quietly, "and it would be very hard for your mother indeed."

He looked at Jan dispassionately.

"I am Jan Pasek," Jan said.

The man in the trench coat wrote something in his notebook and then closed it, putting it into his pocket. He studied Jan's face for a moment. He, too, looked as though he wanted to yawn.

"You have caused me great inconvenience," he said, and then he swung his fist in a high arc over the bed and hit Jan squarely on the nose.

Jan felt an explosion of pain followed by numbness. Another blow struck his face. Dully, he looked up to see that the two uniformed cops had moved to the bed. The man in the trench coat stepped back. The uniformed men began to beat him methodically, raining blows on his ribs and stomach. He tried to roll into a fetal position. They struck his head and legs. One of them pulled him to the floor between them, and they began to kick him.

Through a curtain of torment that was lowering him to

unconsciousness, Jan heard the man in the trench coat tell them to stop. He heard the word "dinner." Turning his head, he saw through one nearly closed eye the man in the trench coat leave with one of the uniformed men. The other sat on the bed, trying to light a cigarette with an uncooperative lighter.

Jan attempted to sit up. The uniformed cop put his lighter aside on the bed. "Feel like fighting?" he laughed, dipping his boot toe into a sore spot in Jan's side, rolling him over onto his back.

Jan felt another deep push of pain in his side and then blacked out.

When he awoke they were carrying him through the lobby of the hotel. Edward, the proprietor, had another sandwich of sausage and bread in his hand. He turned his face away from Jan as he was dragged through the front doorway, his shoes scraping over the flagstones outside. Jan caught a glimpse of the roses through nearly closed lids. He could smell the flowers; their sweetness was mingled with the odor of his own blood.

He was carried a long way. They dumped him once on the way to rest. Jan heard one of the cops grunting, the other making fun of him for being out of shape.

"You would be too if you relied on using your head instead of your fists," his partner replied. The other mocked him in return until the man in the trench coat told them to stop bickering.

They dragged him to the town square, near the statue, where a dark sedan was parked at an angle. The blind woman was still in her accustomed spot. She cocked her head up and smiled at Jan as he was taken past her.

"You found your way to the hotel?" she said, giggling throatily, but Jan didn't know whether she spoke to him or the policemen.

He was thrown into the back seat of the car. One of the uniformed cops got in heavily beside him. The other drove, the man in the trench coat beside him in the front seat.

The car wouldn't start. The driver cursed, the other uniformed man, next to Jan, mocking his friend's ability as a chauffeur. Sharply, the man in the trench coat told them to shut up. The engine turned over, the driver shouting in triumph as they pulled away.

Jan lay on the back seat, watching the slate gray of the sky go past through the rear window, mingled with denuded trees. The face of the uniformed cop hovered over him. "Enjoy it now," the cop smiled. He nodded at the sky with his head. "You won't be seeing that where you're going."

They turned the car from the square onto the tree-lined road. It was then that Jan remembered. The cop's face rose over him again, the pink, stiff bristles on his face spreading into a grin. He put his hard-nailed foot on Jan's chest to keep him from rising. Through the window Jan saw the flower pot outside the inn as the car turned into the lane. He smelled the flowers. Again he smelled the blood in his grandfather's cellar. He saw the knife in his grandfather's hand, felt his own four feet slip on the cellar steps, heard his mother's barren cry at the top of the stairway, begging for a son her dead husband had never given her.

And, finally, as they led him from the car to the attic, he saw once more the look in his lover's blank huge eyes as he was lifted squealing away from her, the lover who now waited for him within, the look that promised, "Someday."

Richard's Head

Around five o'clock Richard began to moan, and Marjorie rolled her jacket up and put it beneath his head. They were two hours out of Boulder, off Route 70, doing eighty miles an hour. There had been a pile-up on the Interstate, and Carl had immediately gone to the meridian, keeping his foot to the pedal, until they got to the next exit.

"Fucking sun'll be down in an hour," Carl said. It came out as a statement of fact, but Marjorie could read the fear in his voice. "Think he'll...?"

"I don't know," Marjorie answered, immediately. Knowing that Carl would ask another question, she added, trying to add her own fear, "I don't know anything anymore."

Carl drove, and for a while there was silence in the car. Marjorie pulled all the way over to her side of the back seat, snugging up against the window. She felt the cool flat of the window glass against her cheek, and concentrated on that. They were driving straight into the sun, and she watched it turn dark orange as it hit the mountain horizon and purpled the sky above it.

The purple made her eyes close, and she slept for a little bit.

At eight o'clock, Richard began to moan again.

Marjorie came up out of a dream, something about driving into the sun, angling straight up off the highway, heading straight to consumption....

The dream was gone and she blinked her eyes open. She saw Carl's frantic head in the front seat, swiveling around toward her and then back toward the road. "Marjorie—" he was saying, hissing it.

"Yes, I'm awake."

"He's—"

"*Okay,*" she snapped, turning to adjust the jacket under Richard's head.

His head had elongated, changed shape. It lay at an odd angle, back over the rolled jacket and slightly to the side, resting over the back of the seat partly onto the rear window shelf. It was the color and shape of an eggplant now, had darkened and grown longer. The features had elongated with it, as if a normal face had turned to taffy, and been pulled lengthwise. The eyes, when they opened, were the same dark color as the skin, pupil, iris and lid.

"Jesus, he was...." Carl waved his hand at her helplessly.

"I—" she began.

A ripple of red sparking fire spread over Richard's head in the darkened car interior. The faint smell of ozone tickled Marjorie's nostrils.

"*—That,*" Carl finished.

Marjorie pulled her hand away, watched the network of tiny red lightning sparks cover Richard's head, dissipate with a faint *snap*.

Richard began to moan again.

"*Do* something!" Carl said.

"I—"

Again the red fire spread across Richard's features; a coat of yellow fire mixed in with the red and there was a slight burning smell.

The fire went away.

Tentatively, Marjorie put her hand out to adjust the rolled jacket under his neck. Her fingers found his head cold, the skin taut and unyielding.

Red fire snapped, moved around her fingers, dispersed.

Suddenly his moaning stopped; his breath evened, his eyes closed. Marjorie's hand stayed against his skin for a moment before lifting.

She was attracted to him because he was a boy. Not in age, but in physical essence, his long, soft sad face, his full mouth. His slow huge deep brown eyes, large for any boy or man, were set too deeply into the lines under his brow, made him appear to be looking at the world from some faraway place. His thin hair was never combed, falling in a thin brown-blonde lick across his forehead.

He was a genius, and she knew, deep inside her somewhere, that it was a mothering instinct and not sexual attraction that made her want to know him.

"I don't understand," he said to her quietly one day as she stood in the doorway of his dormitory room, his soft voice puzzled more than kind, his face like long, sad, fleshy dog's, the full mouth downturned. She felt a brief ethereal chill, looking at that alien face, and then a pang of need filled her and she overcame her reluctance and said again, "I'd like to go out with you."

"He doesn't date," Richard's roommate Carl remarked matter-of-factly from his bed, where he lay reading.

"But—" Marjorie began.

Carl lowered his book, looked at Marjorie stonily. "He doesn't."

"Not until now," Marjorie said resolutely, taking Richard by the arm and drawing him out of the room after her.

"But—"

"I'll have him back after our date," Marjorie said.

"Jesus," Carl said from the front seat. "We need gasoline."

"We can't stop," Marjorie said.

"We have to."

The statement hung in the air between them; Marjorie listened to the hard roll of the tires against the pavement. "Keep going."

Carl became suddenly frantic; holding the wheel hard with one hand, he turned around and stared into Marjorie's face. "The fucking gauge is on E! If we don't stop, we'll run out of gas!"

Marjorie waited until Carl had turned around and was paying attention to the road again. She leaned over the front seat and looked at the gauge.

It was on E.

"All right," she said. "Find a station with a self-serve. You'll have to keep the attendant away from the car. I'll pump the gas. I'll yell the amount to you and you pay him." She put her hand on Carl's shoulder. "You hear me?"

He looked like he was going to hyperventilate, but he said, "Yes."

They found a station a mile and a half later. Carl pulled the Dodge Aries hard into the island, stopping it in front of a self-service pump. Already the attendant, a lanky boy in a grease-monkey's suit, was rising from his chair inside the pay booth and walking out to greet them.

"Keep driving!" Marjorie yelled. "Go on!"

Carl keyed the engine back to life, threw the sedan into gear and left rubber pulling out of the island. The lanky attendant stood staring after them, hands at his sides.

Barely back on the road, the car began to sputter.

"Shit!" Carl shouted. "Shit! Shit!"

He threw the car into reverse, angled it back into the station.

"What are you doing!" Marjorie yelled, seeing the attendant still standing outside his booth, regarding them.

"Just get the gas!" Carl hissed, braking the car abruptly at the pump they had just left.

Carl bolted from the car and ran toward the attendant, who had started toward them. Marjorie watched Carl waving his arms, motioning the attendant back toward the booth. The lanky boy hesitated, looked out at the Aries with curiosity, then let Carl take him by the arm and steer him inside.

Marjorie threw open the back door of the car and yanked the gas nozzle from its mooring. She twisted the gas cap off, shoved the nozzle into the tank and flipped the switch on the pump. Nothing happened. She looked back helplessly toward the booth; Carl was gesturing wildly at the attendant, keeping his attention away from the car.

Marjorie flipped the switch up and down. There was a hollow click within the pump, but the numbers did not relay back to zero and no gas flowed when she pulled the lever on the nozzle.

She studied the pump furiously, looking for instructions, but there weren't any.

"I've got it!" Carl yelled from the pay booth. He had a desperate, frozen smile on his face. He held up a twenty dollar bill for Marjorie to see, then shoved it at the lanky attendant, who was craning his neck to see what Marjorie was doing. "You have to pay first!"

The attendant took the money, turned away from Carl, did something at his cash register.

The pump clicked back to zero, and, when Marjorie pulled the lever on the nozzle, gas flowed into the tank.

"Come on, come on," Marjorie said. The gas seemed to flow at a snail's pace. In the pay booth, Carl was engaging the lanky attendant in a furious conversation. The attendant nodded distractedly, his attention focused on Marjorie again. Suddenly he smiled and winked.

"Jesus," Marjorie said, turning away from him.

The handle on the nozzle shut down. Marjorie pumped gas again until it shut down again. The tank was full. She flipped the switch on the pump off, jammed the nozzle back into its mooring and twisted the gas cap back on.

"Finished!" she called out to Carl, with false brightness. She yanked open the back door of the car and got in.

A moment later Carl appeared, running to the driver's side of the car and getting in. He fumbled in the ignition for the keys, cursed when they weren't there, and fished in his pants pocket for them.

There was a tap on Marjorie's window.

Jumping, her eyes going wide, she turned to see the lanky attendant staring in at her, smiling.

"Forgot your change," he said, his eyes going over her as if she was undressed.

"Shit! Carl!" Marjorie said.

The attendant's eyes wandered to Richard. "Wha—"

Shouting, Carl found the keys to the car, and as they roared off, Richard's head crackling, Marjorie looked back to see the attendant staring after them, mouth open, the dropped change at his feet.

Over the next weeks she began to know him. Everything they did was at her urging, sometimes by the force of her will. But soon, Richard came to accept their outings, even to look forward to them. She could feel him rising minutely from his shell, opening to her, and a great motherly spring of passion, bottomless, was welling within her and, she discovered to her surprise, turning to love.

It was on their third date that she tried to kiss him, turning to his full long face as the credits rolled on a movie and the house lights began to go up. He met her eyes, and a spark she knew was hers alone was shining back there in the depths. Suddenly, she leaned forward, closing her eyes, and tried to meet his lips. But his face had pulled back, with a look of such terror or loathing that she was suddenly afraid, until he abruptly moved his face toward her, his eyes hooded, and brushed her lips with his own.

"No," he whispered, and she realized he was speaking not to her but to himself.

Carl drove very fast for the next hour. The night turned cloudy. Finally, as a few wet pellets of rain began to hit the windshield, a tension broke and Carl eased his foot off the pedal.

Suddenly, he began to cry.

"We'll never get there in time!" he wailed.

"Just drive," Marjorie said, noting with alarm that Carl had taken his foot all the way off the accelerator and that the car was slowing to a stop. Behind them, a truck flashed its lights, pulled around them with a roar, blaring its horn angrily.

"Drive, Carl," Marjorie repeated.

He turned around in the seat, panic and despair etching his features. "Why?" he said. "Do you really think they'll be able to stop it?"

"We don't have a second choice." She began to climb over the seat next to him. "Get in the back."

He sat unmoving in the driver's seat, weeping, his face in his hands. Marjorie pulled at him, trying to cajole him into the back seat, but he wouldn't move.

"I won't go back there with him!" he said hysterically, fighting her when she tried to force him with her hands.

"Then slide under me," she said harshly, trying to keep her own panic from surfacing.

In the back seat, Richard moaned. His head was larger now, wedged up between the window and the shelf beneath it, conforming slightly to the plane of the glass. Marjorie had the feeling that if she put her hand on it now, it would disappear magically into the hard purpled flesh and not come out again. Thin red veins of fire moved over the surface, flashed to tiny, brilliant points.

"Move!" Marjorie ordered, and now, finally, Carl slid across the seat to the passenger side as she threw herself over him, under the wheel, and jammed her foot on the accelerator pedal, throwing them forward.

A truck coming up fast on them flashed its brights, honked, swerved hard around them, passing close, but she ignored it. For the next half hour she drove in the left lane, with her foot flooring the gas.

Carl sat unexpectedly with her in the cafeteria one day. He was short and solemn, sometimes nervous, with dark hair, a physics major.

"I don't think you should see Richard anymore," he said.

"I don't remember asking you."

"There's a lot you don't know about him," Carl said. "He's a genius."

"I know that. I don't care."

"No, I don't think you understand. He really is a genius. His IQ is the highest ever recorded. And the Defense Department wants him badly."

When Marjorie didn't respond, he said, "I was picked to be his roommate."

"Picked? You mean you're a spy for the Pentagon?"

Carl shrugged. "It's a scholarship thing."

"You're supposed to soften Richard up so he'll go to the Defense Department when he's through here. My God, are you the best they can do?"

Carl reddened slightly. "They want to keep it low-key. I'm supposed to take care of him. There's a research facility eight hours east of here where they've studied Richard closely and where they want him to work. If I can convince him to do physics there, that's fine. If not, I get a college education and Richard does what he wants."

"You're a pimp for the government."

Carl ignored her anger. "Like I said, I don't think you should be seeing him."

"Because I'm distracting him from what the military wants?"

"Because it's not good for either of you." Carl leaned forward, over his food tray. "Look," he said, lowering his voice, "let's just say he's not going to be able to give you what you want."

Marjorie felt anger rising. "What do you mean?"

"He...." Carl began, and then he started again. "He'll never love you."

Marjorie felt herself wanting to hit him.

"Listen," Carl said, "they've done a lot of tests on Richard, ever since he was little. Besides his astounding IQ, he has an incredible amount of self-absorption. He literally lives inside himself. That's why he's been able to solve such difficult problems in physics."

"I'm in love with him."

"But he'll never love you. And that's what you need, isn't it? You won't get that from him, Marjorie." He looked straight into her, his eyes hardening. "You're a strong girl, but you can't make him love you."

"What are you, a pimp and a psychologist?"

Carl looked down at his tray. "The Defense Department did a background check on you. You were...." He reddened with embarrassment. "You were abused as a child. You spent some time with a therapist. The reports say you're starved for affection, and obsessive in your pursuit of it."

"You bastard," Marjorie said.

"In a way, you're a lot like Richard. The psychologists say something bad happened to him when he was young, only he overcompensated in the other direction. He's incapable of loving anyone, because he's afraid of being hurt." Again, he looked straight at her. "He's obsessed with something, too, Marjorie, and it's leading to marvelous discoveries. The government doesn't want that jeopardized."

"I won't stop seeing him."

"But—"

She got up, pushing Carl's tray onto his lap as she left.

Eventually, she passed the truck that had winged them. The driver recognized them, tried to block them by pulling out in front, but Marjorie jerked the wheel hard right and flew past him, ignoring his lights and horn. In the seat next to her, Carl had lapsed into shocked immobility, hunched down against the right door, eyes closed, shivering.

It occurred to Marjorie that she didn't know where to get off the highway, couldn't remember the name of the town where the research facility was. For a moment, the panic that had seized and disabled Carl caught hold of her, tried to bring her to a screeching halt. But she fought it back, suddenly remembering the name, and concentrated on the dark road pulling beneath them, the black starry sky, their essential flight.

She looked in the rear-view mirror, saw Richard's head huge in the back, pulsing out as she watched it, filling half the seat, nearly filling the rear-view mirror. He moaned, a tiny, constricted sound that seemed to come from a separate place. His mouth had become very small, along with his eyes, turned inward, lost in the great mass of that head, tiny insignificant appendages in what he had become, his eyes, his mouth, like appendixes, no longer needed for converse with this world.

She pushed everything from her mind but flight, calming her hands on the wheel, willing her foot to stay pressed to the accelerator, watching the night rush by....

● ● ●

Marjorie and Richard's next date started as usual, with a movie and then pizza. But this time she steered him to the bar next to the pizza parlor, sitting with him in a dark corner booth under a dim amber light. Carl followed as always, coming into the bar behind them, sitting four tables away, but she ignored them.

She got Richard to drink beer. He was not used to drinking, and after a second mug his face, all long, solemn angles in the bare light, softened perceptibly. His deep, huge eyes, which often watched her but, she felt, seldom looked at her, seemed to draw his mind to the front. He almost seemed to be staring at her. A slight, fleshy smile touched his lips, and for a moment she shivered, reaching her hand out to brush his errant long lock of hair back from his forehead.

"I love you, Richard," she said.

He reached his hand out tentatively to cover hers on the table, then suddenly drew it away, taking his beer mug and bringing it to his lips, finishing it. When his hand left the mug it rested not on her hand, but beside it on the table.

"I understand," he said. His voice was close to her and yet distant, and though he leaned in to her, she felt that he was still beyond her, on his own island, standing at the shore, now, perhaps, but still landlocked. His eyes were fierce, distant, beautiful brown lamps.

An ache rose in her so strong she suddenly wanted to cry. She saw herself in those eyes, her own aloneness, and wanted, more desperately than she had ever wanted anything, for him to mirror her love.

"Tell me what happened to you," she whispered, afraid of him, but wanting to pull his long sad soft head to her breast and stroke his hair, tell him everything was all right, that his loneliness, and her own, was over.

He leaned closer, the lamps moving with him, distant hot beacons infinitely clear. "One day, when I was three years old," he said, his hand moving farther away from hers on the table, until it fell into his lap, "I tripped on a toy by the coffee table in my mother's living room. I remember this very clearly, struggling for balance. I began to fall and reached for support, grabbing a knick-knack from the top of the table, and pulling it toward me. I fell, dropping the knick-knack on the floor, and it broke. I began to cry, and then my mother came into the room. She saw the broken knick-knack, and she slapped me."

Though his hand had pulled from her, his eyes were still on her. She realized his hand was back on the table, groping for more beer. She poured what remained in her own mug into his and watched him drink it.

He put the empty mug down. "At that instant, at the age of three, I vowed I would find a way so that no one could ever hurt me again."

He smiled, a distant, wan gesture. He talked as if in pleasant recollection, to a looking glass or empty room. "In the 17th Century, George Berkeley came nearest the idea. *Esse est percepi*, he said, 'To be is to be perceived.' He stated that material objects do not exist without the mind, but that since material objects do exist, they must be manifestations of the mind of God."

He turned his eyes on her, the lamps as close as they had ever been, and said, "You see, physics is the way to the answer. I'm very close, now." Again the wan, knowing smile. "Carl and his research facility, they think that it can be controlled."

Suddenly he became mute; she saw that as close as he had come to her, again was he that far beyond her. His hands lay like flat, dead things in his lap, and his eyes were blank, controlled, empty orbs.

"You're going to love me," Marjorie said to him.

"I won't," he said, a whisper, and when she looked at his hands again they were alive, and trembling.

Forty minutes later a police cruiser, siren wailing, red and white lights flashing madly, pulled out behind them from a cul-de-sac next to the highway.

She knew she could not outrun the police in the Dodge. But still she kept the Aries floored, reaching ninety, hoping that somehow the cop driver would give up or fly off the road or go away.

But he didn't. He stayed patiently behind for five minutes, pacing them, pushing his siren to make her understand that she had to slow down. She could see him in her outside mirror, his angry features in his flashing lights, his partner next to him speaking into his radio.

After another beer, she took Richard back to his room. He seemed very drunk when she led him to the bed, and he made no protest when she removed his shirt and began to kiss him.

She lay him back, and soon she had taken off her clothes and the rest of Richard's and had straddled him, watching the faraway look on his features as she brought him to hardness and guided him into her. It seemed, as she arched tight above him, the advent of the fulfillment of her dreams, the attainment of her secret wishes.

"I love you!" she shouted, pulling him deep within her.

She looked down at him, studying his flat features desperately. "Do you love me, Richard?"

His eyes focused on her, coming part-way to her from his distant place. "Do you?"

"I—"

Once again, she saw that he was trembling.

She cradled him deep within her, held him like a baby, ached to pull the words from his lips with her body. "Richard, tell me you love me!"

His face flushed with wonder, and he rose toward her from within; his features filled in with life and astonishment.

"Tell me!" she screamed, pulling his inner core toward her, out of his eyes which stared at her like those of a child seeing the world for the first time.

"Tell me!"

"I...love—" he began, but suddenly he gave a tiny, whispered moan, like a puppy, and clenched his teeth, going to stone beneath her. The light in his eyes receded into that other place, and his iron control rose from inside.

"Richard!"

"No," he said.

"Love me!" she screamed. She pulled him deeper, trying to make him come, but instead his penis began to soften, slipping out of her.

"Richard!"

"No."

"Damn you!" she screamed.

A strangled wail emerged from Marjorie's throat, a mixture of rage and pain. She rose up, bringing the flat of her hand down across his face.

There was a loud knocking on the door, and she heard Carl, demanding that she let him in.

Richard moaned.

For the briefest moment, on the bed beneath her, Richard's face pulled back toward her from that far place. His hand went to the place where Marjorie had slapped him. The light of his inner self burst into his eyes, his face reddened in shocked surprise, and his features twisted into a grimace of sobbing.

"Why, Momma, why?"

"Dammit, Marjorie, let me in!" *Carl demanded, pounding on the door with his fists.*

Richard moaned, a trailing sound. Beneath her, his face changed again. The light sucked back out of his eyes, leaving them flat and calm. A single tear tracked down his face to fall on the pillow.

"Richard?" *Marjorie asked, frightened.*

"I have the answer," *Richard said, in a distant, chilled voice.* "Berkeley didn't go far enough. The only question is," *he said, his open eyes turned in on themselves,* "what kind will I be?"

Carl pounded frantically on the door. "Marjorie!"

Richard lay still on the bed, his eyes open and unseeing, his face darkening from flushed red to blue. Marjorie thought he was dead. She pulled away from him, dressed quickly, and when she had opened the door for Carl they both saw that Richard's head, a horrible purple shade, had begun to grow.

"My God," *Carl said, panic already filling his voice.* "Get him dressed and into my car."

Marjorie pulled into the right lane, leading the police car to think she was pulling over. But she kept the accelerator pedal floored. The cruiser roared into the left lane, pulling even with her. The cop in the passenger seat rolled down his window and motioned angrily at her to pull over.

Marjorie ignored him, and now the police cruiser began to veer into her, trying to force her onto the shoulder of the road.

"No! Please!" she shouted, trying desperately to ward the patrol car off.

In the back seat, Richard began to moan, a low mewling electrical sound. Marjorie glanced quickly in the rear-view mirror to see that the soft oval vegetable thing that was his head filled the shelf under the rear window; in one corner, the window had cracked in a network of tiny lines in accommodation.

"Carl!" Marjorie screamed. "Carl!"

Carl curled tighter into his corner of the front seat, whimpering.

Richard's head crackled with tiny shafts of lightening, tiny red explosions of fire.

"PULL OVER!" the police cruiser's bullhorn warned.

The back window of the Aries pushed out into the darkness. Marjorie could feel Richard's head expand, out through the back window opening, and in toward her, the cool, snapping vegetable-like pulse of it molding around her neck, pushing into the front seat to partially cover Carl in the seat next to her.

She turned her head to see the cop in the passenger seat of the patrol car's eyes widen; heard him shout something, saw him elbow his revolver up over the rim of the window as the car he was in compacted end to end. Its matter squeezed and lengthened, and then was pulled with a snap into Richard's head leaving a blank hole behind. Marjorie felt the slight bump of its entrance, before the mass that was Richard's head pushed all the way into the front seat, forcing her hands from the wheel. She heard Carl cry, and knew that they would not get to where they were going.

She had a momentary, final look at the disappearing world, a small sliver of the Moon as it squeezed tight and was pulled toward her.

Somewhere close by her ear, Marjorie felt the tiny round opening of Richard's mouth.

And, as she went in, was sucked popping into the purple thing and heard endless screams, among them her own, she heard Richard say, in a tiny, sad voice that became huge, "I fear I will not make a loving God."

The day grew late. It grew late as an old man grows late: slowly at first and then with quickening steps. The shimmering front of Selene's shimmerglass house moved down the color chart from ROY to G to BIV, settling finally on a winter purple-gray slipping inevitably to gray-black. The clouds had scudded off, leaving a few hardy stars to blossom into view as if attached to dimmer switches. Star-pictures appeared, making stories of their own in the heavens.

"One more toy to play with," the Toyman said. Noting Selene's frown he added: "But this is a very special one. The toybox's own."

He handed her a tiny silver box. "Play with it carefully...."

BOXES

They went to see the man who collected boxes.

There were two of them, Nathan and Roger, and they went in the afternoon after lunch and armed with flashlights and code kits. They carried Boy Scout Handbooks in their ski coat pockets, and candy bars and a railroad flare which Roger had stolen from his father's workbench. Nathan had a whistle ring and two sticks of gum which he hoarded to himself.

They went in October, when the sun was orange-red and large as a hanging jack-o'-lantern, and they went in the afternoon when the leaves danced circles at their feet in the curt wind and when the chill of winter death was beginning to settle in on porches and doorsteps. They went with caps on their heads, and the energetic joy of the young bloomed in their cheeks and in their bright angel eyes.

Sidewalks disappeared under their running feet. Nathan leaped at the near-nude branch of a tree, missing it with an ooof. Roger leaped behind him and touched it.

The wind whistled the dark day's passing.

The man who collected boxes lived at the far end of the farthest block. His house—lonely, square, and brooding—suddenly reared up before them, and they skidded to a halt.

Roger looked at Nathan.

This was the dividing line, the place where innocent adventure stopped and the breaking of rules began. Bicycles were not even allowed to be ridden to this spot. Cats shied away. The lawn around the house of the man who collected boxes was immaculately trimmed, green even in this late time of the year. No dog did his business here.

No tree grew here.

Nathan and Roger shied away from this perfect, straight front walk, crept instead across the forbidden lawn. Breathing lightly, they drew up to the side of the house. Gingerbread brown it was, and seemed still wet to the touch it looked so freshly painted. So fresh that Roger found himself reaching to touch it. Nathan slapped at his hand and motioned for him to be quiet. Roger smiled.

Around to the back they crept, stopping underneath the one window. Shivers went through them both.

They raised their heads.

Inside, dimly lit, were the colors of Christmas morning. Red and green, gold and bronze, silver, blue.

Boxes.

There they were. Stacked one upon the other, butted up against walls, on tables and chairs, filling almost every inch of space. Boxes. Enameled and lacquered, painted in watercolor, pastel, and crayon, of wood, of cardboard, of tin and beaten brass, round, square, oval, triangle, large, little, tiny, nested, oblong, flat, high, decorated with stencils or drawings, some plain, some elaborately carved, lidded, unlidded, hinged, fitted, some with brass pulls, some with brass handles, some with moldings of party colors, others green felt-lined, red felt-lined, violet felt-lined, black felt-lined, flat-topped and dome-topped, pyramid-topped, untopped, some with secret compartments, keys, spring locks, one with a tiny steel padlock, with stained-glass insets, clear-glass insets, round peek holes, false tops, one with stubby teak legs, one with the face of a monkey tattooed to its front, one with the head of a camel carved from its lid-pull, one with trick eyes set into its side that seemed to follow you back and forth, one with a knife spring-jacked into its bottom, ready to fly up on opening, one with tactile poison along its ridged lip, one with the face of a happy clown on its cover that changed to a frown when you turned it upside down. A bright pink one with peeling paint. A chocolate-colored one with a crack in one corner. One that had never been opened—and never could be. One that had never been closed. One encrusted with precious gems: rubies, a topaz, sapphires, a thumb-sized diamond, eight-sided.

Nathan and Roger stared, fascinated, into the room and their eyes made a glue bond with these boxes. This was part of the dream of their plan. To see these boxes. To peer into this forbidden window and witness the treasures of the man who collected boxes.

To be among them.

There was no communication between Nathan and Roger. Their souls were united and separate in this decision. They had come to observe and now they must touch. Boy Scout Handbooks were fumbled out of slick ski parka pockets and paged through. How to open a closed window? As expected, there was nothing on how to open a closed window, especially one that did not belong to the scout doing the opening. Handbooks went back into pockets, and Roger, in a sudden and triumphant flash of thought, produced a small scout knife, attached to his keychain. It pulled open into a one-inch blade. Nathan was doubtful, but Roger overrode his doubt with enthusiasm.

Eyes peered over the window ledge again.

Boxes beckoned.

With care and the special skill of an amateur, Roger slipped the knife blade under the rubber seal of the outside window and tried to pry it out. Nathan suddenly grabbed his arm, stopping him. He pointed. There was a catch on the horizontal window, and it was in the open position.

Roger pocketed his tiny knife and pulled the window to the side.

It opened with a smooth hiss.

Nathan and Roger exchanged glances.

Behind them, the wind whipped up. An early moon had risen, and shone a pale crescent at their backs. The red sun was sinking. The sky had deepened a notch on the blue color scale, toward eventual black. The air bit cold.

Nathan looked at Roger and thought suddenly of home. Of Dad at six o'clock, coming home with a quart of milk, of the paperboy, of television, of the warm couch and the sharp smell of supper and Mom moving about in the next room. Of sister upstairs, playing her records too loud. Of an apple or late-peach pie, cooling by the kitchen window; the window open a crack to cool the pie but keep the chill out. Of his schoolbooks waiting in his room, neatly stacked; the neon lamp waiting to be buzzed on. Dad reading his paper and the smell of coffee. A warm bed with a crazyquilt coverlet Mom made last winter. The ticking sound of heat coming up in the baseboard. Thoughts of Halloween coming and Thanksgiving coming and Christmas coming. Kickball at recess tomorrow. Late-peach pie and cold milk.

Nathan turned to go and Roger took his arm. A look of reproach crossed his face. Somewhere at the other end of the block a dog barked once, twice. Roger held on to Nathan's arm, pulled his gaze back to the window.

To the boxes inside.

The dog barked again but Nathan did not hear it. Roger looked at him and smiled. Nathan made a step with his hands, locking them together and cradling Roger's foot, hoisting him up and over the ledge. There was momentary silence, and then Roger's face appeared on the other side. He was still smiling. He reached down for Nathan, who now locked his hands in Roger's hands and pulled himself up, over, and in.

Nathan righted himself and heard Roger sliding the window shut behind them.

There was almost nowhere to turn or step. There were boxes to the ceiling. Nathan tried to move deeper into the room and nearly knocked over a large box with carved pull knobs and black polka dots painted on its yellow surface. It tilted and began to fall toward a pile of black lacquer boxes which were stacked upon a cardboard storage box with rope handles. Nathan grabbed at it with both hands, noting its smooth and dustless finish, and righted it.

Roger, meanwhile, had found a pathway of sorts through the boxes and was disappearing behind a bronze-cornered trunk. Nathan hurried to catch up to him.

They both found themselves in a hurricane eye in the center of the room, a tiny cleared out spot walled in on all sides by boxes. It was very dim here, since the fading outside light was cut off by a row of bloodred cubes of diminishing size, starting at the bottom at about three feet square and finishing at the top with a pyramid topper of a tiny box a half inch on a side. There was enough light to see, though, and Roger cut off Nathan's attempt to snap on his flashlight, indicating that it would ruin the effect by having their own light infringe on this treasure room.

Nathan demurred, then agreed.

They sat, Indian style, in their spot and reveled in the boxes. Roger leaned over to his right, plucking at an oval tin circled with painted swans. He opened it, gazed into its bright reflective insides, and closed it again. Nathan stared up at the skyline of boxes around them, and thought how wonderful a dream this would make. There were more colors and pleasing shapes here than anywhere on earth—there must be—and he could think of no place that was more dreamlike. Roger brushed his fingers over the mottled surface of an ebony shoebox-sized box and sighed.

Light became a little dimmer.

There was a sound, and Nathan and Roger were startled. They had forgotten that they had broken into the house of the man who collected boxes; they had forgotten altogether that there was a man connected with these boxes. That had been part of the original adventure—to see the boxes, but above all to see the man who collected them. This they would be able to tell their friends—that they had not only seen the boxes but, most of all, that they had seen the man in the perfect house who kept them.

The sound came again.

It was almost a scrabbling sound—like tiny fiddler crabs loose in a wooden boat and ticking all over its inside surface. An ancient and wheezing sound—old age with claws, moving with slow careful grace and constant, inevitable movement toward its destination.

Nathan and Roger were trapped.

The sound was all around them—slow, inexorable—and, though they were on their feet and fingering their Scout Handbooks, there was nowhere to turn. Nathan could not locate the pathway back to the window; indeed, that pathway had seemed to disappear and even the line of bloodred pyramid boxes no longer stood in quite the same line. The tin box Roger had handled was nowhere to be seen.

There was the sound of a box opening.

Somewhere behind them, or in front of them, or to their left or right, a large box with a large and ponderous lid was being opened. There was a heavy, wheezy breathing. A rattling, dry cough. Another wheezing breath, and then a whispered grunt and the closing of the box lid.

A shuffling sound, the click of a light switch, a shuffling sound once more.

The room was suffused with a dull amber glow, like that in a dusty antique shop. The colors of the boxes deepened and softened.

A dry cough and the shuffling continued.

Abruptly, from behind a box with the gray-painted form of an elephant on it, the man who collected boxes appeared.

Nathan and Roger drew back.

The man who collected boxes shuffled toward them and lifted his heavy head. There were wrinkles there, so many that his eyes were almost lost to view behind them. His hair was the color of white dandelion and looked as though it would, like dandelion, fly away if breathed upon. His hands were veined and trembling, his bones gaunt.

He lifted his head, slowly, and looked out at them through the black shadows of his eyes.

He tried to speak.

He lifted his hand, painfully, and opened his mouth, but only a rasp emerged, dry as yellowed newspaper.

His hand lowered itself to his side.

Nathan looked at Roger.

At that moment, the dog at the end of the block barked again, and Nathan heard it, muffled as it was. He looked at Roger. It was six o'clock.

Late-peach pie would be cooling.

Nathan felt Roger's hand on his arm, but he pulled away. In the pale yellow light he found the slight opening between a dull blue nest of boxes and a charcoal-colored case; he slipped sideways between them and made his way through the maze of boxes to the window, sliding it open. It showed a dark rectangle of the outside world.

He climbed quickly out, hesitating on the ledge.

The dog barked once more, sharply.

He jumped down onto perfect grass.

Behind him as he ran, he heard the shuffle of shoes, and then the clean sound of one lid closing, and then another.

Selene closed the cover of the little silver box.

The shimmer-glass house had turned into a shimmer-glass palace, with a million shining star chandeliers overhead. Selene yawned, feeling an odd, rough tactility to her hands as she rubbed her eyes.

She yawned again.

The Toyman gathered all the toys into his great hard white hands and put them carefully into the toybox. Then he called to Selene to come look.

Down in the toybox, in the toyshop that was there, all the toys had resumed their places on the shelves. It was night in the toybox, and the amber glow had deepened to Halloween orange.

"Do you see," the Toyman said, "way down, that little shelf?" He pointed to an empty space under a pale rose skylight, a space where the rest of the orange glow was softer, more opaque.

Selene nodded, sleepily.

"That's yours," the Toyman said.

"NO!" Selene shouted, looking down now at her body: her black-yarn hair, her cloth skin, her black buckle shoes that hurt the eyes, they shone so bright.

"You knew all along, didn't you?" the Toyman continued. "A Toyman brings toys, but he must also get them from somewhere." His voice softened. "It won't be so bad. No more boredom...."

Selene was silent, staring up at him with her butter-brown eyes.

"Up now with you," the Toyman said. He lifted her gently, like a plucked flower, and placed her into the toybox. She looked up, and the world above her, the shimmer-glass house, receded to a dark rectangle. Around her shelf was a warm dusty glow, and she saw now that the toyshop was as wide to either side, with row after receding row of aisles, as it was long. And on each shelf in each aisle there were toys, of every kind imaginable.

"Not...boring," a corner of Selene's mind thought, and then she heard from somewhere in the distance the voice of the Toyman say, "Come, we have other stops to make."

Then, suddenly, like the wink of a blackbird's eye, darkness fell—

And from far, far away came the sound of the lid—

Closing.

THE LONGEST SINGLE NOTE
PETER CROWTHER

A shape-shifting serial killer in a dead-of-night police station . . . two survivors of an apocalyptic plague wandering the near-deserted highways . . . a student who unlocks a doorway to another world—but gets his arm stuck . . . a dust-bowl werewolf traveling the shantytowns of the Great Depression . . . These are just a few of the startling characters you will meet in this collection of stories by one of horror's most original talents.

From all-out horror to fantasy, from ghost stories to vampires, the tales in this collection are hard to categorize and harder still to forget. And each world could only have been born in the mind of Peter Crowther.

Dorchester Publishing Co., Inc.
P.O. Box 6640 __5078-1
Wayne, PA 19087-8640 **$6.99 US/$8.99 CAN**
Please add $2.50 for shipping and handling for the first book and $.75 for each book thereafter. NY and PA residents, please add appropriate sales tax. No cash, stamps, or C.O.D.s. Prices and availability subject to change.
Canadian orders require $2.00 extra postage and must be paid in U.S. dollars through a U.S. banking facility.

Name_____
Address_____
City_____ State_____ Zip_____
E-mail _____
I have enclosed $_____ in payment for the checked book(s).
Payment <u>must</u> accompany all orders. ❏ Please send a free catalog.

CHECK OUT OUR WEBSITE! www.dorchesterpub.com

COMING IN MAY 2002!

SHADOW DREAMS

ELIZABETH MASSIE

Meet the folks in Elizabeth Massie's world. They're normal, everyday people, living mostly in small towns, growing up or growing old and handling all life's problems just like you and me. Except for one thing—these people are about to be touched by the cold shadow of fear, enveloped by a dark nightmare laced with dread.

Elizabeth Massie has twice won the Bram Stoker Award and has been nominated for a World Fantasy Award for her brilliant horror fiction. This chilling collection, containing her best stories from the past ten years, is proof positive that Elizabeth Massie can see the terror lurking in the familiar and the darkness waiting in our dreams.

Dorchester Publishing Co., Inc.
P.O. Box 6640
Wayne, PA 19087-8640

4999-6
$5.99 US/ $7.99 CAN

Please add $2.50 for shipping and handling for the first book and $.75 for each additional book. NY and PA residents, add appropriate sales tax. No cash, stamps, or CODs. Canadian orders require $5.00 for shipping and handling and must be paid in U.S. dollars. Prices and availability subject to change. **Payment must accompany all orders.**

Name: _____

Address: _____

City: _____ State: _____ Zip: _____

E-mail: _____

I have enclosed $_____ in payment for the checked book(s).

For more information on these books, check out our website at www.dorchesterpub.com.
_____ *Please send me a free catalog.*

STEPHEN LAWS
DARKFALL

A massive storm is raging, filled with lightning, power... and terror. But inside one high-rise office building, all is silent. Moments before, the building was filled with Christmas parties and celebrating employees. Now it is empty. Everyone has vanished, disappeared into thin air. The only thing left behind—a severed human hand.

Detective Jack Cardiff and his squad are about to discover the living hell that is Darkfall, where the impossible becomes all too real, and where things that were once human become living nightmares. As the investigation proceeds, the full extent of the horror emerges, a horror more fearsome than the howling storm that spawned it.

Dorchester Publishing Co., Inc.
P.O. Box 6640 __5218-0
Wayne, PA 19087-8640 $6.99 US/$8.99 CAN

Please add $2.50 for shipping and handling for the first book and $.75 for each book thereafter. NY and PA residents, please add appropriate sales tax. No cash, stamps, or C.O.D.s. Prices and availability subject to change.

Canadian orders require $2.00 extra postage and must be paid in U.S. dollars through a U.S. banking facility.

Name_____
Address_____
City_____ State_____ Zip_____
E-mail_____
I have enclosed $_____ in payment for the checked book(s).
Payment <u>must</u> accompany all orders. __Check here for a free catalog.

CHECK OUT OUR WEBSITE! www.dorchesterpub.com

RICHARD LAYMON
DARKNESS, TELL US

It starts as a game. Six college kids at a party. Then someone suggests they try the Ouija board. The board that Corie has hidden in the back of her closet and sworn never to touch again. Not after what happened last time. Not after Jake's death. . . .

They are only playing around, but the Ouija board works, all right. Maybe too well. A spirit who calls himself Butler begins to send them messages and make demands. Butler promises them a hidden treasure if only they will follow his directions and head off to a secluded spot in the mountains . . . a wild, isolated spot where anything can be waiting for them. Treasure or death. Or Butler himself.

Dorchester Publishing Co., Inc.
P.O. Box 6640 __5047-1
Wayne, PA 19087-8640 $6.99 US/$8.99 CAN
Please add $2.50 for shipping and handling for the first book and $.75 for each book thereafter. NY and PA residents, please add appropriate sales tax. No cash, stamps, or C.O.D.s. Prices and availability subject to change.

Canadian orders require $2.00 extra postage and must be paid in U.S. dollars through a U.S. banking facility.

Name _____
Address_____
City_____State_____Zip_____
E-mail _____
I have enclosed $_____ in payment for the checked book(s).
Payment <u>must</u> accompany all orders. ❏ Please send a free catalog.

CHECK OUT OUR WEBSITE! www.dorchesterpub.com

NIGHT IN THE LONESOME OCTOBER
RICHARD LAYMON

Everything changes for Ed that day in the fall semester when he gets a letter from Holly, the girl he loves. Holly is in love with someone else. That night, heartbroken and half mad with despair, Ed can't sleep, so he decides to go for a walk. But it's a dark, scary night in the lonesome October, and Ed is not alone. . . .

There are others out there in the night, roaming the streets, lurking in the darkness—waiting to show Ed just how different his world could be. Some of them are enticing, like the beautiful girl who wants to teach Ed about the wonders of the night. Some are disturbing and threatening. Some are deadly . . . and in search of prey.

Dorchester Publishing Co., Inc.
P.O. Box 6640
Wayne, PA 19087-8640

_5046-3
$5.99 US/$7.99 CAN

Please add $2.50 for shipping and handling for the first book and $.75 for each additional book. NY and PA residents, add appropriate sales tax. No cash, stamps, or CODs. Canadian orders require $5.00 for shipping and handling and must be paid in U.S. dollars. Prices and availability subject to change. **Payment must accompany all orders.**

Name: _____

Address: _____

City: _____ State: _____ Zip: _____

E-mail: _____

I have enclosed $_____ in payment for the checked book(s).

For more information on these books, check out our website at www.dorchesterpub.com.
____ *Please send me a free catalog.*

IN THE DARK

RICHARD LAYMON

Nothing much happens to Jane Kerry, a young librarian. Then one day Jane finds an envelope containing a fifty-dollar bill and a note instructing her to "Look homeward, angel." Jane pulls a copy of the Thomas Wolfe novel of that title off the shelf and finds a second envelope. This one contains a hundred-dollar bill and another clue. Both are signed, "MOG (Master of Games)." But this is no ordinary game. As it goes on, it requires more and more of Jane's ingenuity, and pushes her into actions that she knows are crazy, immoral or criminal—and it becomes continually more dangerous. More than once, Jane must fight for her life, and she soon learns that MOG won't let her quit this game. She'll have to play to the bitter end.

___4916-3 $5.99 US/$6.99 CAN

Dorchester Publishing Co., Inc.
P.O. Box 6640
Wayne, PA 19087-8640

Please add $2.50 for shipping and handling for the first book and $.75 for each book thereafter. NY, NYC, and PA residents, please add appropriate sales tax. No cash, stamps, or C.O.D.s. All orders shipped within 6 weeks via postal service book rate. Canadian orders require $2.00 extra postage and must be paid in U.S. dollars through a U.S. banking facility.

Name_____
Address_____
City_____ State_____ Zip_____
I have enclosed $_____ in payment for the checked book(s).
Payment <u>must</u> accompany all orders.☐Please send a free catalog.
CHECK OUT OUR WEBSITE! www.dorchesterpub.com

FACE
TIM LEBBON

When a family picks up a hitchhiker during the worst blizzard in recent memory, they think they're doing him a favor. But he becomes threatening, disturbing, and he asks them for something they cannot—or will not—give: a moment of their time. They force him from their car, but none of them believes that this is the last they will see of him.

The hitchhiker begins to haunt the family in ways that don't seem quite natural. He shows them that bad things can sometimes feel very good. He infiltrates their relationships, obsesses them, seduces them and terrifies them. Bit by bit he shows them that true horror can have a very human face.

Dorchester Publishing Co., Inc.
P.O. Box 6640 __5195-8
Wayne, PA 19087-8640 $6.99 US/$8.99 CAN

Please add $2.50 for shipping and handling for the first book and $.75 for each book thereafter. NY and PA residents, please add appropriate sales tax. No cash, stamps, or C.O.D.s. Prices and availability subject to change.

Canadian orders require $2.00 extra postage and must be paid in U.S. dollars through a U.S. banking facility.

Name_____
Address_____
City_____ State_____ Zip_____
E-mail _____
I have enclosed $_____ in payment for the checked book(s).
Payment <u>must</u> accompany all orders. ❏ Please send a free catalog.

CHECK OUT OUR WEBSITE! www.dorchesterpub.com

MONSTROSITY
EDWARD LEE

Blue skies, palm trees, and flawless white-sand beaches. Clare Prentiss thinks her new home is paradise, and her brand new job as security chief at the clinic almost seems too good to be true. It is. But the truth is worse than she could ever imagine.

Lurid dreams, erotic obsessions, and twisted fantasies aren't the only things that abruptly invade Clare's life. Is someone really peeping into her windows at night? Yes. Could those grotesque things in the woods possibly be real? Yes. Is Clare being stalked? Yes. But not by anything human. By a monstrosity.

Dorchester Publishing Co., Inc.
P.O. Box 6640 ___5075-7
Wayne, PA 19087-8640 **$6.99 US/$8.99 CAN**

Please add $2.50 for shipping and handling for the first book and $.75 for each book thereafter. NY and PA residents, please add appropriate sales tax. No cash, stamps, or C.O.D.s. Prices and availability subject to change.

Canadian orders require $2.00 extra postage and must be paid in U.S. dollars through a U.S. banking facility.

Name_____
Address_____
City_____ State_____ Zip_____
E-mail _____
I have enclosed $_____ in payment for the checked book(s).
Payment <u>must</u> accompany all orders. ❏ Please send a free catalog.

CHECK OUT OUR WEBSITE! www.dorchesterpub.com

EDWARD LEE
CITY INFERNAL

Hell is a city. Forget the old-fashioned sulphurous pit you may have read about. Over the millennia, Hell has evolved into a bustling metropolis with looming skyscrapers, crowded streets, systemized evil, and atrocity as the status quo.

Cassie thought she knew all about Hell. But when her twin sister, Lissa, committed suicide, Cassie found that she was able to travel to the real thing—the city itself. Now, even though she's still alive, Cassie is heading straight to Hell to find Lissa. And the sights she sees as she walks among the damned will never be in any tourist guidebook.

___4988-0 $5.99 US/$7.99 CAN

Dorchester Publishing Co., Inc.
P.O. Box 6640
Wayne, PA 19087-8640

Please add $2.50 for shipping and handling for the first book and $0.75 for each additional book. NY and PA residents, add appropriate sales tax. No cash, stamps, or C.O.D.s. All Canadian orders require $5.00 for shipping and handling and must be paid in U.S. dollars. Prices and availability subject to change. **Payment must accompany all orders.**

Name _____
Address_____
City_____ State_____ Zip _____
E-mail _____
I have enclosed $_____ in payment for the checked book(s).
❏Please send me a free catalog.
    CHECK OUT OUR WEBSITE at www.dorchesterpub.com!

THE DECEIVER
MELANIE TEM

The Devil, they say, is in the details. The small decisions we make every day. But for the Harkness family, this expression is all too literally true. For many years the members of this family have gotten seemingly helpful advice at key moments in their lives from a mysterious—and very persuasive—stranger.

He doesn't always look the same. But he's always around whenever some sort of decision needs to be made. And what he says makes so much sense. His influence on the Harkness family seems slight at first. But before anyone realizes it, the strange man is leading them down some very dangerous—and terrifying—roads indeed.

Dorchester Publishing Co., Inc.
P.O. Box 6640 __5097-8
Wayne, PA 19087-8640 $6.99 US/$8.99 CAN

Please add $2.50 for shipping and handling for the first book and $.75 for each book thereafter. NY and PA residents, please add appropriate sales tax. No cash, stamps, or C.O.D.s. Prices and availability subject to change.

Canadian orders require $2.00 extra postage and must be paid in U.S. dollars through a U.S. banking facility.

Name_____
Address_____
City_____ State_____ Zip_____
E-mail _____
I have enclosed $_____ in payment for the checked book(s).
Payment <u>must</u> accompany all orders. __Check here for a free catalog.

CHECK OUT OUR WEBSITE! www.dorchesterpub.com

MOON ON THE WATER
MORT CASTLE

It's a strange world—one filled with the unexpected, the chilling. It's our world, but with an ominous twist. This is the world revealed by Mort Castle in the brilliant stories collected here—our everyday lives seen in a new and shattering light. These stories show us the horror that may be waiting for us around the next corner or lurking in our own homes. Through these disquieting tales you will discover a world you thought you knew . . . and a darker one you'll never forget.

Dorchester Publishing Co., Inc.
P.O. Box 6640
Wayne, PA 19087-8640

5032-3
$5.99 US/$7.99 CAN

Please add $2.50 for shipping and handling for the first book and $.75 for each additional book. NY and PA residents, add appropriate sales tax. No cash, stamps, or CODs. Canadian orders require $5.00 for shipping and handling and must be paid in U.S. dollars. Prices and availability subject to change. **Payment must accompany all orders.**

Name: _____

Address: _____

City: _____ State: _____ Zip: _____

E-mail: _____

I have enclosed $_____ in payment for the checked book(s).

For more information on these books, check out our website at www.dorchesterpub.com.
_____ *Please send me a free catalog.*

DONALD BEMAN
AVATAR

When Sean MacDonald first meets sculptor Monique Gerard, he is fascinated. Her work is famous—some would say notorious—for its power, sensuality . . . and unbridled horror. But Sean didn't expect the reclusive genius to be as compellingly grotesque as her creations. Something about her and her work draws Sean in like a moth to a flame . . . or like a lamb to the slaughter.
_4376-9 $5.50 US/$6.50 CAN

Dorchester Publishing Co., Inc.
P.O. Box 6640
Wayne, PA 19087-8640

Please add $2.50 for shipping and handling for the first book and $.75 for each book thereafter. NY and PA residents, please add appropriate sales tax. No cash, stamps, or C.O.D.s. Canadian orders require $2.00 extra postage and must be paid in U.S. dollars through a U.S. banking facility.

Name_____
Address_____
City_____ State_____ Zip_____
I have enclosed $_____ in payment for the checked book(s).
Payment <u>must</u> accompany all orders. ❏ Please send a free catalog.
        CHECK OUT OUR WEBSITE! www.dorchesterpub.com

BEDBUGS
RICK HAUTALA

From the subway tunnels of Boston to the rain-swept streets of Quebec City to the deepest snow-filled forests of Hilton, Maine, no one in these chilling stories by horror master Rick Hautala is safe from the darkness or the dangers that lurk in the shadows. Waiting for us. Reaching for us...

Over the years, Rick Hautala has terrified and captivated millions of readers around the world. *Bedbugs* is a career-spanning collection of stories that whisks you away on a guided tour of the darkest reaches of the human mind and soul.

Dorchester Publishing Co., Inc.
P.O. Box 6640   __5074-9
Wayne, PA 19087-8640 $5.99 US/$7.99 CAN

Please add $2.50 for shipping and handling for the first book and $.75 for each book thereafter. NY and PA residents, please add appropriate sales tax. No cash, stamps, or C.O.D.s. Prices and availability subject to change.

Canadian orders require $2.00 extra postage and must be paid in U.S. dollars through a U.S. banking facility.

Name_____
Address_____
City_____ State_____ Zip_____
E-mail _____
I have enclosed $_____ in payment for the checked book(s).
Payment <u>must</u> accompany all orders. ❏ Please send a free catalog.

CHECK OUT OUR WEBSITE! www.dorchesterpub.com

ATTENTION BOOK LOVERS!

Can't get enough
of your favorite HORROR?

Call **1-800-481-9191** to:

— order books —
— receive a **FREE** catalog —
— join our book clubs to **SAVE 20%!** —

Open Mon.-Fri. 10 AM-9 PM EST

Visit
www.dorchesterpub.com
for special offers and inside
information on the authors you love.

 We accept Visa, MasterCard or Discover®.